C000137567

# MARISSA FARRAR

# Author's Note

Dear Reader,

Please pay attention to this content warning.

This book contains scenes of self-harm and suicide ideation. If you're struggling with this yourself, please seek help. Reach out to someone and tell them how you're feeling. Contact a Samaritan. As someone who self-harmed through my teenage years and have been left with the scars, I understand how you're feeling.

As well as those CWs, there are also scenes of SA (not by any of the heroes), of laying a parent to rest, and of scenes that are tab00 in nature.

This is the final book of the Immoral series, and I hope I've managed to deliver for Laney and her men the ending they deserve.

Thanks for reading!

Marissa

# 1

## laney

FLASHING LIGHTS BLIND ME AS I CLIMB DOWN THE HELICOPTER'S steps and onto the landing pad. The lights appear as bright circles, as though I've stared at the sun too long. I blink to try to clear my vision.

In front of us stretches a sea of reporters.

Over the deafening roar of the helicopter rotor come the shouts of 'Darius, over here,' and 'Darius Riviera, how did you survive?' all jostling to be heard.

We're surrounded by people, so many people, layers thick. After the solitude of the wilderness, I'd almost forgotten there could be this number of bodies in one place.

The air smells different, too. Gone is the piney scent of the forest, and instead my nostrils are filled with engine oil, smoke, and chemicals. It's far stronger than I remember even in Los Angeles, though I'm sure Ottawa must be less polluted.

I'm overwhelmed, my heart racing, my palms growing clammy. It takes all my strength not to back up into the relative safety of the helicopter and beg the pilot to take me back to the cabin.

Reed must sense my hesitation. He places his palm to the small of my back and leans in closer.

"It's okay, baby-girl. We're right here with you."

His words should comfort me, but instead I jerk away, adrenaline shooting through my veins. What if someone heard what he'd called me? What if someone thought the way he'd touched my back was inappropriate? There are cameras everywhere, filming and photographing every move we make, every word we say.

I remind myself that all these reporters aren't here for me. They're not even here for Reed or Cade. There's only one person they want gracing the front pages of their newspapers and magazines, and that's Darius.

I glance over at him. He's used to media attention, but not at this level, and he's been isolated from it all, too, over the past month. I wonder how much he's even aware of. He must be able to hear the volume of voices, but how much of an understanding does that give him of how many people are here?

His expression is impassive. I can't read him at all. I assume he used to enjoy the attention before the accident, but does he now? Or is he as overwhelmed as I am?

I let the back of my hand brush Darius's. It's not much, just a slight touch to let him know I'm here. I'm telling myself I want that contact for him, but it's for me. What I really want is for them all to huddle close, to put their arms around me, allow me to hide against their chests, so they can create a shield from the real world, but we're all horribly conscious of the new distance that needs to exist between us, especially when we're in the public eye.

We all look like shit. We're painfully thin. The loggers' clothing we've been given to replace our old, torn items hang from us like dress-up clothes on a scarecrow. We're covered in bruises and scrapes and cuts from our perilous journey. Our hair is too long and matted. The men all have beards covering their faces. I can't imagine what the reporters must think of us all. I'm grateful that I got to shower at the loggers' camp before we were picked up. It's not much, but at least I don't smell bad—at least, I hope I don't.

As well as all the reporters, we also have police and paramedics waiting for us. I have no idea how it will work with us being Americans in Canada, and the two pilots and the flight attendant who'd died in the crash also being from the States. I assume there will have to be some kind of cooperation between the two countries to find out exactly what happened.

One of the police officers—at least, I assume that's who he is, though he's in plain clothes—steps forward. He's around Reed's age, maybe a little older. His expression is stern, and I find myself shrinking back. I've never been great with authority figures, and now I'm drowning in guilt. The crash might not have been our fault, but we're about to lie about almost everything that happened to us.

Being the eldest, Reed is the one to meet him, his hand out. The two of them shake.

"Mr. Riviera," the officer says, his voice raised to be heard above the commotion. "I'm Sergeant Moore. I'm sure I'm speaking on behalf of everyone when I say that we're so pleased to find you safe and well."

Reed gives a small nod. "Thank you, Sergeant. We're relieved to be alive. It was looking a little precarious for a while."

"I can't even imagine what you've been through." His gaze slips across the rest of us. "All of you. We will get you all checked out by paramedics, and then transported to the hospital."

"My eldest son, Cade, suffered a bad head injury." Reed glances over his shoulder at us. "But as for the rest of us, other than being underweight and dehydrated, and covered in insect bites, we're all in good shape—at least as good as we can be, considering the circumstances."

I fight the urge to run and hide. If doctors check me over, will they spot signs of the sexual assault? I don't want them to know. I don't want *anyone* to know. Just the thought of it floods me with a kind of heat that leaves me nauseated and lightheaded, my cheeks burning. Since we've agreed to stay quiet about the gunrunners in the hope they'll remain lost out there, the authorities will question who has assaulted me. There are only three options, since, apparently, we were alone, and then I'll be forced to either let one of the guys take the blame or else tell the truth.

Neither option seems like a good one.

As much as I don't want to spend any time in the hospital, I suspect we're going to need a little more than just a quick checkup from the paramedics. Cade's blow to the head will need monitoring. He'll probably need to have an x-ray or CT scan, or whatever else doctors use to diagnose skull fractures or swelling on the brain. He seems almost back to normal now, but he'd been worryingly ill not that long ago. What if he suffers long term effects from the head injury? I've been through a lot, physically, but so has he.

I wonder if I'm being too hard on him. Is it possible that the way he'd acted toward me was partly down to the blow to the head? Cade is big and strong, and his injury had left him defenseless and unable to protect me. Maybe he hadn't been thinking straight.

My heart yearns to believe it.

I can't help myself; I look over to him. There's a distance between us now. We lock eyes, and I see the hurt in my heart reflected in his gaze. I can't bring myself to forgive him for how he reacted when he'd learned I'd been raped. The first thing he did was think of himself. He didn't even consider the sort of trauma I'd been through—how, more than anything, I'd needed him to hold me and tell me nothing had changed. That he still felt the same way about me as he always had. But he hadn't done that. He'd taken his rage and aimed it directly at me. It was the last thing I'd needed or deserved.

I'm so fragile right now, I don't feel as though I can trust him with my heart. What if I do, and he takes it and smashes it into a million pieces?

Reed had been worried I'd come between them all, and now it looks as though he was right.

That, in part, is the reason I've decided to go back to the trailer, to put a little space between us. There's too much at risk. Reed could be torn to pieces by the press, have his whole reputation left in tatters if anyone finds out what happened between us. He's still my stepfather, and they will make it look as though he'd groomed me at the age of seventeen. They won't listen if I tell them nothing happened between us until I was eighteen and that I'd been the one who'd instigated things.

We've agreed to stick to a version of our story that would have been right if we hadn't been intercepted by Smith and his gang. That we'd come to the decision we'd never survive over winter and had no choice but to try to walk to safety. Will the authorities find the cabin? They very well may. They can follow the river upstream, though there are breaks and forks in it that will throw them off course. But we're not going to tell them about how we followed the river the whole way. We're also going to alter the days and times it took us to walk certain distances.

The authorities won't just give up. There are three bodies—or at least what remains of them after over a month in the wilderness, exposed to the wildlife and the elements—to be found. It'll be important to the families to have their remains returned so they can bury them. There will also be an investigation into what caused the plane to crash. People will want to point a finger, have someone to blame.

"We will need to speak to each of you individually," Sergeant Moore says, "and I'm afraid you'll be asked to go over everything several times, as there are a number of different authorities involved. We'll let you get reacclimated first, though, and like I said, have the paramedics and doctors check you over."

Am I going to be separated from the others?

I glance up at Reed, widening my eyes. "Please, I don't want to go on my own."

One minute, I'm telling Reed that I need some space, and next I'm hovering on the brink of a panic attack at the thought of being led to a different ambulance.

"It's okay, Laney," he assures me. "I'm right here." Reed checks with the sergeant. "We can ride together, can't we?"

He gives a brisk nod. "I'm sure that's okay. I'll catch up with you all at the hospital."

Technically, I'm eighteen now, and no longer need to have a legal guardian, but Reed is still my next of kin, so he comes with me in one ambulance, and Cade and Dax ride in the other one.

The paramedic is a theatrical man, who won't stop talking, even as he checks our blood pressure, and hooks us up to drips to rehydrate us.

"How did you guys survive out there all this time?" he asks. "You must have been terrified. What did you eat? Did you have to hunt? Fish? Like mountain men or something."

"We did a lot of foraging," I tell him. "Ate a lot of berries and roots. That kind of thing."

"It's a good thing you crashed at the time of year you did. Imagine if you'd crashed in winter and the place had been covered in snow. You'd have probably been reduced to eating each other to survive."

I share a glance with Reed, who arches an eyebrow at the man's comment. I almost blurt that the guys ate me plenty of times, just to see the paramedic's reaction. It's one of those intrusive thoughts that seem to want to get me in trouble, but I manage to bite my tongue.

The paramedic catches the look between us but misreads it. "Oh, God, I'm so sorry. That was completely insensitive of me, wasn't it? I mean, people actually did die. You must have seen dead bodies and everything."

"It's okay," Reed tells him.

I guess we're going to have to get used to this kind of questioning. Everywhere we go, people are going to want to talk about what we went through. They're going to want all the gory details.

Once more, the impulse to run and hide flashes through me.

# 2
## laney

AT THE HOSPITAL, WE'RE ALL GIVEN PRIVATE ROOMS—COURTESY of the airline, apparently. They probably want to do whatever they can to stop us from suing for damages. I don't know the exact financials of the Riviera family, but I don't think they're desperate for money. Then I remember Cade, and my heart sinks. He needed money. It had gotten him in trouble before the crash. If he gets a big payout for this, will it help or hinder him?

As for me, I've never had money. I have no idea what it's like to live with it. It doesn't even seem real. The truth is, I don't need it. That month out in the wilderness has proven that. There were moments when I'd experienced true happiness for the first time in my life, and we had nothing—a roof over our heads, but that was all.

I'm not so naïve to think living in the cabin is anything like real life. I bet if I told someone who was drowning under debt that they didn't need money, they'd probably smack me around the head, and rightfully so. Money could be an evil in its own right.

I'm relieved to be away from all the crowds, but I miss the guys already. I haven't been without them for any length of time since I came into their lives. I'm going to need to get used to it, though. We're back in the real world now, and, somehow, we're going to have to figure out how to get on with our lives. I have no idea what that even looks like. We're not all going to be able to live in the same space anymore. Dax is going to want to get his career going again, make the most of the elevated celebrity status the crash has given him, and use it to propel him into a whole new level of fame. He needs Cade by his side for his day-to-day life, and Reed manages him, so they'll be involved as well. There isn't room for me to be just a hanger-oner.

Besides, I have things I need to deal with as well. I haven't had the chance to bury my mom yet, and I've got no idea what sort of condition the trailer will be in now. All my belongings are still there, since I never got the chance to collect anything before the crash.

As much as I want to cling to the guys, I need to go home.

Doctors and nurses flutter around me, making a fuss. I'm given a hospital gown, and the oversized logger's clothes are bagged and taken away. I'm hooked up to a drip and try to remain patient while lights are shone in my eyes, and every inch of me is checked over, despite me telling everyone I'm fine.

All I want is to be left alone and allowed to sleep. The hospital bed is narrow and hard, but it's clean, and still feels luxurious after what we've been through.

After an hour or so of being poked and prodded, I'm brought a tray of food—if you can call it that. It's a bowl of some kind of beige slop, and a bowl of Jell-O. My expression makes what I think of the offering clear.

"Sorry," the nurse says as she sets the tray on the table that swings over the top of the bed. "You don't want to overdo it on these first few days back to normal eating. You can make yourself sick if you eat too much, especially if you try to eat high fat or high sugar foods."

"No chance of getting an Uber Eats to bring me a Big Mac and fries, then?"

"Sorry, sweetie. Not for a good few days yet."

I don't tell her that we ate far better back at the loggers' cabin. I wonder what the guys will think of the food. They won't be impressed. Cade might even throw it at someone. They're all bigger than me, though, so perhaps they've been given something more substantial.

I force myself to eat what I've been given. I know I should be grateful, after almost starving to death, but my lack of appetite isn't only down to the unappetizing meal. I miss the others, and I'm fearful of what's to come next. We're safe, and we all survived, and I should be celebrating that, but instead it's like I have a weight in my chest, and it's dragging me under.

All I can think about is all the secrets we're keeping and what will happen if we're caught out on our lies.

A hospital orderly comes and takes away the tray.

I lie on my side and stare at the wall, lost in thought. Maybe I doze a little, or perhaps I just reside in that dark place that exists inside me now.

A man in a suit, holding a clipboard, knocks lightly at my hospital room door. I jerk back to wakefulness.

"Miss Flores?" he says. "I wondered if I could ask you some questions."

I'm self-conscious in my hospital gown, and I sit up, pulling the bedsheets closer to my chest. "Oh, yes, the sergeant warned us that we'd be asked a lot of questions."

He smiles warmly at me. "I imagine you're going to get pretty sick of repeating yourself by the time all this is over."

Over? Is it ever going to be over? It doesn't feel that way to me. I'll always carry what I've been through inside me. I'll forever relive it. It's never going to be truly over for me.

Instead of saying what I think, I just give a small smile. "You're probably right."

He gestures at a chair beside the bed. "Do you mind?"

"No, of course not."

He drags it around so it faces my bed and sits down, his right leg crosses over his left.

"Right," he says. "Let's start at the beginning, shall we?"

"Sure."

"Your mother died recently, is that right?"

His question surprises me. I'd expected him to talk about the plane crash, but I guess he needs to get all the background info, too.

"Yes, right before the accident."

"And that's how you found yourself in the care of Reed Riviera?"

I hesitate, still unsure what this has to do with the crash. "Yes."

"How did you feel about that? It can't have been easy, suddenly being dependent on a man who abandoned you when you were only three years old."

"I couldn't really remember him, so it didn't seem like much of a big deal." I find myself bristling, sitting up straighter, my shoulders tensing. "I was just grateful someone was prepared to be there for me. Without him, and my stepbrothers, I'd have been all alone in the world."

"But Reed Riviera was supposed to protect you, to keep you safe, and instead he puts you on a plane that crashes, and you end up lost in the wilderness for more than a month."

"Is there a question in that, Mr....?" I realize he never gave me his name, or even where he's from. "Who did you say you're with again? The airline, or the police, or..."

I let my words fade, waiting for him to fill in the space I leave in the air.

"I simply wanted to ask some questions, Miss Flores. If you don't like this particular subject, we can always move on."

I look around, searching for the emergency cord I know is here. If I pull it, will someone come and help me?

I raise my voice. "You need to leave."

"Really, Miss Flores, or may I call you Laney? There's no need to be like that. I don't mean any harm. I just wanted to talk to you."

I'm such a fucking idiot. This man is clearly a reporter. I don't know how he sneaked in here, but he used my naivety against me. What if I'd said something I shouldn't have?

"I said get out!" I've raised my voice now. "Get out."

Movement comes at the doorway, and suddenly Cade is standing there. His face is a rigid plane of fury. He doesn't even pause long enough to ask what's going on. All he sees is me in distress and a strange man in my room.

He looks almost comical in the hospital gown that hangs down to his knees. He grabs the reporter by the front of his shirt and hauls him out of the chair. The clipboard falls to the floor with a clatter.

Cade lifts him and slams him against the wall. The back of Cade's gown is open, flashing his perfect peach of an ass and the tattoos running down his back. "Who the hell are you, and what the fuck did you say to her?"

"Nothing! I just asked some questions, that's all. I didn't mean any harm."

Cade continues to pin him up, but he turns his head to look at me. "Did he put his hands on you, Laney? Did he hurt you?" He turns his attention back to the man and gives him an extra shove. "Did you touch her, you fucking prick?"

I'm worried this is giving the reporter something else to write about.

"Put him down, Cade. It's okay. He didn't come near me. He was just asking some questions I didn't want to answer."

"I'll go. I'll go," the man says, holding both hands up in surrender. "Jesus Christ. You're fucking insane."

"You haven't seen the half of it," Cade growls, but he lets the reporter go.

The man scurries for the door and vanishes off down the corridor.

I'm shaking, and my heart's going a thousand miles an hour.

Cade shuts the door and comes to sit with me on the side of the bed.

"Are you okay?" he asks.

I want to thank him, but at the same time, I don't want him getting in trouble. That reporter is probably going to write about this now. He'll probably say that Cade is unstable or unhinged or something. Plus, this won't be the last time something like that happens. We're all going to need to get used to a little unwanted attention.

"Yeah, I'm fine, but you can't do that every time a reporter tries to talk to me. You're going to end up with an assault charge."

"You think I fucking care?"

"*I* care. I don't want you to get in trouble because of me."

He shakes his head. "Laney, I'm already in trouble because of you, and it's got nothing to do with the law or any damned reporters."

I want to hug him, to have him wrap his arms around me and hold me until my shaking subsides, but what if the reporter comes back? What if he brings a photographer with him this time and snaps a picture of us like that? Will people be able to see that there's more between us than just sibling love? The possibility terrifies me.

"I don't give a fuck what anyone else thinks," Cade continues. "Let them write their stories. Let them gossip. None of it means anything to me. All I care about is you."

"That's not true. You care about your brother and your dad. Think about what that will do to them—Reed in particular. And what about Darius's career? If the press get wind of our relationship, it could end things for him. People might not want to book him if they think he's involved in some kind of..." I'm not sure how to describe it. "…immoral relationship with his younger stepsister."

I can tell my words have made him think.

I take his hand. It's so big compared to mine, though it's not like I even have particularly small hands. My nails are ragged, and what remains of them has dirt embedded deep.

I lean into him. He smells so good. I don't think any of us realized what we actually smelled like back at the cabin, but now we smell of soap and shampoo, I can tell the difference.

"I want to protect you, Laney." He shakes his head and glances away. "I didn't before, and I hate myself for it."

I squeeze his hand. "It's not that you didn't—you *couldn't*. Those are two completely different things. You were unconscious, Cade. What were you supposed to do?"

"It doesn't change what happened."

I let out a sigh and close my eyes. I'm suddenly exhausted. "I don't want to go over this again," I tell him. "I can't. I don't have it in me."

He leans in and kisses my forehead, and a well of tears tightens my throat.

A flash of red catches my attention, and I jerk back. I turn Cade's arm to see the inside of it. Blood runs from the inside crease of his elbow, and I realize he must have yanked his drip out when he heard me shouting. He really is a little bit crazy, at least when it comes to me.

I gasp. "You're hurt."

"I tore out my drip. It's fine."

"Jesus, Cade."

He shrugs like it's no big deal.

"Out of all of us, you need the most medical attention. Go back to your room and call the doctor back to redo your drip. You won't be any good to me or anyone else if you end up unconscious again."

"I'm not going to end up unconscious," he insists. "I'm fine."

"Have they even done a CT scan yet? If they haven't, and you haven't had the all-clear, then you don't know you're fine. Go back to bed, Cade." I'm angry at him now, and angry at myself, too.

It's like we need each other so much, we're happy to hurt ourselves as long as it means the other person stays safe.

He lets go of my hand and gets to his feet. He turns and flashes his butt at me as he goes.

"You know everyone can see your ass," I call after him.

"They can all kiss it, too," he replies and saunters out of the room.

Despite myself, I smile and sink back down into the pillows. I don't think I'll sleep. I'll be too paranoid about another reporter coming back, but my eyelids are heavy, and I can't help myself.

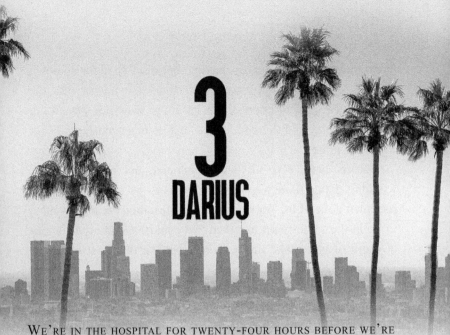

# 3
## DARIUS

WE'RE IN THE HOSPITAL FOR TWENTY-FOUR HOURS BEFORE WE'RE all given the all-clear.

Before I'm allowed to leave, a nurse dresses my wounds and applies ointment and an antihistamine for the insect bites.

I run my fingers over my skin, feeling the bumpy raised flesh. The bugs made a meal out of me, and I bet the others, too. It's strange how quickly I'd grown used to these things. Just one of those bites only a couple of months ago would have driven me crazy, but now I barely noticed them.

My hands feel empty without my violin. I hadn't given it too much thought while we'd been literally fighting for our lives, but now the imminent threat is gone, I'm aching to hold it. Then I remember I'll never get to hold that particular instrument again.

It's lost to me now.

I shouldn't mourn an inanimate object, but a part of me does. That violin has been an extension of me for so long that it feels like losing an arm or a leg. Will a replacement feel the same? Play the same?

The thought of playing brings me instantly to Laney. I want to play for her. I want to encase her in the music, to wrap her in the notes, to carry her along with me. I've never played with the intention of trying to impress anyone before. I've always known I had talent, and simply wanted to share the music with the world. But I want to impress her. I want to wow her. I want her to hear me play and think to herself that no other music will ever live up to mine.

I hate that we've all been separated, but of course they wouldn't expect Laney—a grown woman—to want to stay in a room with one of us. But even back at the cabin, we'd all wanted to be in the same room together. We could have chosen for one or more of us to take the bedroom, but we didn't. It had been important that we were all together.

Except now everything is going to change.

Laney insists that she wants to go home to her trailer, at least for a short while. She has things she needs to sort out, including burying her mother. We all want to be with her, to support her, but she seems to think she needs to do these things on her own.

I don't want her to be on her own. It doesn't feel right to me, but she's an adult now, and I need to respect her wishes. I'm aware the three of us can be imposing, and maybe she feels like she can't think properly around us. I understand. We're all greedy for her, and it must be a lot, especially after what's she's been through.

Because none of us have passports—they were all lost in the crash—we're reliant on the US government to get us replacements. We've been assured this will happen as quickly as possible, and that we'll be on home soil before we know it, but in the meantime, we're being put up at a decent hotel in Ottawa and have been told the expense is on the airline.

Finally, we're discharged from the hospital.

A minivan is waiting to take us to the five-star hotel.

As we leave the hospital, we crowd around Laney, creating a protective barrier against the reporters, but the moment we step outside, they swarm us. They shout questions at us, and I duck my head, glad I'm unable to make eye contact with any of them.

I keep my hand on Cade's shoulder, allowing him to guide me to the transportation.

It's only a fifteen-minute drive to the hotel, and we're greeted from the minivan like we're celebrities.

We've each been given a small suite, complete with a living area, a large bedroom, and bathroom, and a well-stocked mini-bar. It's not as though we have any luggage to have brought up to the rooms, but they're well stocked with toiletries, slippers, and robes. Cade talks me through where everything is, and together we pace the room so I can create a picture of everything in my mind.

We don't intend to stay apart, so once I've got my bearings, we all convene in Reed's suite. Its layout is identical to mine, which makes things easier.

"This place is amazing," Laney says. "I don't think I'm ever going to take running water for granted again. Is it wrong if I want to shower again?"

Cade agrees. "Yeah, and we have a flushing toilet. Who'd have thought a goddamned toilet would feel like a luxury."

"Clean sheets," Laney sighs. "And a new toothbrush, and shampoo, and conditioner."

"Sharp razorblades," Reed joins in.

None of us have shaved yet. It'll feel weird to have smooth skin again. Maybe I'll keep the beard.

Laney sighs, a breathy sound. "Whatever food we want."

Cade snorts. "If I never eat another berry, it'll be too soon."

We all fall quiet as the realization that we're actually safe, and memories of the cabin sweep back over us. It's going to take some serious adjustment to get back to any kind of normality. I can't envision it yet. It feels completely foreign. A part of me feels as though this is all a dream or a hallucination, and any minute I'm going to wake and find myself back there.

The crazy thought that maybe I died when the boat went over the waterfall, and this is all some kind of afterlife, goes through my head. The intrusive thought is powerful, and it catches my breath, my heart thudding against the inside of my ribs. To that way lies madness, and it suddenly feels both dangerous and alluring.

"You okay, Dax?" Reed asks me.

"Yeah, sure."

"You've gone pale."

I shake my head. "Still in shock, I think. None of this feels real."

Is it harder for me because I can't see my surroundings? Would this be easier to accept if I could?

Laney's small, slim hand slips into mine, and she squeezes my fingers. I'm instantly swamped with guilt. How can I feel sorry for myself after she was assaulted and then raped? She's so brave to even still be functioning, to be able to put one foot in front of the other, to wake up in the morning and face a new day. Every time I think about Smith and the others putting their hands on her, I want to rage against the world. I have to fight the urge to lift my face and roar at the sky like some kind of caveman.

I pull her into me, wrapping my arm around her, and kissing the top of her head. She smells different now, of whatever shampoo and body wash she's used. All I want is to touch her.

It's as though she's my place in the world. Like she grounds me. Chases the unnerving thoughts away just by being there.

I never want to let go of her.

I'm grateful to have my brother and father, too. I could have lost them at any moment.

We've all been starved for so long that it will take us some time to get our stomachs back to normal. We're eating small amounts, but often, but even though our stomachs might not be able to handle much, our heads are still greedy as hell. The knowledge of being able to have whatever we want, whenever we want, is like landing in heaven.

None of us want to risk going out to eat. Even heading down

to the hotel's restaurant is too overwhelming. We're at the height of this media storm, and if we step into public, we're bound to be mobbed.

It's strange that I'm hiding away from public attention now. It's something I'm used to, but after being in the wilderness for so long, I've gotten used to the quieter life. Besides, compared to the sort of attention I got as a musician, this is like attention on steroids. I have little doubt that when I get back to work, my concerts will sell out within minutes, and that I'll be able to charge whatever I want.

The thought doesn't bring me any pleasure. It doesn't seem right for my career to have been given a boost after everything, especially after what Laney went through. It's so wrong. I'd happily retire forever if it meant being able to take her pain from her. Such a thing is impossible, however.

One of the reporters already got into Laney's room and asked her questions. It was lucky that Cade overheard her shouting for the guy to leave, or anything could have happened.

"Let's order room service," Reed suggests. "The whole damned menu."

"Yes, that sounds like an excellent plan."

I smile at the excitement in Laney's voice.

"The tab is on the airline," Reed says. "I say we go nuts."

Cade claps once. "Yeah, let's fucking do it. The hospital food was shit."

He's right. It was terrible. The doctors were conscious of not overloading our systems, aware it could make us sick, so they insisted on us having broths to help rehydrate us, before allowing us too many solids. The dreams I'd had of tacos back in the cabin hadn't come to fruition, but now we're away from the watchful eye of the medical staff and can do whatever the hell we want.

We've all got plenty of eating to catch up on.

Reed gets on the phone to order. "Yeah, one of everything,"

he repeats when they've clearly thought they misheard him. "And we'll take a bottle of your most expensive champagne, too."

None of us will have any kind of tolerance for alcohol right now. In addition to not having drunk anything since the crash, when Cade took those miniature bottles from the plane, our bodyweights are definitely on the low side.

Laney is still beside me on the bed, the waft of her shampoo and body wash filling my senses.

"God, you smell incredible," I tell her.

I can't help myself. I catch her around the waist and lift her into my lap. I'm instantly hard. I press her down onto me and grind up against her. She gives a throaty moan of pleasure and circles her hips. Is she wet for me already?

I make a suggestion. "I say we strip Laney naked, lie her on the bed, and eat all the incredible food straight off her body."

"Hey," she protests. "Then when do I get to eat?"

I sweep her hair from her neck and kiss her skin. "How about we dangle grapes into your mouth like they used to with those Greek goddesses?"

She giggles. "Make it French fries and you've got a deal."

"How long do you think the food will be?" Cade asks.

Reed seems to think for a minute. "It'll take some time, especially considering what we've ordered."

"Enough time to make Laney come, then," Cade says.

I join in. "At least once, if not twice."

"I like the sound of that," she replies.

I cup her breast beneath her t-shirt, and her nipple pebbles under the graze of my thumb. I want to bury myself in her, to taste her, feel her, smell her.

She suddenly stiffens and pulls away from me. "We're safe in here, aren't we? No one's going to have put hidden cameras in the room or be spying on us through a window."

"We're multiple stories up," Reed tells her. "No one is looking through the window."

"You're sure?" she checks.

"I'm sure," he echoes.

Her body softens once more, and I pull her t-shirt over her head and cover her breasts with my hands. She lets out a breathy sigh of pleasure. I find my way around her body by the noises she makes, stroking the places where her sighs and moans grow louder. I sense Cade has come closer and then he must be in front of her as her sigh is swallowed by his kiss.

Together, we strip her naked and lay her out on top of the luxurious king-sized bed. The other two give me a moment to run my hands over her, so I can create the perfect image of her in my mind. I start at her face, running my fingers over her brow, down over her eyes, which slip shut beneath my touch, and then trace the shape of her nose. Then I reach her mouth and linger at her lips. She parts them, and her tongue slips out, and I grow even harder as her hot mouth circles one of my fingers and sucks it like she would my cock.

I give a throaty groan and fight the urge to open my pants and ram my cock down her throat. There's time for that later.

She releases my finger, and I continue down, tracing the curves of her breasts, thumbing her hard nipples. I run my hands down her arms, and then trace the dip of her waist. I lower my face to her navel and tongue her belly button, and then kiss the spot between there and her pussy. She spreads her thighs for me, and I keep going down, covering her cunt with my mouth and suckling on her clit. The sounds she's making grow louder, and she lifts her hips, pressing against my face. I would happily die in this moment.

I squeeze her thighs and picture their length and curve in my mind.

Just as I sense she's on the verging of coming, I lift my head.

She's utter perfection, and I tell her so.

"And you're a tease," she tells me, a smile in her voice.

"I could eat you all night," I reply, "but I'm not the only one who wants a taste."

We all want to make her feel good. We live to give her pleasure. It's the least she deserves.

For me, the sound of her laugh is like sunlight. If she's not in the room, it's like the air is starved of oxygen.

"Roll over," Reed instructs. "I need your ass."

I shift over to give them space and slip my hand down the front of my jeans to rub my cock.

Reed's low murmur reaches my ears. "Is this okay, baby-girl? You're not too sore?"

"It feels good, Daddy," she says. "Oh, yes, just like that."

I wonder how he's touched her to make her whimper like that. Is he fingering her asshole? Tonguing it, maybe? My imagination conjures the sight.

The sharpness of a spank fills the air, and Laney cries out. "Oh, God."

"I like to see you wear my handprint, baby-girl. Your ass is so fucking beautiful."

"Oh, fuck, oh, yes."

I grow harder by the second.

A knock comes at the door. It'll be room service, but of course we don't want anyone coming in, especially not right now. Luckily, the suite opens onto the living area, so we're able to shut the bedroom door, hiding Laney from any prying eyes.

"I'll get it," Cade offers.

Laney falls silent for a moment, and I hear Reed get off the bed, and the rustle of a sheet drawn up to cover her naked body.

From the other room come murmured voices, and the thanks from the room service guy as Cade tips him. Then the door closes again. The wheels swoosh against the thick carpet as he brings in the cart, and then the air grows redolent with the aroma of food.

Cade tells me where everything is so I can find it easily. Reed wasn't joking when he said he was going to order the whole menu.

As promised, I hold a French fry to Laney's lips, and she takes a bite.

"Oh, my God, that's so good," she says. "Almost better than sex."

I grin and pick up a chocolate covered strawberry. "How about food *and* sex?"

"Heaven," she sighs and takes a big bite of the strawberry, her lips brushing my fingers.

I lower my face and lick the juice running down her chin.

"My turn," Cade says.

We take turns feeding her like a princess, taking pleasure in everything she eats.

Then we balance sushi across her stomach, slices of juicy mango above her pussy, so the juices run down, and we lap it into our mouths. We place chocolate covered strawberries between her breasts. We dribble yogurt and cream over her nipples and suck it off.

The three of us consume her.

# 4

*Laney*

I HAVE TO HOLD STILL OR THE FOOD WILL TOPPLE FROM MY BODY and end up all over the sheets.

My legs are spread, and Reed places chocolate sauce on my clit and then ducks his head to suck it off. It takes every ounce of self-control not to arch and buck, especially when Cade sucks one of my nipples into his mouth and then lightly bites.

I can safely say I've never experienced anything so decadent.

I love that they still want me, that—in their eyes, at least— I'm not so damaged and broken as to not be desired. I push the memory of Cade's reaction to the news of my assault out of my head. It wars within me—the desperate need for him, and the fear of him hurting me. I can't afford to let anyone else hurt me right now. I don't know if I'm strong enough to take it.

When they've finished with the food, Reed pops the champagne.

"Spread those thighs, baby-girl," he says. "I want to drink this from the finest vessel there is."

Reed climbs back between my legs, and dribbles champagne over my pussy. It's ice cold and fizzy, and a total contrast to the hot, smooth tongue that laps it away.

I'm building higher and higher, teased to the brink. Though they promised me two orgasms before the food even arrived, what they've done instead is bring me to the edge, over and over. Now I'm squirming with desperation to come.

"I want you to fuck me, please," I beg. "Fill me up. Stretch me."

"How about we play a game?" Cade suggests.

"What kind of a game?" I'm not sure I have enough patience for another game.

"Think you can tell which of our cocks is fucking you?"

I repress a smile. "Oh, that kind of game."

If it means getting fucked by all three of them, I'm all in.

He picks up a large white napkin and wraps it around my head, covering my eyes. He ties it at the back. "On all fours. We're going to take turns."

I do as he says, my knees planted wide. I sense them behind me, Reed and Cade most likely focusing on my exposed, swollen pussy. In the darkness of the blindfold, it occurs to me that this must be what sex feels like to Darius.

The weight of someone behind me dips the bed.

A cock eases inside of me, pumps into me once, and then pulls out.

"You're a tease," I gasp, though I'm not sure I know who I'm talking to.

Then pressure at my pussy again, and I'm stretching as a second dick enters me. I let out a whimper. "Oh, fuck."

This time, whoever is inside me takes it super slow. He pushes in deep and holds himself there, while rocking his hips slightly. My pussy clenches around the mystery cock. Who does it belong to? It must be either Dax or Reed, as I'm sure I'd feel the cold metal of Cade's piercing.

Cock number two pulls out, too.

The moment the third cock presses against my pussy, I can

tell it's Cade. I was right about feeling the piercing. But I'm enjoying myself far too much to spoil the game now. There's something filthy and wanton about me being on my hands and knees while three men take me in turns. All I think about is how each one feels inside me, the way they make my toes curl and my eyes slip shut with pleasure.

He pulls out again, leaving me empty and desperate to be filled.

Suddenly, an image jumps into my head. It's no longer Reed, Cade, and Dax behind me, but Smith and his men. The idea that they've done something to the guys, and it's them who've been taking turns penetrating me fills my mind. Though I know such a thing is impossible, it fills me with terror, and I lunge away, yanking the blindfold from my eyes.

Reed reaches for me. "Laney, what's wrong?"

I jerk away. "I'm sorry—"

"Hey, it's okay. It's okay."

"No, I just—"

I can't even bring myself to form the words properly. To my horror, I realize I'm crying.

I've ruined the moment.

"It was too much," Cade says. "Fuck. I'm the one who's sorry. I should never have suggested it."

"It's not your fault. None of it's your fault."

I'm going to leave them with blue balls, but I can't go back to what we were doing. I pick up the sheet and wrap it around my body. I'm shaking all over. Fuck, that was horrible. It was like being propelled back in time.

"It's okay, Laney," Darius says, putting himself away, though it's a struggle with his hard-on. "None of us are ever going to make you do anything you don't want to. You're safe with us. Always."

I sniff and nod. "I know. I love you."

He pulls me in for a hug and kisses the top of my head. "We could all use some sleep, anyway."

I'm pretty sure he's going to go back to his room and jerk off, but I seriously can't blame him.

"There'll always be another time," Cade says.

"I'm sorry I ruined your game."

"Don't be silly." He kisses my mouth. "We love you, no matter what."

The two of them leave the room and go back to their own suites. I curl up on my side on the bed, the sheet covering my body.

"Can I hold you?" Reed asks.

"Yes, please," I reply.

He fits his body into the back of mine, the sheet a barrier between us. His arm is a reassuring weight across my waist.

"Do you think we'd have ended up together if the plane hadn't crashed?" I ask.

"I don't know how to answer that. I can't predict the future… or not future, but an alternate future."

What I want him to say is that of course we would—that we're destined to be together, and he'd have seen and recognized that in me the first moment he saw me.

I can't picture my future at the moment. What's going to become of me?

I'm more lost now than I was in the wilderness.

I don't want them to see that side of me. The side that's pulling me down, that's dragging me into darkness, and whispering sweet nothings to encourage me to stay there. I want them to get on with their lives, to not have to worry about me. I don't want to be a burden.

I can feel myself starting to doze and jerk myself out of it.

"I should go back to my room," I tell him.

I don't want to accidentally fall asleep and have the maid or someone else walk in and catch me here. I reach for my clothes and pull them on.

"Laney, wait." Reed cups my face in his hands. "Are you going to be okay on your own?"

I force a smile. "Of course. I'm a big girl now."

"You can pick up the phone and dial this room any time you need me, okay?"

The only time we've slept apart since the night before we got on the plane was in the hospital. We've always bundled ourselves into the same room. But now with people with smart phones everywhere, it feels unsafe, like we're constantly being spied on.

I offer him a half smile. "Are you sure you're worried about me being on my own, or is it actually that you'll miss me?"

"I will miss you," he says. "The second you walk out of that door, I'll fucking miss you."

"I'll miss you, too," I admit.

He walks me to the door and opens it. As I slip out, he goes to kiss me goodbye, but I'm aware we're in a public corridor, and I yank out of his grip.

He frowns. "Try not to be too paranoid, Laney."

"You were the one who told me off for touching your knee back at the loggers' cabin," I remind him.

I'm still smarting from his rebuke, though I understand the reason behind it. It felt like rejection, and I know I'm insanely sensitive right now, but I can't help it.

"There were others around then. There's no one here but us right now." He gestures down the empty hotel corridor.

"You don't know if there are security cameras," I point out. "Or maybe a member of the paparazzi is hiding somewhere nearby waiting to snap a photo."

He sighs. "Okay, Laney. Point made. I'm sorry."

I appreciate his apology, but I'm still hurt, and, no matter what he says, paranoid.

I slip away, hoping no one has seen me leaving the room. It doesn't matter that he's still my stepfather, that we're allowed to spend time together, especially after what we've all been through. I can't even look at them without feeling as though everyone knows exactly how our relationship changed over the course of the past month.

# 5
## laney

I BOLT UPRIGHT WITH A GASP, YANKING MYSELF FROM THE GRIP of a nightmare where I'd been back at the waterfall and all I could see were the guys' bodies floating face down on the surface of the pool. No matter how hard I tried, I couldn't wade through the water to reach them, and I knew, with every second I wasted, they were all dying, and I'd be completely alone.

When I come fully conscious, I have no idea where I am. The big white bed, the floor length drapes, the thick carpets… then it comes to me. I'm in the hotel in Ottawa. I wonder how long we'll be here before we get to go home.

My heart thumps, and anxiety washes over me.

It isn't only the thought of going home again that's affecting me, it's also the idea of getting back on a plane. Maybe we should refuse, and drive instead, but that'll take days. Besides, I know I need to get over this fear. Darius is bound to need to fly for his work, and I can hardly have a panic attack every time.

Statistically, I believe, flying is far safer than driving, and I doubt there are many people in the world who survive one plane crash only to end up in another. Common sense says that I'm safer now than I've ever been, but convincing my heart of that is something else.

I wonder if the others are awake yet. My stomach gurgles, and I realize I can order room service. I don't, though. The thought of ordering someone to come to my room makes me uneasy. What if they take advantage of me being here alone? What if they're not who they say they are? What if they try to hurt me?

I don't want to be frightened of the world, but I am.

Instead, I make sure the door is locked and the additional latch on, and then I go to the bathroom and take another shower. Hot water pummels my neck and shoulders as I stand there, my head bent, my eyes half-shut. Fragranced steam fills my lungs. I want the water to scald away the layer of my skin Smith and his men touched, and for it to do the same for my insides. I want to be able to step out, reborn and renewed, but that's impossible.

I seem to be missing a lot of time while lost in thought. By the time I step out, the skin of my hands and toes are as wrinkled as an old lady's, and a strange, bloodless white. It instantly pulls me back to both my nightmare and the time after we'd gone over the waterfall. My breath catches, and I struggle to draw another.

Will life be this way from now on? With every tiny thing affecting me like I've been hit by a train?

I manage to dry myself off and dress in the clothes that have been provided—in this case, a pair of black sweatpants, a white t-shirt, and some sneakers. There's underwear, too, which I put on, reluctantly. It's not a style I'd normally choose for myself— too plain and practical, like something someone's mother might wear. One thing I am looking forward to about getting back to the trailer is being able to wear my own clothes again.

A knock comes at the door, and I jump.

"It's me." Reed's voice comes through the wood.

I exhale a shaky breath and hurry over to open it.

I let him in. "Hi."

"You sleep okay?" he asks.

I shrug. "Nightmares."

"I know how you feel."

His reply surprises me. "You have them, too?"

"Sure. I expect Darius and Cade do, too, though Cade would never admit to it."

I let out a sigh. "I just want to go back, you know." I correct myself. "I mean, not back to before you came into my life, but back to the person I was before the crash. I feel like I hardly even know who I am anymore."

My confidence is at an all-time low. I'm wrung out with anxiety. I'd had a hard time growing up with my mom, but being forced to be independent had given me a kind of strength. I wanted that back.

"It's really soon yet, Laney. Be gentle with yourself. Things will get easier."

"I hope so." I turn my thoughts to the brothers. "Are Darius and Cade awake yet?"

"I'm not sure. I came to check on you first. You hungry? Thought we could get some breakfast."

Fresh nerves fizzle through me. "What? In the hotel restaurant?"

"We're going to need to face the public again at some point."

"You just said it was really soon." Panic heightens my tone.

He lifts a hand in a stop sign. "It's okay. We can order room service again. It was only a suggestion."

"Thanks. The thought of sitting in a restaurant and having everyone stare while I'm trying to eat is horrifying."

He smiles, but it's tinged with sadness. "It's something we're all going to need to get used to, though."

"Is it? Maybe I can just live on takeout for the rest of my life. Or I could move into a hotel room and order room service every day. I'll make the airline pay as a result of traumatizing me."

"You don't need to do that. I can cook for you at home."

I jolt at his words. "At home? In the trailer?"

He gives a small, confused laugh. "No, of course not. Why would I cook in the trailer?"

"Because that's where I'm going. I need to go home. I already told you."

"Well, sure, to pick up some stuff, but not to stay for any length of time."

My frustration mounts. "You haven't been listening to me. I need to figure out who I am now. I need some time and space to do that."

I'm definitely not the same person I was before the crash, but I'm also not the same person I was at the cabin. I have to learn how to live with the person I need to be, but right now she's a stranger to me.

"Anyway," I continue, "don't you need to go home, too? Back to Maine."

They have a house in Maine. I know nothing about the place. I've never seen so much as a picture. But I don't expect them to live out of hotels for me.

He stares at me. "No. Are you crazy? You think we'd leave you and go and live thousands of miles away?"

"I…" I hadn't really known what I'd thought. But yeah, I guess that's exactly what I assumed would happen. Darius would get on the road again, make the most of his moment in the spot-light, and he'd need Cade with him.

"Home is wherever you are, baby-girl."

My chest tightens. "You can't all come and live in the trailer. There's nowhere near enough room."

He laughs. "No, but we can rent somewhere nearby. I know you say you want your space, but we're not giving you thou-sands of miles worth of space. I want you to know that we'll be near if you need us. If you need any of us."

The well of tears behind my eyes breaks, and I wipe them away. "Thanks, Daddy."

He pulls me into a hug and kisses the top of my head. "Silly girl. You're family now. We're not going to abandon you."

I appreciate that he's not trying to pressure me into returning to their house in Maine with them, either. I know they're used to being on the road, but they must want some normality, too. Maybe stuff like their own clothes and own bed aren't as important to men.

Reed orders more room service—to my room this time—and Cade and Darius come and join us.

"We're going to need to speak to the cops soon," Reed says. "Is everyone happy about what we're going to say? We have to make sure we all stick to the same story, or at least close enough that it's not going to raise any red flags."

Darius tightens his lips. "We didn't do anything wrong. None of what happened was our fault."

"I know that, but if we don't want there to be any chance of them finding the cabin and rescuing Smith and his men, then we have to make sure they don't find either the cabin or the plane, at least not until after winter. There's no way they'll survive a winter out there with no stores or preparation. We can help the police and search and rescue teams locate the bodies of the pilots and the flight attendant come spring so the families will be able to say their goodbyes. The police aren't going to make this easy for us. They will separate us when they're questioning us, and they'll go over things again and again, trying to trip us up."

"Why?" I ask. "It's not like we're the criminals."

"It's simply how they question people to make sure they're telling the truth." Reed takes a breath. "Remember, we mustn't mention the river. We say we came across it after several days of walking. We don't want them to know the cabin was anywhere near it."

"They're going to ask where our water source came from," Cade says.

Reed thinks for a minute. "There was an old well on the property that was still usable."

I don't like the idea of being questioned, though I know I have no choice. I've never been a good liar. My cheeks always flare red, and I'm always certain I'm going to get called out on it. Guilt wedges inside me that we won't be helping the families to recover the bodies of their loved ones, either, but then I think of Smith and his gang, and my heart races, and I grow short of breath. My fear of them finding us again is far greater than any guilt I might feel.

If they make it back to society, they will find us and kill us, I have no doubt about it. And they'll probably gang rape me first in front of the guys just to prove that they can. We could send the police after them, tell them exactly what had happened, but men like that will have contacts on the outside they'll be able to send after us.

It's safer all round if we do everything we can to ensure they die out there, just like we would have done if we hadn't been able to escape.

Our breakfast arrives, and we fall silent as we feast on pastries and crisp bacon, orange juice and coffee.

A part of me wants to apologize to them all for what happened last night, but I'm also too embarrassed to bring it up again. What if I freak out every time we have sex? I tell myself that's not going to happen. It was the blindfold that flipped me into a dark place, not the men fucking me.

The hotel room phone rings, and we all turn to stare at it. Who could be phoning me here?

"I'll get it." Reed gets to his feet and answers it. "Laney Flores' room."

He listens for a moment, his ear pressed close to the phone, and then nods. "Yes, of course. I understand. We'll be down shortly."

He puts the phone back down and turns to us. "Looks like they're ready and waiting for us downstairs."

"Who are?" I ask.

"The police, the airline, the lawyers."

"Shit," Cade swears.

My stomach tumbles with nerves, and Darius reaches out and takes my hand. "Let's get this over with," he says.

I blow out a breath. I'll feel better once it's done.

Together, we leave the room and catch the elevator down to the first floor.

People in suits are waiting for us in the foyer.

I recognize a couple of them—a woman from the airline called Amanda Greer, and the police sergeant, Moore, who'd met us off the plane. They're all wearing the same strange smiles that I can't read.

We still have a lot of formalities to deal with before we can get our replacement passports and get on a plane home.

I'm pleased all the various authorities have come to us, instead of making us travel to their offices. I guess they figure we've done enough.

They've made use of the hotel's conference rooms to set up in. We're separated, and I'm taken to one of the rooms, where I'm seated in front of a long table that contains a panel of similarly dressed men and woman. The room is windowless, and airless, with patterned mauve carpets and uncomfortable chairs with the same pattern on the seats that's on the floor. There are jugs of water, and practically shot-sized glasses.

One of the suited men clears his throat.

"Miss Flores. My name is Frank Turner. I'm a representative from the company who manufactures the plane you were on. Can I start by saying what a relief it is to learn you survived the crash."

He's careful about how he words things. They won't want to say something that sounds like they admit any kind of responsibility for the crash. The company will try to make the crash out to be pilot error rather than admit to there being any fault with the aircraft itself.

"Thank you," I say, my voice small.

I wish the guys were with me, but I expect they're in identical rooms, going through the same questions.

"I realize this is difficult," he continues, "but can you run me through what happened during the flight? You can start before you even got on the plane. Was there anything unusual you noticed?"

"I—I have no idea what would be considered unusual. I'd never even flown before."

His hands are folded on the table primly. "It doesn't matter how small the detail. Anything that stood out in your mind?"

I don't feel as though he's really listening to me.

I take a shaky breath and twist my hands in my lap. "Honestly, I can't remember much about it. I know that in your mind it's only been a matter of weeks, but to me it feels like a lifetime ago. So much has happened since then."

"I understand that, but I really do need you to try to remember."

I tell him what I recall, about how there was turbulence, and bad weather, and then the pilot announcing equipment failure and needing to make an emergency landing.

The suits all exchange glances and write things down. I doubt the equipment failing is what they were hoping to hear.

I don't care either way. The crash happened; it makes no difference to me who they want to point the finger at. I guess the only reason I care is that I don't want anyone else to have to go through what we did.

They move on to what happened after the crash—the distance we walked, where we found the other half of the plane, discovering the flight attendant's body.

Sometimes, they reword the question so it sounds different,

but it's essentially asking the same thing. I know they're doing it to try to catch us, as though instinctively they know we're not telling the whole truth about something.

Eventually, exhausted and frustrated after repeating myself once more, I lose my temper. "Stop! Just stop. I can't do this anymore."

"We only want to find the plane and the bodies of those poor people," one of the suits says in response. "I'm sure you understand how important that is."

"If it was that easy to find," I say, "you'd have found us before now, wouldn't you? It's hard being lost in a place where everything looks the same. Where all the days seem to blur into one. When you're terrified, and half-starved, and dehydrated, and exhausted. I'd like to see one of you give an accurate description of exactly what directions you took and what distance you'd walked."

I'm aware I sound a little hysterical, but I don't even care.

"You're right, and we're sorry. Perhaps it's time for a break?"

I put my head in my hands. "I just want to go home. Why is that so hard to understand? I want to go home and sleep in my own bed. I want to bury my mom. I want to say goodbye to her."

I'm half expecting Cade to launch himself into the room and demand to know who's upsetting me, but he's dealing with his own assholes.

"It's okay, Miss Flores. I think we've got enough for today."

For today. It means they're not done. There will still be more lawyers and police officers and people from the airline wanting to ask questions in Los Angeles. Then there will be the reporters to deal with, and just the regular guy on the street who'll recognize us and want to know everything.

They excuse me, but I'm in no way done. I still have people from the airline to speak with, plus police from both the United States and Canada.

I manage to grab a coffee before I have to head into the next session. Cade catches up with me.

"How was it?" he asks.

"Brutal," I reply.

"Yeah, I know what you mean." He takes my hand and squeezes it. "Stay strong, Laney. If you can handle us in the wilderness for a month, you can definitely handle a bunch of overpaid suits."

"Thanks, Cade."

He kisses my cheek, as chastely as possible, and then we're ushered into our next sessions.

The day feels as though it's never going to end. We break briefly for lunch, and then meet with yet more people. I don't understand why they can't see how exhausted I am. My throat is sore from all the talking. I've repeated my story so many times now it almost feels as though that's all it is—a story.

Of course, none of us mention Smith and his men.

By the time the evening arrives, and the interviews have been completed, we're all silent and numb from being made to relive our trauma over and over.

# 6
## REED

A KNOCK COMES AT THE DOOR.

It's the second morning in the hotel. I'm hoping we might get news on our passports today. Yesterday was long and exhausting. It had felt as though the questions would never end. The interviews had taken all day, with breaks only to eat, and we'd all crashed not long after dinner.

I get up from where I've been lying on my back on the bed, arms folded behind my head, still reveling in the softness of a good mattress, and go to answer the door.

On the other side stands the woman representing the airline, Amanda Greer, a fake smile plastered across her heavily made-up face.

"Good morning. I hope you slept well."

"Like a log," I lie.

I actually slept like shit. I'm not used to having Laney and the boys sleeping in separate rooms from me. Every time I'd dropped off, I'd jerked awake again, my heart pounding against my ribs, the feeling that something was very wrong lodged deep inside me.

I wonder if they'd had the same disturbed sleep, and for the same reasons. We're all grown adults, and it would have looked strange for us to have insisted on staying in the same room, but being apart feels wrong, too.

"That's wonderful," she replies, that same saccharine smile not budging. "We actually have a treat arranged for you all this morning."

"What kind of treat?"

I'm automatically suspicious.

"We've organized for the four of you to have use of the hotel's hair salon and spa facilities for the day, and we've also arranged for several local boutiques to bring in their personal shoppers and a range of clothes for you all to try on. Whatever you like is yours—all on the airline, of course. It occurred to us that you don't have…anything."

She's right; we don't. The hotel has provided all the toiletries we need, plus towels and robes, but other than that, we have the clothes we're standing in, which are the same items the loggers donated to us. A new wardrobe sounds great, and I'm sure a decent shave and haircut will make me more human again. I scrub my fingers through the length of my beard. I've never allowed it to grow so long before. I've almost forgotten what my face looks like beneath it.

"When is all this happening?" I ask.

"Whenever you're ready. The whole team is waiting for you."

"Have you told the others yet?"

"Not yet," she says.

"Leave them to me. I'll gather everyone together, and we'll meet you down there."

She clasps her hands together. "Wonderful."

I close the door again, if only to give her time to leave, and then go to Laney's room.

"You okay?" I ask.

"Of course," she replies, but her expression is pinched, and there are dark shadows beneath her eyes. I have to keep reminding myself that just because we're out of the wilderness doesn't mean everything is automatically all right again. Laney —and most likely the rest of us too, but mainly Laney—have been traumatized, and that's going to take time, and an expensive therapist, to get over.

"Did you sleep?"

She shrugs. "A little. The room felt weird. Everything was too loud—the traffic outside and other people moving around the hotel."

"I know what you mean. It's going to take some getting used to." I fill her in on what Amanda told me.

She holds out both arms, displaying the way her t-shirt hangs off her like a cloak.

"I could definitely do with some clothes." Her hands go to her hair, lifting a clump and letting it fall again. "And this is in desperate need of attention."

"You always look beautiful to me," I tell her.

I mean it, too. Every time I look at her, my heart seems to stop. Her beauty doesn't come from fashionable clothes or a good hairstyle. It's purely natural and comes from her heart.

I gather the others together.

Darius and Cade aren't quite so impressed by the idea of a day at the salon, or spa.

"No one's touching my hair," Darius grumbles.

Cade scrubs his chin. "And I'm keeping the beard."

"Do what you want," I tell them both, "but you both definitely need clothes."

They can't argue with that.

Together, we make our way down to the first floor, where we discover a whole team of people waiting for us. We're taken to the salon located on the same floor. The entire place has been dedicated to us. Staff stand around, waiting to get started.

The women and men who work at the salon are all dressed in

identical whites, an emblem of the hotel on the breast of their shirts. We're each handed over to a different hairdresser.

Laney shoots me a worried look.

"I'll be right here," I reassure her.

Within minutes, I find myself at a sink, in a chair that gives a massage, as my hair is washed several times and then given a conditioning treatment. The hairdresser massages my scalp like it's the place he thinks I'm carrying most of my tension, and I have to admit, it feels good.

Before I know it, I'm whisked in front of a mirror, a fresh gown placed around me, and then the hairdresser is snipping away at my hair. Strands fall to the floor.

The whole time, I'm conscious of where Laney is. She has a female hairdresser who seems to be chatting to her easily. I watch for every smile, each flit of her gaze toward me that signals she might be uneasy. All I want to do is protect her. It's as though I have no other reason to exist on this Earth now.

When my hair is cut and styled, I'm moved to a different part of the salon. Now a Turkish barber soaps my face, and the chair is reclined while he takes a razor blade to my throat. It's unnerving to think he could kill me right now, if he chose to, and I have to question my own mind. Only a matter of a couple of months ago, I'd never have entertained such a thought, but now it feels more than possible. I find myself clenching the arms of the chair, my knuckles white, until he's done, and a hot flannel is placed across my newly bare skin.

I feel half naked without my beard. The skin beneath it is paler than the rest of my face, after being hidden from the sun from all that hair. I do feel more like my old self, though, more in control.

Automatically, I look for Laney again. She's had a cut and a blow out, and her hair is now a silky soft sheet. The sight of her catches my breath, and I know I'm staring, but I can't help it. Cade and Dax equally have their mouths open.

She spots me watching and touches the ends of her hair self-consciously. "Do you like it?"

"You look...incredible." I have to remember that I'm playing the role of her stepfather when others are around. It's not easy when all I want to do is drag my fingers through her newly cut locks and crush my mouth and body to hers.

Cade's jaw hangs. "Well, fuck," is all he can manage.

"Can I touch it?" Darius asks.

"Sure," she replies.

Perversely, I'm almost jealous of my son as he gets to run his hands over her hair, pausing to twirl the ends around his fingers.

"I don't think I've ever touched anything so soft," he says.

She smiles, and I can tell how hard it is for them not to kiss. Everything that's come so naturally between us over the past few weeks now needs to be curtailed, and we're all struggling.

She leaves Darius to come over to me.

"You shaved," she says.

"Technically, I wasn't the one who did it."

Laney places her fingers to my jaw. "I'd forgotten what you looked like without a beard."

I angle my head. "Better or worse?"

"I like both."

We hold each other's gaze. "That's good, then."

Amanda Greer clears her throat, getting our attention. "The boutiques are ready for you now."

The clothes have been brought to us, rather than us trying to fight our way through the reporters and general public and their cell phone cameras.

"Whatever you want is yours," she tells us.

We'll be traveling soon—I hope—so there's no point in selecting more than we can pack to take with us. My style is smarter than either of the boys, and I'm aware that I might need to make a public statement to the press at some point soon. Darius tends to keep his clothes simple, and all in plain colors—

it means he won't accidentally choose something to wear that clashes—whereas Cade is purely casual, all t-shirts and jeans.

I check out what Laney is going for. She's kept it casual, too —jeans, tank tops, sneakers. They've also been subtle about providing her with underwear, and even a swimsuit.

I wonder what the boutiques will get out of this. Will they use it as a promotional opportunity? The stores that dressed Darius Riviera and his family after being rescued from a plane crash? There must be something in it for them, aside from the payment of the clothes, to make them go to all this extra effort.

Laney emerges from the dressing room. Her arms are spread wide, and she does a little twirl. "What do you think?"

She's only in jeans and a top, but she looks beautiful. More like her old self—not that I ever really got the chance to know her before the crash. I remember sending a personal dresser to her room the night we saw Darius perform, all the dresses and heels I'd insisted she wear. Why had I done that? She'd been grieving for her mother, and I'd made her dress up? What the fuck had I been thinking? Now, looking back, I wonder how I could have been so coldhearted. All I'd thought about was the impression others would have of her, how I'd wanted her to fit in. I hadn't wanted others to judge her outfit. I could kick myself for it now. What a selfish prick I'd been. I don't think I'd even asked her what she wanted to do.

"You're perfect," I tell her.

I can tell the boys think the same.

Amanda approaches. "We'll have everything wrapped and sent up to your rooms," she says.

"Thank you. How's it looking as far as us getting home?" I ask. "The hotel is a luxury, but we just want to get on with our lives now."

She ducks her head in a nod. "We're doing everything we can, but you understand that this is an unusual situation, and we have to make sure we have covered all angles."

I continue to press her. "What other angles can there be, other than us getting home? We've spoken to the cops and the lawyers, and everyone else out there, it feels like."

She clears her throat. "There's still the matter of us having not yet located the plane."

I raise my eyebrows. "You can't expect to keep us hostage here until that happens. After all, I assume there were search teams looking for us straight after the plane went down, yet you still didn't find us. Why would you think things are different now?"

"No, no, not at all." She's newly flustered. "We'd just been hoping with your descriptions of your journey to safety that it might help narrow things down. We're under a lot of pressure to locate the plane so we can learn exactly what happened to make it crash, and of course to find the bodies of those still missing so their families can lay them to rest."

"I understand all of that, but you don't need us here. If you have more questions, you can contact us by phone, or send someone to speak to us in person. My family have been through a lot—more than you could ever imagine—and we're ready to go home."

She gives a tight-lipped smile. "Of course, Mr. Riviera. We really are doing everything we can." She clears her throat. "Now that you're all looking and feeling—I hope—more like your old selves, I'd like to gather the four of you in the conference room."

"Okay," I say cautiously. "What's this about?"

"Our lawyers would like to speak with you."

It would probably be sensible to have lawyers of our own, but I can't think about that right now. If it looks like the airline is trying to screw us, I won't hesitate, but for the moment I'm willing to hear them out.

I tell the others, and together we go to the room allocated for us. A long table runs down the middle, identical chairs positioned around it. There are at least thirty chairs, but only three are filled with two men and one woman, all dressed in suits. They rise as we enter.

"Mr. Riviera." One of the men shakes my hand, and then moves on to my sons and stepdaughter. "Cade. Darius. And this must be Miss Flores. I'm Brett Matthews. Take a seat, all of you. Can I get you anything before we get started?"

There's already a jug of water on the table and small glasses set around it. We'd had our fill of coffee that had been brought to us while we were having our hair cut, so we all shake our heads.

The lawyer gives a smile that doesn't quite reach his eyes. "Let me first just say how well you're all looking."

"Thank you," Laney mumbles.

Cade and Darius don't respond. Cade already has his walls back up, defensive. I can tell by the twitching of the muscle in his jaw.

"We've all been talking," the lawyer says, "and we've decided, considering the circumstances, that we'd like to make you an offer for any…inconveniences you may have sustained."

Cade barks laughter. "Inconveniences? You've got to be shitting me? You mean almost dying?"

He clears his throat. "Well, yes. We've come up with a figure we believe will be agreeable to you all."

"Let's hear it," I say.

He continues, "I'm sure, after everything you've been through, that a lengthy court battle where you're made to relive what happened to you isn't what any of you want."

"Let's hear it," I repeat.

"We'd like to offer you all the sum of twelve-point-six million US dollars."

I glance over at the others. Darius's expression is unreadable. Laney's jaw has dropped. Cade's eyebrows lift.

"Between us?" Laney asks.

The lawyer shakes his head. "No. Each."

Her mouth drops farther. "Holy shit."

"Do we need to make a decision right away?" I say.

It's a hell of a lot of money, but I don't want to rush into anything. Cade glares at me, like he's questioning what I'm doing.

"The offer will stand for twenty-four hours," the lawyer replies.

"That's enough time for us."

I stand, and we shake hands again. "I'll be in touch."

We all leave the room.

Laney spins to me and grabs my arms. "Twelve million dollars? And we're thinking about it?"

"I know it seems like a lot of money, but they'll go higher if we push them."

They're fearful of us suing for damages and want to keep us quiet so we don't destroy their reputations, though I imagine they've already taken one hell of a knock as it is, what with the amount of publicity that's surrounded Darius Riviera's disappearance. They'll want to settle higher rather than us going through court. I don't care about the money, but I don't want to go through a court case either. They can tie you up for months, and I don't have the energy for that. I don't have the energy for much at all.

She shakes her head. "It *is* a lot of money. I don't need any more than that. It's enough to let me live more than comfortably. And he's right about not wanting to make this a lengthy court case. I don't want to take the stand and be grilled by lawyers about what happened, especially considering…"

She doesn't need to finish. We all know what she means. Especially considering we haven't told the full story. I know Laney doesn't want the assault and rape to come out. It would kill her to be made to tell a whole courtroom about it.

"What about you, Cade? Darius?"

Darius shrugs. "It's not like we're desperate for the money. All I ever wanted was for us to be safe. I say we take it and put this all behind us."

"Yeah, let's take it," Cade agrees. "It's still a shit load of cash."

"Okay. Let's break the news to them, then. I'm sure they'll be happy to hear it."

Unsurprisingly, the airline lawyers *are* happy to hear the news.

"There's one condition," Reed adds.

I glance at him in surprise. We hadn't discussed a condition.

"Laney gets her portion of the money right away. She needs it more than the rest of us."

"I'm sure that can be arranged," comes the reply, and the men shake on it.

They insist on buying us lunch to celebrate, though with the amount of money we're about to get, we're more than capable of paying for our own.

After we've eaten, we retire to our rooms. After the poor night's sleep, I'm in need of a nap.

Just as I'm dozing off, the phone in my room rings. It's Amanda Greer again.

"Mr. Riviera, I just got word that your new passports have come through, so we've arranged a flight for you back to Los Angeles first thing tomorrow morning. I thought you'd want to know right away."

"That's excellent news, thank you."

Los Angeles isn't home to us, but it's home for Laney, and wherever she is, we'll be.

"Can I ask you to do something for me before you go?" I ask Amanda.

"Of course. Name it."

"We're going to need a short term rental in Los Angeles— somewhere decent—and we all need cell phones, too."

If Laney is going to insist on going back to the trailer, I want to know I can get in touch with her, and she can contact us.

"Consider it done," Amanda replies.

# 1

## *Laney*

WE'RE GOING HOME. PROPERLY HOME.

A flight has been arranged for us—a big commercial plane this time, not like the smaller one that crashed—but I'm still anxious about flying again. We could have driven, but it's thousands of miles and would have taken days. I don't think I'm strong enough yet to handle that amount of time in a car.

Going back home also means leaving the security of the hotel, and that also makes me nervous. People are going to recognize us, and ask questions, and maybe even try to take photos or videos. I'm not used to this kind of attention, though Darius and the others are, maybe to a lesser extent.

I want to hold Reed's hand, but I'm still conscious of how people might interpret our relationship. I know how important it is that no one finds out what happened between the four of us out there. We'll all be judged for it, but Reed worst of all.

We've been given small suitcases in which I've packed everything from the hotel room, including one of the towels, and the robe, and all the toiletries. They're far better than anything I have back in the trailer.

I have to remind myself that I'm not poor anymore. I've never lived a life where I've had money, and old habits are hard to break. After being in the cabin for so long, I can't quite wrap my head around the idea that food is no longer scarce, and I can eat whenever I want. As a child, I'd always been hungry and scavenged for food. It had felt like there was never enough, and I never knew where my next meal was coming from. That had gotten easier as I'd grown up and been able to earn some of my own money, but the hunger I'd experienced at the cabin had thrown me back to those times. Even now, I find myself wrapping a pastry or bread roll in a napkin and slipping it into my pocket or bag.

I don't trust my current position. I know I can be thrown back into starvation and poverty at any minute, and the child in me is always preparing for that.

We leave the hotel together, heads down, and are ushered into a private car with blacked out windows so the numerous paparazzi and curious public can't get a good look at us. It's strange leaving the hotel. It's only been a couple of days, but the place has been a refuge, and leaving means I'm exposed all over again.

"You okay?" Reed asks me.

"You don't have to keep asking me that."

"Yes, I do."

He doesn't do the same with Cade and Dax, though I guess they didn't go through what I did.

At the airport, we're allowed to use a private entrance reserved for celebrities, so we don't have to mix with the general public. I still feel like everyone is staring and talking about us behind their hands. My anxiety causes my heart to beat too fast and I'm lightheaded, my stomach swirling with nerves. I know we can't hide away forever and that we need to figure out a way to get on with our lives, but that doesn't mean this is going to be easy.

We get through passport control and are taken through to

boarding. We have first-class tickets—another luxury I'm unused to—and are boarded first.

On the plane, I sit bolt upright, my back practically glued to the seat, my hands gripping the armrests. It feels like it takes forever for the other passengers to be seated.

Everything about this is throwing me back to the previous and only other flight I've ever been on. The one that almost resulted in our deaths. I'm wishing we'd taken the ground route option. A flight attendant comes around, offering refreshments, but I can barely even look at her, never mind take anything from her. She probably doesn't look anything like the poor woman who lost her life in the crash, but she's wearing the same uniform, and all I can think about is her.

We're finally ready for take-off, and I'm on the verge of running screaming to the door, so I can get off this thing as fast as possible. I'm shaking all over, my palms slick with sweat. I'm worried I'm going to puke in front of all these first-class passengers and make a scene.

"Laney, baby," Reed says. "I know you don't want me to keep asking you, but are you all right?"

"Not really," I whisper.

He stretches out a hand and takes mine. "It's going to be okay. You need to breathe. Take in one breath and count to three, and then blow out to four. You're safe. We're all safe. Nothing bad is going to happen again."

I know the chances of a second plane I'm on going down must be so remote they're not even calculable, but it doesn't stop my brain panicking. I do as Reed instructs, even as the engine roars loudly and the plane picks up speed, forcing me back in my seat.

But I don't puke, and I don't go screaming to the door. I breathe and squeeze Reed's hand, and before I know it, the plane has leveled out and we're cruising. I'm never going to enjoy flying, but the all-encompassing panic that has gripped me finally eases its hold.

"You okay, Laney?" Dax asks.

"Better now. How about you?"

"I don't think I'm ever going to be able to fly without thinking about it," he says.

"What about you, Cade?" I ask his brother.

He doesn't look over at me but stares out of the window. "It's only flying. No big deal."

He might be saying that, but I can tell by the tension in his neck, shoulders, and jaw that he's struggling, too. Sometimes I get caught up in my own pain and trauma and forget about theirs. Maybe I had it worse, but what I went through doesn't make what they experienced less. I know my being hurt also hurt them, but especially Cade. Him being out of action and helpless while I was raped has undermined his sense of self.

We might be physically safe now, but we've all still got our struggles ahead of us.

I manage to zone out for the remainder of the flight. I'm incredibly relieved when we touch down in Los Angeles without incident.

Word must have been leaked about us landing, as there are yet more press waiting for us. One thing Los Angeles has more than its fair share of is the paparazzi.

I'm happy to step out onto U.S. soil, though. There had been a time I'd believed I'd never do it again.

"Let us take you back to the trailer," Reed says.

"Yeah, if you insist on going back to that place," Cade adds gruffly, "the least we can do is make sure you get there safely."

"I can get a cab," I tell them. "I'll be fine."

Darius catches my hand. "Laney, we want to be with you."

I squeeze his fingers. "I know you do, and I want to be with you, too, but right now we have press following us everywhere, and we have to be careful. Besides, this just feels like something

I have to do on my own. I know you won't get it, but I need some time to process everything that's happened."

"And you can't do that with us around?" Darius sounds hurt.

I give a small laugh, trying to ease the tension. "Absolutely not. You're far too much of a distraction."

"A good distraction, I hope," Cade says.

*Most of the time...* I think but don't say. Things still aren't one hundred percent between the two of us, and I know I've been giving him mixed signals, but I still don't know how I feel. This is part of the reason I need space. I can't think clearly with them around. When the sex is so good, it's hard to untangle my thoughts and emotions from the physical. I also use sex as a distraction, and that isn't healthy either, but then neither was what happened the other night. We haven't tried again since, and I'm still worried I might freak out again when we eventually do.

"I've got some stuff to sort out," I reassure him. "My mom died right before the plane crash. There's so much I haven't managed to organize."

"We can help," Reed offers.

"I know, and I appreciate that. I promise I'll ask if I need it."

He doesn't push me, and I love that he is respecting my wishes. He's treating me like the grown woman I am now.

"Don't forget that," he says. "We're in the city, should you need us, and only a phone call or a message away."

The airline provided us all with new cell phones with U.S. SIMs before we left the hotel this morning. So far, I've managed to avoid Googling our names, in case I read something about us online that I don't like. I'm not mentally or emotionally strong enough to handle that yet.

"I know. Thank you."

I want to hug and kiss them, to pull my body to each of theirs, but once more I'm horribly aware of all the eyes that might be on us, how if anything looks like we're more than just family members, it'll be torn apart and overanalyzed. My biggest fear is the truth about the nature of our relationship being exposed.

I know I've created space between myself and them, a physical space I don't want but feel we all need.

"Laney," Reed says, "come here."

I hesitate. "What?"

"If you think you're walking away from me without a hug, you can think again."

I glance nervously at the press and lower my voice to a whisper. "But what about them?"

"We're still family, Laney."

I step into the circle of their arms, so we end up in a kind of group hug, with me in the middle. Tears threaten like an oncoming storm, but I hold them back. If I start to cry, there is no way they'll let me leave on my own.

"I haven't been able to sleep these past few nights knowing you're not in the same room as me," Reed says. "God knows how I'm going to manage when you're not even in the same building."

I manage a smile. "You're a grown man. You'll be fine."

"I'm going to miss you."

"We all will," Darius adds.

"I'll miss you, too, but we can see each other soon."

I untangle myself, pick up my case, and go straight to the cab. I don't look back, worried they'll see the tears in my eyes. I remind myself that this isn't permanent, that we'll be back together soon.

I just need some space to sort my head out.

# 8

*laney*

I STAND OUTSIDE THE TRAILER THAT HAS BEEN MY HOME FOR most of my life.

It doesn't look any different. The bubblegum pink paint my mother used is cracked and peeling in the bright sunlight. The windows are dirtier, the corners strung with cobwebs. I'm relieved none have been broken, though, and the door appears intact. A part of me had been worried I'd return to squatters, and I don't have the energy—emotional, physical, or otherwise—to deal with that.

We always left a key hidden beneath a plant pot, and I pray it's still there, otherwise I'm going to have to figure out a way to break in. The plant itself is long dead, just a dried-out twig in cracked dirt, but I maneuvere the pot and exhale in relief when a glint of silver flashes at me in the sunlight.

"Bingo."

I pick up the key and go to the door. My stomach flips with nerves, and I steady my breath. I'm not sure why I'm so anxious. This is my home.

My mind conjures the morning when my whole world changed, and I picture my mother's body still sitting on the toilet. I know it's crazy—she was taken away more than a month ago, and there's no possibility I'll find her still sitting there—but my heart pounds.

I wish I'd taken the men up on their offer to come with me. Why had I decided I needed to do this on my own? Then I give myself a mental slap. I need to know who I am without them. I have to stand on my own two feet. I'm an adult now. I want to learn how to be a grownup in my own right, to be an equal player, not someone who can't even do a simple thing like returning to her home on her own.

Placing the key in the lock, I turn it and open the door.

A wave of stench smacks me in the face, and I turn away from the trailer and grimace. "Jesus Christ."

It's clear no one has been here to clean the place out. The stink of rotting trash overwhelms my senses, and the air is alive with the buzzing of flies. They're crawling over everything—the windows, the kitchen surfaces, the ceiling. I've grown pretty used to bugs after living in the cabin for so long, but it still freaks me out. The thought of my mother's body enters my head again, and I push it away. The flies are here because of the trash, not because of her.

I almost turn around and get the hell out of there. I'm going to need to bleach every single surface to even begin to make it livable. But then, what the hell else have I got to do?

The phone the airline bought me beeps, and I check the messages. It's Reed.

**<How's it going?>**

I type out a reply. **<Place needs a clean, but otherwise fine.>**

I want to put a kiss, or say 'miss you,' but I'm paranoid. What if a reporter hacks his phone, or he's in public and someone is reading over his shoulder? It's not worth the risk.

The phone beeps again. **<Sure you don't want some help? Many hands and all that?>**

**<I'm good, but thanks.>**

I slip the phone back in my pocket. I can do this. I'm a woman now. I've survived a fucking plane crash and lived in the wilderness. I can clean a goddamned trailer.

The first thing I do is go around opening all the windows to let the flies out and get some air circulating. I've also left the trailer door open as a way for them to escape. I pick up a hand towel and flap it around, trying to drive the flies out.

I open the refrigerator door and almost gag. It's not as though we ever had a huge amount of groceries, but what little we did have has turned to moldy soup. I can't even recognize the fruit or vegetables the sludge might once have been. I check under the sink for some cleaning products and large trash bags. I wish I had a mask to wear, or even a bandana to wrap around my face.

I get to work, tossing stuff out and scrubbing what remains to within an inch of its life. I take out all my anger and grief on the surfaces, cleaning until my back aches and my arms are stiff. I strip what was once my mother's bed, and what will now be mine, and wash the sheets on the hottest setting available. When they're clean, I pin them up outside to dry in the hot sun.

I go back inside and open the small closet. It's still full of Mom's stuff, as is the tiny bathroom. Seeing her belongings brings tears to my eyes, and my throat constricts. She's never going to wear any of it again, and it's definitely not my style—too hippy-dippy for me—but I can't bring myself to get rid of it. Not yet, anyway.

A light knock comes at the door, and my heart lurches. Stupidly, I hope to find Reed, or Darius, or Cade there, but instead it's a guy I vaguely recognize. He's around my age, maybe a couple of years older, casually dressed in a tee and jeans.

"Can I help you?" I'm defensive, but for good reason. "You'd better not be a reporter, because if you are, you can fuck off right now."

The smile falls from his face. "Err...no. I'm your neighbor. I live a couple of rows over. I saw you were back and wondered if you needed a hand."

A neighbor. That's why I recognize him.

"Shit, sorry. I didn't mean to be a bitch."

"It's fine. I get it. You've been through a lot. It's understandable that you'd be paranoid about random guys coming calling on you."

I experience a flash of heat. What does he mean by 'I'd been through a lot'? For a second, I think he's talking about the assault and rape, but then I realize he means the plane crash. It's like my brain directs every incident back toward that event.

"Yeah, thanks. I need to be careful."

He gestures at the trailer. "Is there anything I can help with? Anything you need?"

I don't want to let anyone in. I don't trust anyone, no matter how nice they seem. "No, I'm fine."

He nods at the black trash bags piled up outside the front. "I can get rid of those for you."

I hesitate. While I don't want to accept help, the bags are heavy, and they stink, and they're going to smell even worse if I leave them in the sun for much longer.

"Okay, yeah, that would be good."

He touches his hand to his chest. "I'm Sonny, by the way."

"Laney," I tell him.

He offers me a cute smile. "I know who you are."

He bends to pick up the closest of the trash bags, and then walks away to carry them to the communal trash cans located on the outskirts of the trailer park. Quickly, I back up and shut the door, my heart beating hard. I don't want any attention, especially not from a male.

All I want is to be left alone.

I'm grateful the power and water were never switched off, though I imagine there are some outstanding bills by now. Not that it matters. I have money to pay them, so I'll just add it to the list of jobs I have to do.

*I have to do this*, I remind myself. As much as I want to run back to the comfort and security of the men, I need to learn to be myself again, or at least a new version of myself. Besides, I have to think about how it would look to the outside world if I continued to live with Reed and his sons. I no longer need to be under his guardianship. I don't want anyone to question the nature of the relationship between us. In time, the heat will die down, and the newspapers will move on to something else, but right now it's just too dangerous.

When the sheets are dry, I make up the bed again and climb onto it. I curl up on my side, exhausted, my muscles aching from all the hard work. I've done a good job, though. The trailer is livable now. I don't have anything to eat, but I can order something in, if I want. Right now, though, I don't have much of an appetite. I'd much rather sleep.

Tucked down the side of the bed, between the bed and the side table, a corner of pink knitwear catches my eye. I reach down and take hold of the soft material and pull it out. It's a knitted sweater my mom liked to wear when the evenings grew cooler. I lift it to my face, bury my nose into the material. It still smells of her.

Something inside me cracks. The dam of tears behind my eyes breaks, and I swallow against the painful lump in my throat. A bark of a sob erupts from my throat, and I hold the sweater tighter. My shoulders shake as I cry.

I cry for the loss of my mother, of the loss of any possibility of her ever changing to become the parent I'd so desperately wanted. I cry for myself, for the person I was before the cabin, before the assault. For the way it's changed me and how I feel about my body—how it no longer truly belongs to me. My sense of safety has been torn from me.

And I cry for Reed and Darius and Cade. For missing them, and wishing things were different.

# 9
## REED

THE HOUSE AMANDA GREER HAS RENTED ON OUR BEHALF IS beautiful.

It has five huge bedrooms, each with its own bathroom and walk-in closet attached. The kitchen is a cream marble affair with an island, and out back is a swimming pool.

There's more than enough room for Laney to be here as well.

No matter how hard I try, I can't get my thoughts off of her. What's she doing right now? Is she okay?

She's eighteen years old, and I'm forty, but I can't help myself. I love her. She means everything to me. I know our situation is far from perfect, and that we have to be careful, but a part of me wants to be reckless. I want to say 'fuck it' and let everyone know what kind of relationship we have now. But I can't, and it's not only about protecting my own reputation. They'll hound Laney as well if they find out. People will judge her, maybe even worse than they'll judge me. They'll call her a slut, and every other name under the sun, and it'll be my fault. She's too good for that to happen, too fragile.

She's not fragile like glass; she's fragile like a bomb.

But I'm worried that by exploding, she'll destroy herself.

I've just got off a call from the director of the same concert hall where Darius played the night before the crash. They heard we're back in the city, and they want him to do a return performance. They've cleared space for him, bumped some other performer to make way for him. It's not all altruistic. They know everyone will want a ticket and that they'll sell for hundreds, if not thousands.

Is Darius ready, though? I'm not so sure.

When we arrived at the house, we found a new violin waiting for him as a gift. It's an exact replica of the one that was destroyed at the cabin, but I haven't seen him play a note yet. He's held the instrument, placing it beneath his chin and raising the bow, but he hasn't let the bow touch the strings.

"I'll do it," he says, when I mention the offer to him. "I need to get back out there."

"You sure it's not too soon? It'll be the same set you played before the crash."

"No, I'll be fine. It'll be good for me. Maybe the music will help take my mind off things."

"By things, do you mean Laney?"

He shrugs. "Just everything."

He's withdrawn. Cade is angry—and that's normal for him—but for Darius not to play isn't normal at all. Perhaps he's right, and being on stage again will help him feel more like his old self. I understand how they're feeling—I'm torturing myself about what happened to Laney just as much as they are—but it's not going to help her any if we all allow it to eat us up inside. She's the one who's truly suffered, and we need to make sure we're here for her to help her heal.

"As long as you're sure."

"It's what I do. I play the violin. Who am I if I don't do that?"

I feel like he wants a fight.

"A son. A brother," I tell him.

He turns his chin, as though those things mean nothing. I

want him to know that those are the most important things in his life, that without the people we love, the rest of it becomes immaterial. He's more than just his talent.

He doesn't reply.

"Fine, I'll let them know you're on board."

"Good."

He doesn't need the money. None of us do. We'll all be getting a big enough payout from the airline that we'll most likely never have to worry about working again. I don't care about the money too much, but I'm happy for Laney. It'll set her up for life. I'm worried about Cade, though. He's already proven he can't be trusted with large amounts of cash. What will he do with it all? Will he gamble it away? Drink it away?

It might be his downfall.

"Have you heard from Laney today?" Dax asks. "How's she doing?"

"How do you think? She's not good. She might act like she's got it all together, but she's hurting."

Darius shakes his head. "I don't know why she's insisting on staying at that shithole of a trailer."

I raise my eyebrows. "Don't let her hear you saying that. It was her home for most of her life. She lost her mom right before the crash. She hadn't had time to process that or come to terms with it. Hell, she didn't even get the chance to bury her mom and say a proper goodbye. It might not be what we'd choose to do, but we need to support what she wants. It won't be forever."

His lips thin. "It had better not be. I hate her being someplace else."

Is that all that's wrong with Darius? He's missing Laney. I get that. I miss her, too.

He lets out a sigh. "You ever think it would have been better if we'd all been able to stay in the cabin? If we'd just carried on living our lives that way—living off the land, swimming in the river, not having to worry about anyone else's opinions?"

I shake my head. "That life isn't possible, Dax. Winter was coming in, and we'd never have survived it. We were wasting away as it was. We had no access to medicines. We were lucky to have made it out alive."

"Yeah, I know. I'm just dreaming. Never thought it would be possible to be homesick for a place that was never actually our home."

I give a rueful smile. "Believe it or not, I know exactly what you mean."

"Sometimes I get this strange feeling like the past month wasn't real. That it was a dream—or a nightmare, depending on your opinion."

"It was real, Dax. Trust me, it was more than real. You've spoken to the cops, to the airline, to the lawyers. Do you think they'd be bothering with all of that if it wasn't real?"

He gives his head a slight shake. "Yeah, I know you're right. It's just a sensation I can't shift."

I wonder if him not being able to see is adding to his sense of…what…disconnection?

"Maybe you should speak to a therapist about this?" I suggest.

He huffs air out through his nose. "I'm not speaking to a therapist. I'm fine. It's hardly surprising that I'm feeling a bit disconcerted, is it?"

"No, I suppose not."

I'm still worried about him, though. I'm worried about all of them.

Laney said she wants to learn to find her own way in the world. I want to tell her she doesn't need to, that we'll be right here for her, for as long as she needs. Forever, I hope. But I know there's still tension between her and Cade, and I can't see an end to that right now. Maybe space is what she needs. It's not what I want, though, and neither do my sons.

I wish I could tell the world how I feel about her. I'd stand on the rooftop and yell it at anyone who passed. I don't even care that people know both my sons are in love with her, too. People should know she's ours, that we'll do anything for her—kill for her, if we had to. I want people to know that if they mess with her, then they'll have the three of us to deal with.

What we have together is special. We love her, and she loves us. Why does society feel the need to demean it and turn it into something sordid? Because they will. The first hint that there's anything between us and Laney that traverses what society sees as being improper, and we'll all be skinned alive for it. It won't matter that she's not our blood relation or that nothing happened until she turned eighteen. They'll twist things around to make us look like abusers, and still make Laney out to be a whore. They won't actually care about how she is—it'll all be for the head-lines and the click bait.

# 10
## laney

THE FOLLOWING MORNING, I WAKE EARLY.

There's something I have to deal with, even though the thought of it cuts me to the soul.

I need to reclaim my mother's body and arrange her funeral.

I assume the state will have held on to her body. It's not as though she's an unidentified homeless person who has no known family. She had me, and she had Reed. The authorities know that.

I catch a cab to the coroner's office. It drops me off in front of the imposing red brick building. There's no point in the driver waiting. I have no idea how long this is going to take.

The noise and movement of the city is making my head spin. There's too much, too much of everything. How did I never notice it before? Has the city always been this busy, this noisy? Everyone in a hurry?

Someone on a motorbike zooms past, and I practically leap right out of my sneakers. I'm jostled and knocked by people walking by, and it's almost comical the way I'm practically turned in the wrong direction by the force of everyone around me.

Putting my head down, I hurry toward the building, desperate to get inside and off the street.

The office is air conditioned, and a shocking chill compared to outside. I wrap my arms around myself, partly to keep warm, and partly for comfort.

I've never had to do something like arrange a funeral before. I really have no idea where to start, but I'm hoping someone here will point me in the right direction. There can't be much to it—buy a burial plot in a cemetery, have someone say a few words over her grave. For the first time in my life, I actually have money in the bank, and I want to spend it on her. I want to get her a pretty headstone, too. She wasn't a religious person, but I know she'd like that. Besides, it's partly for me as well. I want somewhere I can go to visit her.

I think she'll be a better listener in death than she ever was in life.

A man in a collared shirt sits behind the counter.

Are people staring at me? I'm horribly self-conscious. Do they recognize me? Are they talking about me behind their hands? I resist the urge to turn and bolt and hide back inside my trailer. I wish I'd taken Reed up on his offer to come, but then it'd be even worse. I'd be worrying that people would be questioning the relationship between us. I'd be conscious of every word spoken, of every glance, of every touch.

"Good morning," the man says. "How can I help you?"

"Hi. I need to reclaim my mother's body."

"What's her name, please?"

I tell him, and he types it into his computer.

He looks up at me. "And your name?"

My cheeks heat. I'm going to have to explain who I am, or he's going to wonder why I'm only just coming in now. I don't want him asking questions about my experience. It feels as though nothing I say will be right.

"Laney Flores. My mom died a little over a month ago."

"A little over a month ago?" he repeats. "I'm afraid we don't hold on to bodies for that long."

His words send a jolt of alarm through me. "What do you mean? Where is she? I want to bury her, to give her a funeral."

"I'm sorry, but the state took care of disposing of her."

"Disposing of her? You make her sound like she was a bag of garbage you had to get rid of!"

He at least has the grace to appear embarrassed. "My apologies. I didn't mean it to come out that way. What people often do in this situation is a memorial service for their loved one."

"I don't want a memorial service. I want a funeral. I want to bury my mom."

"I'm afraid that's simply impossible. In cases like this, when a person has no family—"

"She had family. You knew she had family. I was the one who found her goddamned body and called in the authorities."

He clears his throat. "Well, yes, but your whereabouts were…unknown."

"You mean everyone thought I was dead?"

"Your whereabouts were unknown," he repeats.

"You could have waited. How long did you hold on to her before you decided to give up."

"Two weeks."

"Two weeks?" I bark my dismay. "That's all? I could have easily been found in that time."

"I'm afraid we simply don't have the funds to store bodies indefinitely when we're unable to locate families."

"Indefinitely?" I'm starting to sound like a parrot. "Two weeks can hardly be considered indefinite."

"I'm sorry. There really isn't anything I can say or do that will change anything for you. We do have her ashes stored at the cemetery, and those can be returned for you to scatter. I suggest you consider a memorial so you can say your goodbyes."

I back away, shaking my head. I'm breathless, like someone

is crushing my lungs in their fist. Why hadn't I even considered the possibility of this happening? It simply had never occurred to me. It wasn't as though my mother didn't have any family. She had me. They knew that, and yet they still cremated her.

I don't know why this has hit me so hard. I guess I always thought I'd see her again, get the opportunity to say goodbye. Being handed an urn of ashes isn't how I'd imagined it would happen.

It's only a ten-minute drive between the coroner and the cemetery, so I grab another cab rather than walk it. I enter the building, feeling as though I'm in a daze, and approach the front desk. I explain the situation to the man behind it.

"Do you have some ID?" he asks.

I nod, numb with grief. I'd brought my new passport with me, just in case, so I hand it over.

"Wait over there," he says, nodding to a bank of plastic seats.

Fifteen minutes pass before a woman in her sixties approaches me carrying a large white box, which I assume contains what remains of my mom.

"Miss Flores?" the woman asks.

I get to my feet. "Yes."

She pushes the box into my arms. "I'm sorry for your loss."

The cannister of my mother's ashes is far heavier than I'd anticipated. I don't know what I'd thought—that it would be a little pot I'd be able to sprinkle somewhere—but instead I have to use two hands just to hold it, the weight straining my arm muscles. I can't believe this is what she's been reduced to.

Where am I supposed to sprinkle these? I imagine other daughters would have happy memories of the times they spent with their mothers on the beach or hiking in the hills, but I never had that relationship with her. She never did any of the things regular moms did. If someone asked me what place had been special to her, I'd probably have said the bar, and it's not as though I can go and tip her ashes under her favorite vodka bottle.

I'm instantly hit by a wave of guilt for thinking such a thing. I'm sure I can conjure up somewhere special to do a memorial. Who would come, though? Reed, obviously, though Cade and Darius never even met my mom. Who else was in her life? A string of men who were as messed up as she'd been. I definitely don't intend to track any of them down. After the way they treated her, they don't get to come and act all upset about her death. Besides, I don't even know how to contact any of them outside of hanging around the same bars she did, and with my newfound notoriety, I don't plan on doing that either. We have neighbors here at the trailer park, but I doubt any of them would want to pay their respects. The complaints we got about her late-night parties, and the screaming fights that followed, were enough to mean they're probably glad she's gone.

I leave the building, grab yet another cab, and take her home with me.

I take her out of the box and place her on the fold-out table. I sit opposite and stare at the urn. My mom wasn't the greatest of parents—I'm sure even she would have admitted to that—but it isn't as though all I have are bad memories. Her mood swings had sometimes been frightening, but when she'd been on a high, she'd been vibrant and alive. She'd seemed to glow from the inside, and anyone who was nearby would notice her. Wherever she went, she drew every eye in the room.

I remember being small and staring up at her, and thinking she was the most beautiful person in the world. But then the light and the happiness would vanish, like a curtain drawn down, and the anger would take over, and the dark moods, and the staying in bed for days at a time.

It kind of reminds me of myself now. I wonder what she went through in her life that I never knew about. How much had she protected me from? I guess I'll never know now.

Fresh tears slip down my cheeks.

It feels as though all I'm doing is crying.

# 11
## CADE

I PRESS MY FINGERS INTO MY TEMPLES, WILLING THE THUDDING in my skull to abate. The x-rays and CT-scans I'd had in the hospital showed no damage to my skull or my brain, but that hasn't stopped the headaches.

I'm relieved, but it also troubles me. If there's nothing physically wrong with me, why was I unconscious for so long, and why am I still in pain now?

Is it possible I'd been unconscious out of choice? What if I'd simply not wanted to face up to what was happening and took the coward's way out instead? The idea makes me want to tear my own brain from my skull. What if there was something I could have done to prevent what happened to Laney, and instead I'd remained buried inside my own body?

I'll never forgive myself.

I haven't told any of the others about the continuing headaches, or the ringing in my ears, or how, sometimes, my vision grows blurry at the edges. What would be the point? The doctors have already said I'm fine, so all it will do is make them worry. I'm the last person I want them fretting over. I don't deserve for them to waste a single thought over me.

I'm telling myself the headaches will fade over time. It's

probably some kind of stress reaction. The drinking doesn't help either, at least not the day after, though initially a few drinks make me feel like I'm halfway normal again. Halfway back to being the Cade I was before the crash—the Cade who didn't give a fuck about women except for them to fill a need. Now I have Laney living rent free in my head, and I can't evict her, no matter what I do. And it's not even about the sex, though I do miss fucking her, and my body craves to be inside her. I'd be happy just to be near her, to have her close. She's the only thing that quiets the thumping in my head and the whirlwind of fury in my chest.

But she doesn't want me. She thinks I'm going to hurt her, and maybe she's right. Perhaps it's better if I do stay away, but fuck, it's hard. Every cell in my body wants to go to her.

I walk into the living room to find Darius on the sofa, his violin between his knees. He looks as though he might have been practicing, but I haven't heard him play a note.

"You're going to play, then?" I ask my brother.

Reed has already set up Darius's big return performance.

"Sure. It's what I do. What's the problem?"

"It just feels too soon."

I'm annoyed with our father for setting the show up for Dax. It's his job to protect Darius, and he should know this isn't right. Darius is in no way ready.

But Darius shrugs as though it's no big deal. "What's the point in waiting?"

"So you can get some fucking practice in?" I suggest, unable to hide the sarcastic note to my voice.

"I don't need practice. I've been playing the violin practically my whole life."

Dax acts cocky, but I know it's just an act. It's his way of building himself up against the world. I know him well enough to know that nothing I say is going to make the slightest bit of difference. Once he's made up his mind, that's it.

I shake my head. "This is bullshit. I'm going out."

I half expect him to ask me where I'm going, but he remains silent, his head bowed over the as yet un-played violin. The instrument is brand new, and I can't believe he's considering stepping out in front of an entire audience of people without putting in some kind of practice first.

Even worse is that our father is letting him.

I briefly consider going to Laney and telling her of my concerns, but Darius would fucking kill me. He'd probably think I was telling tales on him, like when we were kids. Maybe he'd be right.

Deep down, I know if I went to Laney, it wouldn't really have anything to do with Dax. I'd just be using it as an excuse to see her.

I'm desperate to fucking see her.

She's like a drug, and my body is craving a hit.

Since I can't have her, I'll find something else instead. Booze is easy to come by, and now I have plenty of money to buy it. I don't give a shit about the paparazzi or any of that crap. They can photograph me if they want to. I'm not hiding inside this goddamned house.

Without saying another word to either my brother or father, I slam out of the door and head to the nearest bar.

# 12

## laney

BANGING AT MY FRONT DOOR SENDS ME ROCKETING UPRIGHT in bed.

It's late, the world dark outside my bedroom window.

I can't say I'd been sleeping. I'd been dozing at best, my head filled with the promise of the nightmares I knew would come. Each time I started to drop off, my brain had taken me back to the time down on the beach, Axel's body pressed heavily on mine, and I lurched to wakefulness again, my heart hammering.

Now that same hammering is coming from my door. I sit up in bed, the covers pulled around my body. I stare in the direction of the noise.

Who's there?

Instantly, my thoughts jump to Smith and the others. What if they'd made it out of the wilderness and tracked me down, wanting to finish the job? It's not as though I'd have been difficult to find. Our names and faces have been plastered over every newspaper, magazine, and online article across most of the country over these last few days. Smith would have been able to find me easily.

"Laney?" A shout. A man's voice, gruff and deep.

83

I recognize it instantly and let out a breath, my shoulders dropping. It's Cade. What's he doing here?

"Laney, let me in. I know you're in there. I need to see you."

He's shouting loud enough to wake up half the trailer park. I have images of my mother and her stream of boyfriends, how they'd often fight in the middle of the night, loud enough for everyone to overhear what was being said. I don't want to become her. I don't want people to think I'm the same as her.

The only way I'll get Cade to stop shouting is by letting him in.

I hop out of bed and hurry to the front door to unlock it. I have security chains on, too—several of them—and a deadbolt. I purchased them all after returning to the trailer and installed them myself. I gave myself a pat on the back for being able to do that on my own, and not needing to ask a man for help.

All the chains and locks mean it takes me some time to undo everything. On the other side of the door, Cade lifts his fist and bangs again.

"Come on, Laney, open up. I only want to talk."

"Keep it down," I hiss back at him. "I'm going as fast as I can."

Maybe I should tell him to get lost, but the truth is I've missed him. I've missed all of them. I need this time away from them to heal and grow as a person, but that doesn't stop me wanting them. I take some pleasure in Cade being here. It means he's missed me, too. He's been thinking about me as well.

I get the door open and step back to let him in. As well as his huge body, a wave of alcohol fumes enters.

My heart drops. He's drunk, and I'm not sure what drunk Cade is like. Right now, I'm wary of everyone, even him, and that he's been drinking doesn't help to ease my nerves.

"Jesus. Cade," I say, wrinkling my nose. "Did you bring half the bar with you?"

His eyes widen slightly, his gaze sliding past me, as he takes in my trailer. "Why are you living in this dump?"

"Fuck you, Cade. This is my home, remember? We can't all have famous brothers who have a shit load of money so we get to live out of five-star hotel rooms."

He jerks back, lines appearing between his eyebrows in confusion. "What are you talking about? Yes, you do. Darius is your family, too. Besides, we don't come from money either."

"Then stop being so fucking judgmental," I snap. This has gone wrong pretty fucking fast. "What are you doing here, anyway?"

"I had to see you."

"Why?"

My question seems to confuse him further. "Because I love you. Because it's killing me being away from you. My whole head is full of you, Laney. There's no room for anything else."

His size dwarfs the inside of my trailer. He's big and tough, and covered in tattoos, but the pain scrawled across his features makes him look younger.

I sigh and cover my face with my hands. "I can't do this, Cade. You've been drinking, and I'm exhausted."

He twists his lips and turns his head. "Darius is going to fuck everything up."

My heart lurches. "What do you mean?"

For one second, the thought that Darius is sleeping with another woman jumps into my head. He wouldn't do that, would he? What if he's been drinking, too? I bet he's been surrounded by female attention since we got back. Why would he stay faithful to me when he has the choice of every other woman in the country? All those perfect hourglass bodies, with their big tits and butts, when I'm practically a stick, especially since the crash. I know I should be feeding myself up now we're back, but, after the initial rush to be able to eat whatever I wanted, I seem to have lost my appetite again. Nothing is appealing, and the thought of actually grocery shopping and cooking feels like too much effort. I can't seem to find it in myself to get out of bed, and instead just lie there, staring at the wall, hour after hour.

"He's going to do a concert, but he's not ready."

I shouldn't be relieved, but I am.

"Is he okay?"

Cade's gaze darkens. "You care about him but don't give a fuck about me."

"That's not true, Cade."

He's draining me, and I don't have the strength for this.

"Yes, it is. I can tell by your reaction. You still haven't forgiven me for what happened back in the forest. But I've forgiven you."

My eyes pop wide. "*You've* forgiven *me*? I hope you're fucking joking right now." I pause and think again. "No, actually, I don't, because even joking about that is totally unacceptable. You don't have to forgive me because I didn't do anything wrong. I was the one who had things done to her, not the person who made it happen."

"Don't twist this, Laney. You know what I'm saying."

My nostrils flare, and I shake my head. "Get the fuck out. I don't want to speak to you, especially not when you're like this."

He squares his shoulders. "I'm not going anywhere. You're mine, Laney."

My vision shimmers through unshed tears. Is this how it's going to be? "Not right now, I'm not."

"Bullshit. We belong together. You know it as well as I do."

"No. I told you to leave." I shove his chest.

He grabs my wrist. "No, and you can't make me."

He's restraining me, taking away my freedom, and it sends me right back to the cabin and those men. Panic grows in my chest, swelling like a balloon until I'm sure it's going to suffocate me. All I know is that I need to be free, and my body goes into pure fight or flight. With nowhere to go, it chooses fight, and I batter at him with my free hand until he finally releases me. I throw myself backward, desperate to put space between us.

"Get out, get out, get out, get out, get out!" I scream at him.

It's all I can do to stop clawing at my hair. My spine curls as I hunch over.

"Laney?" His voice is distant. "Fuck, Laney. I'm sorry. I'm sorry."

I don't want to hear it. I can't hear it. How is this ever going to work? Every time I let myself soften toward him, he fucks up again. He's too damned selfish.

"Get out," I repeat. "Get out."

Still, he hesitates. "I can't. I can't leave you like this."

I can't even look at him.

Finally, he says, "Fuck," and the trailer door slams in his wake.

The neighbors have probably been wondering if they should call the cops, but it's not like it's the first time they've heard a fight coming from this trailer. It would normally be my mom and some random man she'd picked up in a bar, though. Am I becoming like her? Is that going to be my destiny, to live out my days in this place, getting drunk and high, and picking up violent men?

Tears pour down my cheeks. I can't even bring myself to get up off the floor. I have no energy. The tug into darkness is overwhelmingly powerful, and I can't even bring myself to fight it. At least there's peace here—a strange kind of peace, anyway. I'm so lost inside my own head that I don't notice the cold floor or how hard it is. I don't even think about the fact the trailer door is still unlocked, and that I haven't put any of the chains on.

# 13
## laney

I have no idea how long I've been lying on the floor when the door opens again. I jerk upright, gasping. Is it them? Has Smith found me? Maybe it'll be better if he finishes the job and puts me out of my misery. I'm not even sure if I care if he kills me. I only know that I can't go through the sexual violence again.

"Laney?"

It's Reed's voice.

I blink, and his face comes into view. He's crouching beside me, his hand outstretched, but not making contact, as though he's afraid of touching me.

"Reed?" I say, my voice small and distant.

"Cade sent me."

I push myself upright and throw myself at him, a sob building in my chest.

"Oh, baby. Come here. Are you okay?"

"Why does Cade keep blaming me?" I cry. "How can he not see how much it hurts me? It's like he thinks I wanted to be raped. Like I wanted that gun inside me. Like I wanted another man's mouth on me." *Like I wanted to come with someone else...*

He rocks me back and forth, and I cry against his chest.

"Come home with me," he says. "You shouldn't be by yourself."

"I can't. People will ask questions."

I realize he's come to the trailer, that someone might have seen him.

"You're still my stepdaughter, Laney. You've still been through something traumatic. I'm allowed to help you through that."

But no one else outside of us knows about the rape and the assault. I've kept that to myself. The trauma I've been through, at least to the outside world, is the crash and surviving in the wilderness, but to them, I came out of it just fine. Except I'm not fine, not fine at all.

I create space between us and wipe my eyes. "The only thing that'll make things worse is if people find out about us. I can't stand the thought of the press making you out to be something you're not."

He cups my face in his hands and kisses the top of my head. "You don't need to worry about that."

But I do. I *do* worry about it, just like he should, too.

He brushes my tears away with his thumbs and peppers my face with kisses, gentle, affectionate. I know I should push him away, to stop this going any farther, but I can't bring myself to do it. I need his comfort like a drug. It feels so good having his arms around me, his lips on my skin, the scent of him filling my senses. No one can see us in here. The door is shut, and the blinds and drapes are all closed.

My mouth finds his, and he kisses me deeply and sensuously, our tongues dancing. That spark fires between my legs, and I moan into his mouth, needing him. I pull at the bottom of his t-shirt, wanting contact with his skin. I pull it over the top of his head and throw it to the floor. He does the same to me, whipping off the top I'd worn for bed. I'm not wearing a bra, and he ducks his head to my breasts, sucking on one nipple and then moving to the other. I lace my hands in his thick hair and squeeze my thighs together as the heat builds.

He lifts his face again, then takes my hand and says, "Bed."

I'm not going to argue with him. I'm only in my sleep shorts now, naked from the waist up. He kicks off his shoes on the way, and his hands go to his belt buckle, flicking it undone.

I climb onto the bed and rid myself of my shorts. I'm not wearing any underwear, so I'm now completely naked.

"Fuck, Laney. You're so beautiful."

His gaze rakes across my skin, and I find myself pushing out my tits and sucking in my stomach, wanting him to admire me.

Standing at the end of the bed, he shoves his pants and boxers down his thighs and kicks them away. His cock juts out at a right angle, long and girthy, a slight curve to it. I admire the thickness of his body, the soft hair across his chest, the breadth of his shoulders. He's so solid and real, both physically and emotionally.

"Spread your legs," he tells me.

I do, and he can't take his eyes off me, staring at my pussy. "I wish I'd known the first time we fucked that you were a virgin. I'd have done things so differently."

I bite my lower lip and ask, "How would you have done it differently?"

"I'd have taken my time, that's for sure.

He wraps his hand around his cock and slowly touches himself as he stares down into me. "I'd have licked your sweet virgin pussy, and sucked your clit, and made you as wet and swollen as possible. Then I'd have teased you."

I like this game. "How would you have teased me?"

"I'd have rubbed you with my cock, like this."

He climbs onto the bed to bring himself between my thighs, and, with his hand still around his erection, he places the head between my smooth, wet inner lips. I gasp at the contact and lift my hips, wanting more, but he pulls away. He wants to control the scene, so I force myself to hold still. He uses the head to rub my clit, and then moves down using both our wetness to masturbate with.

"I'd rub you like this," he says, his tone low and growly with lust, "and then I'd push inside you, just the tiniest amount, so we can both feel how good you stretch around me."

He does it, so slowly, and my eyes roll with pleasure.

At least when I'm fucking, I'm not thinking of anything else. It's the one time my brain and heart don't want to crawl out of my body. I'm here, experiencing this. I'm in the present. Maybe I shouldn't want it. Maybe it should remind me too much of what happened, but the two acts feel nothing alike. The body parts might be the same, but the sensations are at complete odds with one another.

Reed continues, "Then I'd pull out again, and pay attention to your clit, building you up, and then I'd push a little deeper."

He does exactly what he describes. I look down, watching the place where our bodies meet. There's something magical about the way he vanishes inside me, at how my body stretches to accommodate him.

"Look at us, baby-girl," he says. "Look at how perfect we are together."

"We are," I gasp. "We're so fucking hot."

Each time he pulls out, he pushes in a little deeper, until finally he sinks his cock deep inside me and holds himself there. His body shadows mine, our faces close. He brushes my hair back and stares into my eyes. I feel him twitch against my inner muscles clamping around him.

"You know this feels like home to me," he says. "Being joined to you like this. Any time I'm not inside you, I miss and crave the connection like nothing else."

"You make me feel safe," I tell him.

He presses his forehead to mine. "I wish I could have kept you safe."

I close my eyes and shake my head. "Don't…"

Slowly, he pushes deeper still. It's as though he's trying to forge us into one being. "I'll take care of you. It's all I want to do. I'll provide for you, and I'll protect you against the world. I swear I will."

He rams himself harder, and I give a breathy yelp.

He kisses my neck, my shoulders. "Just do as I say, be mine."

"I'm yours."

"You need to let Daddy take care of you."

He thrusts his hips, and I moan.

"Say it," he demands.

"You can take care of me, Daddy."

"Good girl. That's my good baby-girl."

He flips us over, so I'm the one on top now.

"Ride me," he commands. "Use my cock to get yourself off."

So I do. I arch my hips and angle my pussy so my clit rubs his shaft.

"Here, let me." He places his thumb over my clit and rubs, slowly at first, but meeting my momentum as I ride him harder.

My ass bounces up and down. I'm getting closer, riding the wave. Words spill from my mouth.

"Oh, yes, Daddy. Oh, fuck, yes."

Right as I'm on the brink, he pushes a finger in my ass. I see stars, and my orgasm explodes over me. I shudder and jolt, and he lets out a strangled groan and jerks inside me.

I fall onto his chest, and he puts his arms around me. Our hearts beat against one another, gradually slowing, together with our breath.

We lie in each other's arms.

"Do you think Cade will ever get over what happened?" I ask.

"He should be the one worrying about you, not the other way around."

I sigh. "In a perfect world, perhaps."

"He's angry, and he doesn't have anywhere to direct that anger, since we left Smith and the others at the cabin. So he's aiming it at you, and himself, and everyone else around him."

I lift my head slightly from his chest to look at him. "I worry about him. I worry about everyone."

He squeezes me. "You don't have to worry about me."

"If people found out about us, things could get very nasty fast."

"We just have to make sure no one finds out."

I realize I haven't even locked the door. Anyone could walk in. I look around, catching sight of the gaps between the drapes. The night beyond. Anyone could be peeping through now, maybe even with a phone camera, recording what we've been doing. What if they posted it on the internet? Reed would be ruined.

I sit up, pulling the covers around myself. "You should probably go."

"What's wrong?" He frowns.

"You can't risk falling asleep here and have someone see you leave in the morning. People will talk."

"Laney..."

"I know, I know. I'm still your stepdaughter, and we're allowed to spend time together, but that should probably be meeting for dinner or going to see a movie, not you being in my bed all night. The trailer only has one real bedroom, and people will talk."

"You don't have to stay here, you know. You can come back to the house."

I shake my head. "And then what would people think?"

"That we're family who are allowed to share a house."

I sigh. "I know, but people will read into it."

"You do whatever is right for you, Laney," he says. "We'll always be here for you, should you need us." He pauses and chews at his lower lip. "Feel free to tell me to get lost, but how would you feel about talking to someone about how you're feeling? I think it might help."

I consider it. "Yeah, maybe, though I'd have to limit what I could say."

"I don't think so. You'd have patient confidentiality."

I grimace. "I'm not sure it counts when someone's been murdered and other people's lives are in danger, no matter what assholes they are."

He kisses my head again. "Just let me do this—for me, as much as it is for you. It'll make me feel like I'm doing something useful."

Maybe it would be good to have someone to talk to outside of Reed and the boys.

# 14
## Laney

I'VE COME TO SEE THE THERAPIST REED HAS ORGANIZED FOR ME.

It's a woman called Sharon Tharp. I'm glad he chose a woman. I don't think I'd have been able to speak to a man.

Sharon is in her forties, at a guess. She's perfected the smart-casual look, in a pair of loose cream pants and a white blouse. Even her jewelry is both understated and expensive.

I feel young and impossibly scruffy in her company. I've slipped off my sneakers and sit with my feet tucked up under me.

We've already gone through what happened during the crash, and the month after in the cabin. I've told her about the terror I'd experienced believing we weren't going to survive, and how I'd thought we were all going to die at various moments during our hike to safety. She's listened intently, asking questions, and nodding at the right times.

The therapist leans forward slightly, her hands wrapped around the knee that's on top of her crossed legs, and offers me a sympathetic smile.

"I've been doing this job a long time now," she says, "almost twenty-five years, and I can tell when someone isn't being fully honest with me. You have secrets, Laney, I can see it in your eyes."

I close the eyes that have betrayed my inner thoughts, trying to hide them from her.

"I don't know what happened to you out there, Laney. I can't pretend I'm not concerned. I've worked with a lot of women who've suffered trauma from abuse, and I've got to say you're showing all the signs. I know you were in that cabin with your stepfather and two stepbrothers…"

I can see exactly where she's going with this. "No! Whatever it is you're thinking, stop it now. Nothing like that happened. They're good men. They'd never hurt me."

She jerks back at the force of my words. Does she think they groomed me? That I'm some victim because of them?

"There's a psychological response called Stockholm syndrome," she says.

My jaw drops. Has she listened to nothing I've said?

"It's not like that!"

She holds up her hand. "Just listen to me, please. It's more common than you think, and many victims of kidnapping or abuse don't see it in themselves either. They believe that how they're feeling is real, that their love for their kidnapper or abuser is as real as any other, when actually it's a coping mechanism to get them through their experience."

"They didn't kidnap me or abuse me."

She tilts her head. "Are you sure about that?"

I grind my teeth. "One hundred percent."

"You understand that everything said in this room is confidential."

I jump to my feet. "They didn't fucking abuse me! I thought you're supposed to be a therapist. Aren't therapists supposed to listen, 'cause it seems to me like you're just creating a whole imaginary situation that never even happened."

The worst thing is that she's also right, just not in the way she thinks. She's right about the abuse, just not the identity of the abusers. I'd always been scared of this happening. By keeping the existence of Smith and his friends a secret, any revelation of the rape I'd suffered would automatically be pinned on my stepbrothers and stepfather. After all, we were alone in the wilderness. Who else could have been responsible?

"Laney, please, take a few deep breaths and sit back down. I never meant to upset you, but burying things you've gone through and refusing to speak about them isn't going to help either."

My reaction probably makes me look even guiltier. But how can I tell her the truth? If she knows we abandoned three men to die, won't she be compelled to do something about it? It doesn't matter what those men have done. We're not the judge, jury, and executioners. We shouldn't be the ones who get to decide if they live or die.

But that's exactly what we've done, and I don't regret it for a second. I want Smith, Axel, and Zeke to be dead. I want them to never be able to hurt another person.

By staying quiet, I might be hurting myself, but I'm protecting the people I love the most.

This was a mistake. I want to walk out, to never come back to another session, but I'm worried about the consequences. If I do, will that make Reed and his sons look even guiltier? Will it break the patient-doctor confidentiality and send the therapist to the cops with her suspicions?

I need to find a way out of this.

Instead, I lie, or at least I tell a half truth. I sit back down and bend my head, unable to look at her in case she sees the misdirection in my eyes.

"I did suffer a sexual assault, but not when you think. Before my mother died, when I was still a child, she had boyfriends. Bad men. They didn't seem to care that I was only thirteen years old. Most of the time, they were drunk or high. I wasn't sure they even realized I wasn't my mother."

She gives me that same sympathetic smile, probably congratulating herself on the breakthrough.

"I'm so sorry, Laney. Thank you for talking about this. Did you ever tell anyone? Did your mother ever know?"

"No, I didn't tell anyone. I didn't have anyone to tell. And no, I don't think she knew, but she was always too out of it to understand what was happening."

"How did it make you feel?"

"Angry, lost, betrayed, hurt. Like my body wasn't my own anymore. Like I wanted to tear off my own skin and crawl out of myself." Now I'm not lying. It's exactly how I feel. "I keep wanting to somehow turn back the clock and go back to the person I was before. It's like I don't understand how that isn't possible, even though I know it's not." I cover my face with my hands. "I know that sounds nuts."

"It doesn't. Not at all."

"I'm angry, too. Angry that—" I catch myself. I'd almost said 'they' instead of 'she.' "Angry that she didn't stop it, even though I know she was incapable. Now she's dead, and I don't want to still be angry at her."

Sharon angles her head to one side. "Sometimes anger can be a necessary emotion. Your mother was the person who was supposed to protect you, and she failed. In fact, she didn't only not protect you, she brought the person who assaulted you into your life. But she's gone, and you have no one to aim that anger toward, so instead you're letting it eat you up inside."

"It feels like everything is eating me up inside. Like I'm a hollow shell of a person, walking around, trying to look like I'm still whole."

"You won't always feel that way. You will heal."

I wonder if I'll stand a chance of healing before that thing eating me up makes me vanish for good.

I glance down at my hands and note how my nails are chewed right down to the beds. The skin around them is a combination of raw and dry, and they're like an outward sign of my tortured interior. I shove them between my thighs, out of view, though I'm sure they've already been noticed.

I don't tell her that I've still got my mother's ashes sitting in the trailer, and that I have no idea what I'm going to do with them.

She watches me, and I can tell she knows that, despite my revelation, I'm still holding back. She lets out a sigh, as though I'm disappointing her. I cringe inside. Why should I even care about that? I'm paying her—well, Reed is paying her—to help me. I shouldn't feel guilty that I'm not living up to her expectations.

"I have a suggestion," she says. "If there are things you don't think you can tell me, how would you feel about writing them down? If you used a password protected document on a computer, so you know no one else can read it, you can get out what's inside of you without worrying about anyone else finding out."

"Writing it down?" Immediately, all my self-doubt floods back to me. "I'm not exactly a good writer. I never even finished school, and when I was there, I didn't pay much attention." I was too busy being hungry, or trying to ignore the kids who were laughing at my dirty, too small clothes. "My spelling and grammar aren't exactly great."

She smiles at me. "That doesn't matter. It's only for your eyes, remember? No one else is going to read it, so no one else will judge."

"What's the point of writing something no one else will read?"

"It can be therapeutic. Help you work through the things you don't want to say out loud."

I consider this. Writing down everything feels dangerous. What if someone else comes along and reads it? But then she's right about me being able to lock it behind a password. Besides, who would even want to read it?

I think of the hordes of journalists. Actually, lots of people would. Even with my shitty grammar and spelling, it is one hell of a story, and not only that, it features Darius Riviera.

Maybe I can write what happened but make out like it's fictional. I'll change our names and ages, maybe even change how we get stranded, write it as a boat sinking, and us ending up on a deserted island instead. But the rest of it will be true. I can write about how it felt to lose my mom, to find out about the family I barely knew existed. I can write openly about how our relationship changed over time.

It's not as though I expect anyone to ever read my story, but I'll still feel I can be more open by changing the details. I won't feel the need to censor myself.

It feels like a good compromise, and one I'm safe with.

"Okay," I say slowly, "as long as you promise I won't have to show it to anyone, I think I can work with that."

Her smile widens. "That's wonderful, Laney. I do think it'll help. You might find yourself able to open up more in these sessions, too."

I highly doubt that, but I don't say so.

She glances at the clock on the wall. "That's our time up for today. We can chat some more about things when I see you next."

I nod and get up from the chair.

Will I even book another appointment? I'm not sure. I do feel a little lighter, though, from talking.

I gather my belongings and leave the office.

I realize I don't actually have anything to write on. I have my phone—the one the airline bought me—but it's not going to be convenient to write anything on at length. I need something with a proper keyboard.

For the first time in my life, I have money, so, on my way

home, I go to an Apple store and buy myself a MacBook Air using the card the airline supplied as part of their compensation. It's the most expensive item I've ever owned by far, and bizarrely I fight against a wave of guilt about the purchase. I don't deserve it.

I get home and shut and lock the door behind me, fearful that someone will have spotted me with the expensive box and want to steal it. I place it on the fold-down table and unbox it, lifting the machine from inside. I stroke the silver casing and carefully open the screen.

It's a thing of beauty.

I spend some time getting the MacBook set up and finding some software I'm comfortable to write with.

"Where do I start?" I say to myself.

The answer comes to me right away. The beginning. The moment in my life where everything changed—the day I came home to find my mom dead on the toilet.

I open a new document, the page completely blank, and start to type.

# 15
## DARIUS

THE CLAP OF HANDS YANKS ME FROM MY REVERIE.

"Right, we've got a date," my father says. "They're rescheduling some things so you can have your return performance in two days' time."

"Great," I say without feeling. "Is Laney coming?"

"I'm not sure. I haven't asked her."

Laney was my light, and now I'm back to living in darkness. It's not as though she's completely out of reach, but it feels as though we're living a lie. She shouldn't be somewhere that we're not. None of this feels right.

I have my suspicions that the other two have been over to see her. It's not as easy for me, though. I could get a cab, but it feels irresponsible. I wouldn't know who was following me or if anyone was watching me arrive.

I can't bring myself to play either. I'd told her I'd play when we were back in civilization again, and here I am, but I still can't bring myself to do it. I don't think my promise was so much about being back in the city, but more to do with us being home.

Us being safe.

Technically, we are, but I can't seem to get the part of me that's a musician to recognize that.

"Do you think she would come?" I ask.

"Honestly, I don't know. She's got a lot on her plate, and placing her right in the public eye so soon might not be her thing."

The worst part is that I know he's right. Laney would hate it, and I don't even want to put her in that position.

Cade's been drinking again. He thinks we won't notice—or perhaps he simply doesn't care if we do. I'm worried he's in self-destruct mode, but what can I say? I probably am too, just in a different way.

Reed lets out a sigh, and the couch cushions sink as he drops down beside me.

"Come on, Dax. Stop moping around."

I twist slightly to face him.

"How can you be so fucking…normal?" I throw back at him. "Like nothing has happened."

"This isn't easy for me either, but we have to get on with our lives. If we don't, we might as well have died in the cabin."

Sometimes, I wonder if that might have been for the best.

"I'm going to play, aren't I?" I say. "What more do you want from me?"

"I don't want anything from you except to see a little of the man I feel like we've left behind."

"Yeah, well, maybe he's gone for good."

He tuts his tongue against the roof of his mouth. "What do you think Laney would say if she heard you talking like that?"

"I wouldn't know. I haven't seen her in days."

The pause is long enough to be loud.

"Is that what's wrong? You're missing her?"

"Aren't you?" I throw back.

"Sure. We just have to be careful."

Is that guilt I hear in his tone? "You've seen her recently, haven't you?"

He exhales. "Cade went around there. He'd been drinking and he upset her. I just wanted to make sure she was all right."

"Did you fuck her?"

"Seriously, Dax?"

I suddenly understand the phrase about a green-eyed monster. That's exactly how I feel—as though I've suddenly been overtaken by a jealous beast.

I get to my feet, my hands balled into fists. "You did, didn't you? Fucking hell. All this talk about us needing to be careful around her, to prevent the paparazzi making assumptions and writing stories about us, and you go over there and fuck her."

"It wasn't like that. She was upset. Things just…happened."

I snort. "Convenient."

I hear the scrub of his hand over his face, the rasp of stubble.

"Okay," he says, "maybe we do all need to spend some time together. It could help us all."

"As a family, right?" My tone is sarcastic.

"Yeah. As a family."

"Okay, fine."

It feels like scraps, but even scraps of Laney are better than nothing.

I'm still jealous that he got to be with her while I've been trying to stay away, for her sake. I can't think of the concert I'm going to be playing in a couple of days. My head is full of her. Maybe spending some time with her will help, and then I can focus on the violin again.

## 16
### *Laney*

It's been a few days since I picked up my mother's ashes, and they're still sitting in the same spot.

For the life of me, I can't figure out what to do with them.

The rumble of a car engine comes from outside, and, a moment later, someone knocks on my door.

I open it to find Darius, Reed, and Cade all waiting outside for me.

"What are you all doing here?" I ask.

I'm delighted to see them.

"We thought we'd take a day trip," Reed offers.

"A day trip? Where to?"

Already I'm thinking of the paparazzi, of being in public with the three guys, and doing or saying something that might give us away as being involved with each other in a way that isn't considered moral.

"Down the coast. Let's get away from the city for a while."

It sounds like exactly what I need, but I still hesitate. "I'm not sure."

He offers me a half smile. "Come on, Laney. We can't hide away for the rest of our lives. It's not right."

"Isn't it?"

"No. You're young, and beautiful, and should be shown off to the world."

I give a strange little hiccup that's somewhere between a laugh and a sob. "I don't feel either of those things."

How can I have such an old heart and head inside such a young body? Eighteen years. It doesn't sound like much, but I've been through more in that time than some people do who live to be eighty. I can't imagine how that must be, just to be able to live out your years in peace. My chest aches for the life I'll never get to live.

"Well, you should," he insists. "Let us take you out. Nowhere too busy. A restaurant on the beach, so we can look out over the ocean. Remember all those times we pined about food when we were in the cabin, but now we're back, it's like we're taking it for granted again."

"People will see us," I say. "They'll recognize us."

He shrugs. "So let them. We're not doing anything wrong. We're only eating a meal, Laney. Spending time together, as a family."

My heart flutters. I love the thought of being able to spend time with them like that. It feels so normal, so…wholesome. Just us as a family, eating dinner in front of the ocean.

"Okay," I agree. "But there's something else I need to do, too."

"What's that?"

"Spread my mom's ashes. Is that weird? I just don't know what to do with them."

"Of course. If that's what you want."

It is.

"What shall I wear?" I ask.

"Whatever you want."

I appreciate that he's not trying to strongarm me into dressing up. It's not as though I have many clothes, anyway, and most of what I do own is old and faded. I don't want to wear what the airline bought me—they still don't feel like they belong to me for some reason. That's okay with me. I want things that'll help me blend in with the background.

I dress in a pair of faded jeans, a sleeveless tee, and push my feet into a pair of sandals. I pull my hair into a high ponytail, slick on a bit of mascara and lip gloss. Finally, I grab a pair of oversized sunglasses. They're not only to shield my eyes from the sun, they're also to give me something to hide behind.

The last thing I pick up is the urn containing my mom. I need to use both hands, and I clutch it to my chest.

Reed has rented a car. I slide into the back with Darius, pressing my thigh to his, and then place the urn down in the footwell, beside my feet and the passenger door. I let out a sigh of happiness and rest my head on his shoulder. He turns slightly and kisses the top of my head. Then he takes my hand, lacing his fingers through mine and squeezing tight.

"I missed you," he says. "So much."

I snuggle in closer. "I missed you, too."

For the first time in forever, something in my chest loosens just a fraction. Maybe this will all be okay.

Reed takes a route out of the city. I'd assumed we'd be going to Venice Beach or maybe the marina, but instead we take the coastal road south.

I watch the scenery go by. None of us feels the need to speak, to fill in any silences. We're all completely comfortable together.

Finally, we arrive.

Reed parks the car, and we all climb out.

The restaurant is set high on the cliff, a bitemark of a white sandy beach far below us. The slow, rhythmical crash of waves on the shore lulls my soul. I breathe in the tang of salt in the air. Seagulls whirl against the blue sky, their mournful cries reaching my ears.

I find myself smiling. "This is beautiful. I don't know how I've never come here before."

"Describe it to me," Darius says.

So I do, leaving nothing out.

The restaurant is more of a shack than an actual building. Food is being grilled outdoors, the fish and chicken charring over the coals. The tables are all set in the open air, too.

I find myself laughing. "This is nothing like I was expecting," I tell Reed.

"What were you expecting?"

"Somewhere a little more…formal."

"It's good to see you smile," he says.

"It's good to have a reason to smile."

We're ushered over to a table and handed menus that are just pieces of laminated cardstock.

I choose a Portuguese chicken, fries, and slaw, and order an iced tea. Darius gets the same as me, while Cade orders the burger, and Reed goes for the steak.

There's a gaggle of girls, all in their twenties, sporting barely there bikini tops and tiny denim shorts. I feel completely over-dressed compared to them. Their laughter penetrates our conversation, and I'm finding it impossible to ignore them.

Our food arrives. It smells great, but once more my appetite has deserted me.

One of the women approaches our table. She leans her butt up against it, a pouty smile on her face.

"Hi, Cade. Hi, Darius. I bet you don't remember me, do you?"

Cade looks disinterested. "Should I?"

She giggles. "Uh, yeah. We spent an interesting night at a hotel a few months ago. The two of you, and just…me."

Darius shifts uncomfortably. Does he recognize her voice?

"I'm so happy you guys are okay. I'd been so worried about you after hearing about the plane crash. I can't believe you went through something like that and survived. It must have been tough out there."

Cade pushes his food around with his fork. "Yeah, it was."

The woman's girlfriends whisper to each other. A couple of them hold up phones and snap photos, or even a short video. My stomach sinks, my appetite fleeing even further. This is exactly what I'd been afraid of—us being recognized.

The beauty of the setting seems to fade.

I need to learn how to deal with this. Reed is right in saying I can't hide away in my trailer for the rest of my life. Darius was famous before this, but now he's practically infamous. I need to expect people to recognize him, and after the sort of press coverage we've had, recognize the rest of us, too.

That doesn't stop me wanting the woman to go away, though.

She carries on, apparently oblivious to the effect she's having on our group. "If you want a repeat performance of that night we spent together, you only have to give me a call. I gave you my number, but I didn't hear from you."

"Maybe that should tell you something," Cade says.

Her lips thin. "You should thank me, you know. All the publicity that's been surrounding you has made people's stories about you worth something. I could get a good payout if I sold my story about how I spent the night with the pair of you. The things you did to me, both of you. You're into some kinky shit. I bet the press would love to hear about it."

I hate the thought of them being with her. It hurts, and I'm filled with jealousy. They didn't even know I existed then, so it's completely irrational, but I can't help myself. I want to be the only woman they've ever touched.

Cade shrugs. "Do what you like. We've got nothing to hide."

She shifts her attention to Reed. "This your daddy? Does he like to get in on the action, too? 'Cause if he did, I'd be game, you know?" She winks at Reed. "Three of you, and I've got three…"

She doesn't fill in her sentence but flicks her gaze up and down her own body, and parts her pretty lips, her tongue sneaking out as though to call attention to one of the places she's inviting them to fuck her.

Reed hardens his jaw. "We're trying to have a family meal. I'd like you to leave now, and take your gaggle of friends with you."

The woman ignores Reed and turns in my direction instead. I'm wondering if she's going to invite me to join the party. Maybe she likes a little girl-on-girl action.

"What about her?" she says. "She the one who went down in the plane with you? Did you go down on anything else, sweetheart? Being lost out there in the wilderness for more than a month with nothing else to do, I bet you had to create your own fun."

Reed gets to his feet, and slams both hands onto the table. "That's my stepdaughter you're talking about. Now, shut your mouth and fuck off."

People are looking. The girl's friends are all laughing and talking about us, taking pictures and videos. My face burns, and I slide farther down in my seat. I want to slide right under the table and vanish.

I get to my feet. "Let's leave."

Reed takes my wrist and tugs me back down with him. "No. We're enjoying our meal. I won't be chased out by a group of women who have no manners."

The owner of the restaurant approaches us, a white napkin wrung between his hands. "Mr. Riviera. Is everything okay?"

"We're being harassed."

"I'll ask them to leave right away."

Cade is staring at me from across the table, but he addresses his father. "I think we should go."

I'm shaking, I can't catch my breath. Behind my dark glasses, tears trickle out and run down my cheeks.

"She *needs* to go," Cade says.

I'm terrified I'm not going to be able to catch my breath. My heart is beating so fast, I think it might just explode. There's a pressure in my head as well. The world seems to have retreated so now I only exist inside this ball of panic my own brain has created.

"Come on, Laney. Let's go back to the car."

Reed throws some money onto the table—probably far more than the bill will actually be. We abandon our half-eaten meals.

In the dark coolness of the car, the air blasting, I finally catch my breath.

"I'm sorry. I ruined everything, didn't I?"

"It's not your fault," Darius says, taking my hand. "We shouldn't have pushed you."

My feet knock against something hard, and I glance down, my heart sinking. My mother's urn is still in the footwell, where I'd placed it when I'd gotten into the car at the trailer.

I'd completely forgotten about my promise to spread her ashes.

# 17

## REED

I DRIVE LANEY HOME.

That didn't go to plan at all. I'm fucking furious at that woman for ruining things, and for her friends for laughing and taking photographs. Will those images pop up online soon? Will she tell her story with it?

Cade and Darius can handle it—after all, they're the ones with that past—but Laney is more vulnerable. I'm worried this experience is going to make her retreat farther into herself.

We arrive back at her trailer, and she climbs out, her mother's urn in her arms.

"Shit," I say, "we forgot to spread her ashes."

Her gaze doesn't meet mine. "Another time. It's not as though she's going anywhere."

I walk her to the door of her trailer. Cade and Dax remain in the car. I wait for her to open the door, and we pause on the step.

"I'm sorry things went to shit," I tell her.

"You don't need to be sorry. It's not your fault."

"You didn't tell me how it went with the therapist the other day."

A hint of a smile touches her lips. "Actually, it went surprisingly well. Thank you for arranging it for me."

"You'll be seeing her again then?"

"Maybe."

I hesitate there, not wanting to leave her. "Laney, why don't you come back with us? To the house. No one is going to bother us there. I know Darius and Cade want you there, too."

"I'm sorry, I can't. Not yet. Not until everything has died down."

I think of something else. "Darius has a performance in the same concert hall as the one we went to. I'm sure he'd love you to be there."

Her face drains of color. "I can't. It's too much."

I touch her upper arm. "It's okay. I thought it would be. I only wanted to ask. I didn't want you to think you hadn't been invited."

I want to make her feel better, and I know I can do that with my mouth, my hands, my cock. But I glance back at the car where Cade and Darius are waiting. There's no way Laney is going to let all three of us into the trailer when it's broad daylight and her neighbors are around, too. Especially not after what that woman implied about how Laney had kept us all busy in the wilderness.

If I go in there with Laney by myself, I doubt Dax will ever speak to me again.

# 18
## laney

I'M STRUGGLING.

It's the day after the shitshow at the restaurant, and I can't seem to get myself out of bed. I debate calling the therapist and asking for an emergency appointment, but I can't even get the strength to do that.

My bladder ends up being the one thing that motivates me enough to slide off the mattress, and I make my way into the bathroom.

I can't walk in here without thinking of my mom, and how it was the last place she ever saw. When I sit on the toilet to relieve myself, I see myself sitting in her ghost, like a shadow or an echo.

I finish up and move to the sink to wash my hands. I open the medicine cabinet—mainly out of a strange kind of apathetic boredom. All her pills are still in there, as are some cheap plastic razors.

Barely even thinking about what I'm doing, I take one down.

I break open the plastic casing around the razor blade. It's harder and more fiddly than I'd anticipated, but I keep going. Finally, I free the sliver of metal and pick it up between my forefinger and thumb. It's cold, a shard of ice, but it quickly warms from my body heat.

Experimentally, I place the sharp side of the blade against my opposite forearm. What will it feel like to cut? Will it hurt? Will it transfer the pain in my heart to an external pain?

I press the blade down. My mouth has run dry, but otherwise I'm calm. The constant undercurrent of panic I've been living with seems to have abated for the moment.

On either side of the metal, pinpricks of blood appear, bright red against the paleness of my skin. It amazes me how quickly the tan I'd acquired while living at the cabin has faded. But then I've been inside almost twenty-four-seven since I've been back in civilization.

I press harder, and the blood droplets swell. It's mesmerizing, and I don't feel any pain. I also haven't thought about all the other shit going on in my life right now. All my focus is on my arm.

The skin parts like petals on a blooming flower. For a second, I glimpse pale flesh beneath before it turns red. Then blood is running down my arm and dripping onto the floor. I stare at it numbly.

Is this why doctors used to do bloodlettings when people got sick hundreds of years ago? Maybe they weren't sick with a physical disease, but a mental or emotional one instead. The release of the blood eased something inside them and made them feel better, if only temporarily. It's a strange thing to suddenly understand, but I feel like I do.

The blood continues to drip. The sight of it against the dirty linoleum brings me back to reality.

"Shit!"

I drop the razor blade into the sink and reach for the toilet paper. Quickly, I gather a ream of it around my fist and press it to the self-inflicted wound. I need it to stop bleeding. What will I do if it doesn't? I don't want to have to take myself to the ER and explain to some doctor what happened. They would probably demand to do a psych report on me.

To my relief, it seems to stop.

I grab a Band-Aid from the cabinet and cover the wound. I swill water around the sink, watching the blood dilute and eventually disappear altogether. I pick up the blade and toss it in the trash and promise myself I'll never do that again.

Then I take myself back to bed, curl up on my side, and go back to staring at the wall.

# 19
*laney*

"Anyone home?"

The male voice calls from the trailer door, and I sit up. How many hours have I wasted just lying here? I have no idea. I've lost track of time, as I seem to do so often these days.

"It's Sonny, from down the way."

What's he doing here? I wipe my face and drag my hand through my knotted hair. I probably look like a disaster, but I can't bring myself to care.

I go to the door and open it. It's bright sunlight outside, but I've had the blinds down and the drapes drawn, so none of it penetrates the trailer. That's not so unusual—it helps to keep the heat out—but that's not the reason I have the place closed up.

"Hi," I say and wait for him to explain what he's doing here.

"Some of us are having a cookout and a few beers. I wondered if you'd like to join us?"

"Oh, thanks, but I'm fine."

"Really? You seem to be here all on your own."

I think of my mother's urn and shrug. "I'm not completely on my own."

"Oh, sorry, you're with someone?"

I glance over my shoulder. "Not exactly."

He catches sight of the urn sitting on the table behind me and pales slightly. "Oh, shit. Is that your mom?"

"Yeah, what remains of her."

"Are you going to do a funeral or something?"

"I don't know yet. I need to scatter her ashes, but I can't think of anywhere special enough to do it."

Under the table of a nearby bar seems most appropriate, but I'm pretty sure the owner won't agree.

"Well, if you need some help…" He leaves the offer hanging in the air.

I bristle at his assumption. "Why would I need help from you? I have people. I have a family."

I've flustered him. "Shit, sorry. Those guys you were in the crash with, right? Your stepfather and stepbrothers? I just haven't seen them round here much."

"I wanted some space. We've been living in close quarters this past month. I needed some time to myself."

Am I destined to be alone? It's how I've always felt. I want to believe what I had with Reed, Cade, and Dax was real, but now we're back, and our old lives are intruding, I'm questioning everything. It doesn't help that our fear of the press finding out has created a barrier between us, emotionally and physically. After being so close for so long, I'm finding it hard. A part of me wants to break, to go running back into their arms, but where would that get us? We'd be watching our backs every second. There are still far too many press around, or even nosy passersby who might decide to take our pictures and sell them to the magazines. My phone rings constantly with offers for me to sell my story. It's all anyone wants to hear—all the gory details of how it was to live out there all this time—but I don't need money, and there's no way I'm speaking to anyone.

The truth will ruin us all.

He shakes his head and glances at the ground, scraping his foot across it. "Shit. You need time to yourself, and here I am trying to get you to come and socialize. Talk about putting my foot in it."

I find myself smiling at his demeanor. "It's fine. You didn't know. And I do appreciate being asked, even if I don't want to go."

He throws me a half-smile. "Maybe I'll keep on asking, then, and one day you'll say yes."

I don't want to lead him on, but it's not like I can tell him I'm already taken. I can't say 'sorry, I can't hang out with you 'cause I'm banging my two stepbrothers and stepfather.'

That night at the hotel feels like a very long time ago, however, even though it's barely been a week. I've had Reed here, but that's it.

I clear my throat. "I'm having a bit of a rough time adjusting, what with my mom, and everything that happened after the crash. I need to be by myself."

He lifts a hand in a wave. "No problem. I get it. If you do change your mind, the offer's always open."

"Thanks, Sonny."

He turns and walks away.

I close the door behind him and turn and press my back to it. Maybe it would be nice to have a 'normal' boyfriend, a regular relationship. To be able to hang out with someone without worrying if you accidentally hold their hand or kiss them in the wrong way.

But I know I can't do it. When you've tasted a five-course meal, cooked by the world's finest chefs, how can you go back to a boring, tasteless burger? Even when you know that five-course meal is going to ruin you, you're always going to dream of it, crave it, fantasize about it.

No one else is ever going to live up.

# 20
# DARIUS

THE EVENING OF THE CONCERT HAS ARRIVED, AND WE'RE ALL backstage.

Well, all of us except Laney.

The familiar rumble of the audience waiting for me to step out on stage is too loud. Shouldn't they have quietened down by now? Everyone is too excited, seeing the newly famous Darius Riviera. Before, I was just a man who played the violin well. Now, I'm the man who survived a plane crash and a month in the wilderness. Is that why these people want to see me? They might not even care about the music.

I feel like a caged animal in the zoo, pacing back and forth, while all the visitors peer in and expect me to perform.

Cade is nearby. I sense the tension radiating from him. I want to snap at him, ask him what the fuck he's got to be nervous about. He's not the one going out there.

I miss my old violin. My new violin feels all wrong in my grip, though it's an exact copy of the one Smith smashed to pieces in the cabin. I can tell it's not the real one, though, and I haven't even been able to bring myself to practice on it. I haven't played in over a month, and yet here I am, about to play for an audience once more.

*This is what I love. This is what I do. This is who I am.*

There's only one person I wish I was playing for, and she's not here. I told her I wouldn't play again until we were back in civilization, back in safety. Now we should be safe, but why don't I feel like I am? My whole body remains primed for flight or fight, as though I'm expecting to come face to face with Smith and his men at any moment.

I know some shrink would say I'm suffering from PTSD, but I feel like a complete fraud even considering that I might be traumatized. I wasn't the one who went through the worst of it. Cade was unconscious for days, Reed almost drowned, and as for Laney…Well, we know what she went through. By comparison, I came out of things unscathed.

I turn my thoughts back to the concert.

Every seat in the house is full, and black-market tickets were being sold online for eyewatering amounts. It all seems crazy to me. I'm exactly the same musician I was before the crash.

Or am I?

I try to conjure up the persona I use onstage. I'm barechested, my long hair hanging free. I assume I must look like the same man, though possibly a little more cut now than I was before because of the weight loss, but I feel completely different. My confidence has all but evaporated.

Earlier, Cade walked me through the stage, making sure I knew the exact dimensions of my surroundings. Normally, once I know the space of a room, I have it committed to mind, but for some reason, I'm struggling to picture it today. When I'm able to conjure an image of the stage in my head, I doubt myself. Is it the same stage Cade showed me around earlier, or have I gotten the picture in my mind mixed up with a different one I've played on?

An orchestra is in the pit in front of the stage. Any minute now, the first notes will be played, my signal to walk out. I'm not used to feeling nervous—I'd normally channel any residing anxiousness into confidence—but this time I am.

"You okay?" Cade asks from beside me, his voice low.

"Yeah, fine," I snap, though my palms have prickled with sweat, and my heart seems to be beating too hard.

"You don't seem fine."

"Leave me the fuck alone, Cade."

"All right, bro. Chill the fuck out."

"You're not the one about to play to hundreds of people, are you?"

I sense him take a step back.

"Okay," he says, "okay."

Maybe this was a bad idea. When Reed came to me saying the concert hall had cleared a night for me to do a comeback concert, Cade had warned me it might be too soon. I'd wanted it, though.

I'd needed it.

How else was I going to stop torturing myself with thoughts of what had happened at the cabin? I couldn't get the thought of those assholes raping Laney out of my head. She'd said Smith had fucked her with a gun. I replay that image over and over, growing more and more furious each time. What if it had gone off? It would have blown her insides out.

The gun isn't even the worst part—at least not for me. A gun is an inanimate object. It isn't hard flesh, and hot skin, and beating blood. That's the thing that eats me up the most. The thought of that filthy bastard, Axel, pushing his cock inside Laney's pussy, touching her skin, putting his mouth on her. And I hate that this is what plays over and over in my mind, that he invaded her most personal and secret place like that, a place that should only ever have been ours.

She was only ever ours, and he took that from us.

It reminds me of Cade's reaction. How he thought of himself. I've always thought of myself as being a better man than Cade.

Maybe that's wrong of me, but he has always been the fuckup. I've bailed him out more times than I can remember.

Now I'm starting to realize the two of us aren't that different. We both want what's ours because her not being ours hurts us. Maybe it's fucking pride, but it makes me feel as though I can't breathe when I think about it.

I wish Laney was here right now. Her being away from us sends my mind spinning. If I could reach out and touch her, I know I'd be able to think again. I remember when I was stranded on the other side of the river, how I'd felt like I couldn't take another step without her by my side. That's how I feel now. I need her here.

Except she's busy, trying to get her own life back on track.

The orchestra is repeating the arrangement I'm supposed to walk out on. I should be making my appearance now, violin held high as I strut on stage.

Cade's hand finds the spot between my shoulder blades, and he gives me a little push. "Get out there, man."

It's all I can do not to turn and swing my bow across his head.

I don't want to do this, but what choice do I have? If I thought I couldn't do it, I should have said no when Reed asked me. It's too late now. Everyone is waiting for me. Hundreds of people, plus all the critics who will no doubt be looking forward to ripping me to shreds in tomorrow's newspaper and magazines and online articles.

I need to give them what they came for.

Sucking in a deep breath, I stride out on stage. My legs are weaker than I'd have liked, but I force them to move. I sense the change in atmosphere as I step into the open. The audience erupts into applause, and I haven't even done anything yet.

I used to love this. It was what I lived for. Why is it that now all I want is to turn and bolt?

I try to picture Laney's face in the crowd. The only way I've ever 'seen' her is through touch, but it's enough for me to create a picture of her in my mind. The long eyelashes, the full lips, her endless limbs and soft skin. But instead of being reassured by the thought of her, all I can focus on is that she's not here. Her absence is like a giant black hole in front of me that draws me in, and I fear I might fall down it.

Will the music help? The orchestra is playing, and I can tell by their hesitation, and the notes they play that they can tell something is wrong. I haven't come in where I'm supposed to and they're having to repeat themselves again. Fuck. I need to do this. The audience has fallen silent, they're waiting, uneasy, growing uncomfortable. I sense Cade in the wings. Reed, too. I should have told Reed it was too soon, that I couldn't do this.

I position the violin under my chin and lift the bow. The first note I play doesn't feel right.

My mind goes blank. My hand stalls. I have no idea what comes next.

The orchestra continues, but I'm no longer playing. Murmurs of confusion rise from the audience.

From the wings, Cade hisses my name. "Dax, what's wrong?"

I take a breath and try to play another note, but it comes out all wrong. It's as though I've completely forgotten how to play. I'm a novice again.

The concert hall feels like it's spinning around me, the stage tilting beneath my feet. I'm suddenly completely disoriented. I need to get off, but I have no idea which way to go to reach the privacy of the wings. I'm terrified that if I take steps in the wrong direction, the stage will vanish and I'll end up in the pit, on top of the orchestra.

Then Reed is by my side. His hand on my back.

"I'm sorry, everyone," he announces. "Darius has been taken unwell."

He guides me offstage. We reach the wings, and I double

over. A hot rush of nausea hits me, cold sweat breaking out across my body. I can't control myself. I vomit onto the floor.

Cade's voice. "Fucking hell."

"I'm sorry, I'm sorry." I've let everyone down.

"Let's get you out of here." Reed's hand is on my shoulder. "Maybe you've picked up a bug or something."

I might be an adult, but I'm grateful to have my father with me now. I cling to his arm as he guides me away from the hundreds of people all wondering what the hell just happened.

I find myself thinking exactly the same thing.

# 21
## CADE

I DON'T KNOW WHAT THE FUCK IS GOING ON WITH DAX.

If I didn't know him better, I'd have said that was a classic case of stage fright. Except I've never seen my brother suffer from stage fright. He's always come to life when he's in front of an audience, like he's somehow bigger, taking up more space.

The man I saw on stage was the exact opposite. He'd withdrawn inside himself, practically vanished before my eyes.

He hasn't wanted to speak to any of us. We're back at the house, and he's gone to his room, slamming the door behind him. It reminds me more of me as a teenager than him.

"What the fuck's going on with him?" I say to Reed.

"Nothing. He's just sick."

"Bullshit. He was fine before he went on."

Had he been, though? I'd noticed he'd gone pale. Was that because he'd been ill but hadn't said anything?

But I know my brother. "I've never seen him act like that before."

Reed scowls. "You're overthinking this, Cade. He's just sick, that's all. Don't make more of this than it needs to be."

I gesture toward the door. "You're fucking joking, right? He just left a whole concert hall of people requesting a refund. You don't think it's going to leave a black mark on his name? Who's going to want to book him when they're risking him walking off stage after barely playing a note?"

"Musicians get sick. People will understand. He's probably run down, which is hardly surprising after what he's survived, and he's picked something up. This was all too soon. I should have known that. It's my fault for giving in to the pressure."

"Darius wanted to get back out there, too." I don't know why I'm trying to make our father feel better. Hadn't I thought the exact same thing when he'd mentioned it the first time?

"Bullshit. I'm his manager. I'm the one who's supposed to make the right decisions for him."

I roll my eyes. I'm the one who watches out for Dax. I'm his big brother. Why the fuck isn't Reed listening to me about this not just being a case of a stomach bug? I was the one who was there for Dax all the years Reed was too busy drinking and womanizing to give a shit about his two young sons. It's pissing me off that he is trying to convince himself that nothing is wrong with Darius when something is clearly very fucking wrong. He's lying to himself.

Deep down, I'm still fucking furious with both him and Dax for letting those men assault Laney, too. I'd been unconscious, but they hadn't. Why hadn't they done more? They should have stopped it, no matter what the consequences. Someone as sweet and brave and beautiful as Laney should never be put through that. Not that anyone deserves it.

"I'm going out," I announce.

"Where?"

"Just out."

"You don't need to walk out whenever we disagree, Cade."

"I can do whatever the fuck I want. I actually have places I can go now. I don't have to be stuck in one room with my family anymore."

There's only one place I want to go, and that's to Laney. She said she wanted some space, but haven't we given that to her already? I hate the tension between us. She's still angry at me, and deep down, I'm still angry with her. I'd still rather have died than her go through what she had. Nothing she ever says will make me change my mind about that. I feel sick that those bastards touched her like that.

No, I'll go to a bar. Have a drink. Maybe I can drown the need to see her.

All the stress has caused my temples to throb again. When I'd been waiting in the wings for Darius to go on, I'd struggled to hear the orchestra over the ringing in my ears.

It doesn't take me long to walk to the nearest bar.

I take up position on a stool and signal the pretty female bartender for a beer and a whisky chaser. She flashes me a flirty smile and passes me my drinks. Only a matter of two months ago, I'd have returned the smile and know I was in for a sure thing. Maybe I'd have even asked her if she had a friend who wanted to join us. Now, however, the pretty face and flirty looks do nothing for me. The only woman I want is the one I can't have.

I knock back the whisky and signal for another. If I can't have Laney, maybe I can drink away my feelings.

A second urge takes me. I could hit the casino. When I'm gambling, I don't think of anything except the win.

A male voice comes from beside me.

"Hey, you're Cade Riviera, aren't you? One of those people who was in that plane crash and survived in the wilderness for a month."

I don't want the attention. "No, you're mistaking me for someone else."

The man barks laughter and claps me on the back. I clench my hand around my beer bottle, holding back the urge to pick it up and smash it around the back of his head.

"You're funny, dude. No one out there looks like you."

It's not often I've wished I looked different, but I do now. All I want is to be left alone to drink myself into oblivion.

The man slides onto the stool beside me and signals to the bartender. "Let me buy you another drink," he says. "What are you having? Whisky?"

I'm torn. I shouldn't drink like this. Bad shit happens when I drink too much. I lose control. I get into fights. I lose the sort of money that would pay off a person's student loans. I'm desperate to go to Laney, but she's asked for space. She wouldn't want to see me.

"Yeah, okay," I relent, accepting the offer. "Make it a double."

He twists to face me, his elbow resting on the bar. "So, what happened to you guys out there? It's incredible you all survived."

I shouldn't talk. I have no idea who this asshole is. He could easily be a reporter and might be recording my every word. The worst part is that I don't even care. Right now, I want to burn the whole world down and take everyone with it.

No, that's not true. I'd hold Laney above the flames, except she would probably tell me to put her down so she could burn.

I tell him about the way the plane went down, the aftermath of it, the realization we were stranded in the middle of nowhere. He hangs on my every word, his jaw open.

I'm partway through how we found the cabin when a voice comes from behind me.

"Well, well, well. It's Cade Riviera."

I lower my head, taking a moment to gather myself before I spin around on the stool. I've already recognized the voice. Maybe a part of me was expecting to hear it—that's why I came to this bar tonight.

The dude I'd been talking to quickly senses trouble. He slides off his stool without another word, grabbing his drink as he goes, and scurries off to find some other source of entertainment.

"I heard you were stupid enough to come back to Los Angeles," the other man continues.

His name is Mateo Cruz. Rumor has it he's connected to the Mexican cartel, but I never got involved with that side of things. He's a man who will happily lend money to idiots like me at crazy interest rates, and if you don't—or can't—pay it back, you'll end up with a bullet in your kneecap, or worse. He's not alone either. He's backed up by two of his men, both as mean-looking as Mateo himself.

These are the same people I'd been hoping to escape the day the plane went down. It had been stupid of me at the time. I see that now, but I'd panicked. I didn't have the kind of money they were after, and I'd known what they'd do to me if they caught up to me.

It seems that moment has arrived, but it's different now. I have what I owe.

I hold my chin high. "I came back because I have no reason to run."

"The fuck you don't," he sneers.

His two men grab me by the arms and haul me off the stool. Mateo shoves me from behind.

What is it with assholes like this? Do they always come in threes?

We're garnering attention from the other people in the bar, but no one steps in or says anything. I understand why. Four big men who clearly look like trouble, who the fuck would want to intervene with that? So many people are armed these days, it only takes a matter of seconds for an incident to turn from a bar fight to a mass shooting, and no one wants to get caught in that.

They haul me outside and down the side of the bar, to the small parking lot situated behind. I wrench my arms out of their grip, but I don't run. There's no point. They'll only catch up with me again.

"I've got your fucking money," I tell Mateo. "I can transfer it right now, if you want."

I have the banking app on my phone. All it will take is five minutes.

"Maybe this isn't just about the money," he says. "You thought you could get away with not paying what you owe. I don't like assholes who think they can get one over on us."

I shake my head. "That isn't what happened."

"Bullshit."

"It's not bullshit," I say, though he's kind of right. "I was in a goddamned plane crash."

I had hoped that going to Canada with Dax was at least going to buy me some time, but I hadn't told Mateo that I was leaving the country. In a way, it had worked, though I hadn't been able to predict what was going to happen.

"We thought you'd pulled some kind of stunt with that plane crash. Good way of never having to pay us back, if we thought you were dead."

"It was no stunt. The plane went down. If I was going to try to stage my own death, I wouldn't take my whole fucking family with me."

Mateo nods slowly. He purses his lips and strokes his chin. "I've seen pictures of your family. You've been all over the newspapers. Never knew you had a sister. She's a hot little thing."

Adrenaline surges up inside me at the mention of Laney. "You leave her the fuck out of this. I already told you that I've got the money now. I'll pay you, and we all go our separate ways. No need for us to ever speak again."

"But it's not just about the money, Cade. It's about you thinking you can get one over on us. I don't like people thinking that."

I brace myself. "I didn't. I had to go for work. It had nothing to do with you."

His eyes narrow to slits. "Do you think I'm stupid?"

"No, but I'm telling the truth." I grind my molars. "Look, do you want your fucking money or not? 'Cause I've got other places to be than standing in the middle of a fucking parking lot."

Mateo jerks his chin. "Go on, then. Transfer the money, and we'll take things from there. You should probably know that the hundred grand has doubled now. It's been more than a month since you were supposed to pay it back."

I could try to argue this, but there's no point. I won't win. It's not as though I don't have the money. I just want these assholes off my back.

I could never have planned for things to happen the way they had, but it worked out, at least as far as the money went. Then I remember what Laney went through, and realize I'd happily give every cent back, and take what's coming to me, if I could erase those moments from her life.

I use my phone and log into the banking app. It makes me jump through a handful of security measures, but within a matter of minutes, the money has been paid.

Mateo checks his phone for the notification of the money going in.

"All done," he says. "I'll admit, I didn't think it was going to happen."

"Well, it has, so I'll be going now."

He holds up a hand. "Just one minute. There's another debt you need to pay."

*What the fuck?*

"You think we're just going to let you walk away from this?"

These men are going to do whatever they want, and there isn't much I can do about it. Fighting back will only make things worse, but my fists are clenched, power surging through my muscles. In their faces, I see the three men from the cabin. The same kind of assholes who think they can hurt an innocent woman and get away with it.

I'm not going to win, and I don't even care. Just the impact of fist upon flesh is enough to give me great satisfaction. I let out a roar and swing almost blindly. My fist connects with Mateo's jaw, but it's three against one. They surround me. I take the blow of a punch in my lower back, right above my kidney, and then another in the gut. As I fold in half, a knee comes up and cracks my jaw.

I find myself on the ground, the asphalt still warm from the day's sun. I have no choice but to curl into a ball, my arms above my head to protect myself the best I can as the kicks and punches keep coming.

# 22

## laney

It's late when my phone rings, Reed's name appearing on screen.

Instantly, I know something is wrong.

I answer the call. "What's happened?"

"Cade's in the hospital."

My heart stops. "What? Why?"

My first thought is that he's had some kind of relapse.

"He's been beaten up. He was found in a parking lot behind a bar."

"Oh, God."

I'm already on my feet, looking for my purse. I wish I had a car. I don't have the patience to wait for an Uber or cab.

Reed seems to read my thoughts. "We're on our way there now. We'll pick you up on the way."

"Okay. I'll see you soon."

I pace anxiously as I wait, my phone clutched in my hand in case they need to contact me again. At this time of night, the roads should be relatively clear, so I hope they won't be long.

*What have you been doing, Cade?* I'm worried this might have something to do with me. The last time he came here drunk,

I sent him away again. I shouldn't have done that. He was reaching out to me, and I rejected him.

It feels like forever has passed when headlights finally appear, and then Reed pulls the car up beside me. Darius is in the passenger seat, so I open the rear door and jump in. I barely have time to pull it shut behind me and do up my seatbelt before Reed is on the move again.

"Has there been any more news?" I ask. "Do we know what happened yet?"

"We don't know," Darius says, twisting slightly in his seat. "All we got was the call to say he'd been taken to the hospital."

I squeeze my eyes shut and shake my head. "If he's not okay..."

Darius takes my hand. "Cade's tough. You know that. I'm sure he'll be fine."

I appreciate him trying to comfort me, but he can't know that. None of us can.

"I just can't believe we're going through this again..." I let my voice trail off.

Reed drives as fast as he can. I know we're all sick with worry.

We reach the hospital. Reed stops the car in a loading bay. We're probably going to get a ticket, but none of us care. We run into the hospital. I still have Dax's hand in mine, and he trusts me to lead the way and warn him of any trip hazards. It's late, but the place is still busy. Reed hurries to reception and gives Cade's name. The receptionist points us in the right direction.

We find Cade's room, and I pull up short, sucking in a breath of shock.

"Oh, God, no."

Seeing him lying in the hospital bed, his face bruised and bloodied, his eyes closed, the skin around them swollen, takes me straight back to the time in the cabin.

Except this time he has medical treatment, something he didn't have before. I grab hold of this tiny bit of hope.

"Tell me," Darius says. "What does he look like?"

My voice cracks as I speak. "Not good. Someone's done a number on him."

"You the family?" a male voice from behind us asks.

A doctor in a white coat holding a clipboard is standing in the corridor.

"Yes," Reed says, "I'm his father. This is his brother and…" he hesitates, and then adds, "his stepsister. How is he? Is he going to be okay?"

"We think so. He was conscious when he came in, barely, but he was able to talk. That's why we knew to call you. We've given him some pretty hefty painkillers, which is why he's sleeping now."

"He's only sleeping?" I check. "He's not unconscious."

"He's sleeping," the doctor repeats, "but that doesn't mean his injuries aren't serious. He has a fractured rib, and he's taken a serious blow to the head, most likely from a kick."

"Who did this to him?" Reed asks.

"I'm afraid we don't know that yet. The police will want to speak to him once he's woken up." The doctor glances over our way and then lowers his voice. "Can I speak to you a minute?" He directs the question at Reed.

"Of course."

The doctor takes Reed to one side, but we can still hear them.

"He can't afford to take any more blows to the head. He got lucky this time, but we could be looking at something called chronic traumatic brain injury, or CTBI, if this happens again."

"What does that mean?" Reed asks.

"It's something we see more commonly in people who do a contact sport, like boxing or football, or in our vets, or people who've suffered from domestic violence. It can manifest in many different ways, depending on the patient. In some, it'll be mild, and they'll only suffer from persistent headaches, memory loss, some slurring of speech, or it might affect their mood. This can get worse as the patient gets older, however. But in others, the effect can be extremely severe. It can change a patient's entire personality, resulting in violent outbursts, and no longer loving the people or things they cared about before the injury. Some lose the ability to speak and walk."

Reed places his hand over his mouth. "My God."

"It really is something to be taken seriously, Mr. Riviera."

"Yes, of course. I understand."

This information makes me sick to my stomach. I want to wrap Cade up in bubble wrap and place him somewhere safe. What was he doing to get beaten up? The possibility I might have had something to do with it refuses to leave my thoughts.

I'll take care of him, no matter what he goes through. We might not be married, but I believe in 'through sickness and health.' We're family.

Reed leaves the doctor to join us again.

"You heard all that?"

Darius and I both nod.

I give voice to my biggest fear. "Do you think it's possible that Smith and the others found Cade?"

Darius shakes his head. "If they had, Cade would be dead now, not just roughed up. Don't forget that Cade had plenty of his own issues even before the plane went down. You learned that for yourself when you found his phone."

"Do you think that's who did this? The same people he'd been hoping to hide out from?"

"Most likely, yeah, or else Cade has been mouthing off in a bar somewhere and someone took a disliking to him. You've seen how angry he's been since we got back. I bet it would only take someone looking at him the wrong way to set him off."

"Cade can handle himself, though," I say.

"Maybe there was more than one of them."

Cade's been angry because of me, at least in part. Things have been so tense between us, and I haven't given him any definite answers as far as what our futures hold. Seeing him like this again, however, has made up my mind.

What would I have done if he'd died? I'd have never forgiven myself for the distance I've put between us. My heart would have shattered, and I'd never have been the same again. Maybe loving Cade—allowing myself to love Cade—will be a risk, and he might well hurt me again. But not having him in my life is unthinkable.

He's worth the risk. Every single second of it.

Tears are streaming down my cheeks again. Darius must hear the hitching of my breath, as he reaches out his hand, takes my fingers in his, and pulls me to his chest. He holds me tight as I cry, easing my pain, though I know this must be just as hard for him. Cade is his brother, and Reed's son, and they witnessed what happened to Cade back at the cabin. They almost lost him, too. Going through it again is difficult for them.

"He's going to be okay," Darius reassures me.

I manage to pull myself together. I don't want to make this about me, because it isn't.

I go to get coffees for us all from a vending machine. They're bad, but they're caffeinated. I know none of us are leaving Cade's side until he's woken up and we know he's going to be okay.

The night passes slowly, and painfully. We all try to doze in the chairs beside his bed, but it's not easy.

By the time hazy morning light filters through the slats in the window blind, my eyes are sore and gritty, my back stiff from trying to sleep in an awkward position, and there's the threat of a headache looming in my temple. All my attention is on Cade, however.

His eyes flutter open. "Laney?"

My heart leaps.

"Hey, you're awake." I take his hand. "Your dad and brother are here, too."

Cade turns his head slightly, and winces. "My head hurts."

"You have a head injury," Reed says. "Another one."

"Fuck."

"Yeah, fuck." Reed's lips thin in disapproval. "What happened, Cade?"

His gaze slips away. "Nothing. Just a run-in with some old friends."

"Did these old friends have something to do with the money you owed?"

He lifts one shoulder. "Maybe."

"You're going to need to tell the cops."

"No, I'm not doing that. If they ask, I'm just going to tell them I was jumped and I didn't see anything."

Reed's nostrils flare. "These people need to be behind bars."

"If I go after them, it'll only cause more trouble. We're done now. They got what they wanted, and they've been able to walk away feeling like big men. It's over."

Reed studies him for a moment. "Okay. As long as you're sure."

"I'm sure," Cade insists.

I hope he's right.

# 23
## laney

CADE IS IN THE HOSPITAL FOR THE NEXT COUPLE OF DAYS.

One thing I'll say for the man is he's a fast healer, and, thankfully, he's not showing any signs of permanent damage from the beating. We take turns visiting him, sneaking him takeout because he's refusing to eat the terrible hospital food.

Within the first twenty-four hours, he started getting antsy and wanted to be discharged, but we managed to convince him to stay. I'm worried about the men who beat him up. What if they're still out there and decide to finish the job?

Cade insists the business has been settled, but that doesn't stop me worrying. Then again, worrying seems to be my middle name these days. I hate how anxious I am about everything. When I go to bed at night, I repeatedly check the door and all the windows, making sure they're all shut and locked tight. Even when I'm in bed, I lie there, my ears straining to pick up on any sound, and then start to worry I forgot to lock something.

I've just left the hospital. Reed's taken over sitting at Cade's bedside, though Cade is rolling his eyes and insisting he doesn't need to be babysat. We're all still concerned about him, though, especially after what the doctor said about chronic traumatic brain injury. Cade might not be showing any signs of it yet, but that doesn't mean he won't.

I stop by the store on the way home. My refrigerator is empty, and while I haven't been home much to cook, I still need the basics of milk and bread.

I grab a basket at the entrance, but my thoughts aren't on my grocery shopping. There are times I feel as though I'm sleep-walking through my life, no longer present in my own reality. A part of me is still trapped in the cabin, and it's as though I'm reliving those days over and over in my head.

For the life of me, I can't think of what I need, and I alternate walking aimlessly up and down the aisles, to standing and staring at a shelf. The basket hooked over my arm remains empty.

It feels crazy that, back at the cabin, I used to daydream about being in a store, being able to choose whatever I wanted and gorge myself on it. Now I'm here, my appetite has deserted me. Perhaps it's because I got used to not eating much, but I keep realizing I've missed entire meals—getting to lunchtime and not having eaten breakfast, or going to bed, only for it to dawn on me that I never ate dinner. I know the lack of food isn't good for me, and that I need to put on some weight, but it's hard to force food inside me when I rarely have any appetite.

"Excuse me?"

A female voice yanks me from my daydream, and I turn to find a woman a little older than me standing behind me.

"Oh, sorry," I say, assuming she wants to get to the shelves, and stepping out of the way.

Her forehead furrows. "You're Laney Flores, aren't you?"

Do I know this woman? I don't recognize her, but she clearly knows me. My stomach sinks. I hope she's not another reporter. I thought they'd given up already, moved onto some other story, exploited some other poor victims.

"Who are you?" My tone is brusque.

"My name is Stephanie Hawkins."

The way she says it is as though she expects me to recognize her. A bell rings in my head, but I still can't quite place it.

She must see my confusion as she adds, "Kirsty Hawkins' sister."

Kirsty Hawkins. Shit. The flight attendant, the one whose body we'd found hanging half out of the rear part of the plane. The one who'd died in the crash.

My cheeks flare with heat. "Oh, my God. I'm so sorry I didn't recognize you."

She waves a hand dismissively. "It's fine, honestly. I imagine you've had a lot to deal with."

Now I look at her, I can see the resemblance. But her eyes are bloodshot—from crying, perhaps—and her skin is pale. She's slender, on the verge of underweight. Has she always been this thin, or is it weight loss caused by grief?

"I wondered if I could buy you a coffee?" she asks.

I glance down at my empty basket. I still haven't managed to get what I came in here for. "What, now?"

"If that's okay? I'd really love to talk to you."

I have no idea what she'd want to talk to me about, but I don't feel as though I can say no. Don't I owe this woman something? We could have done more to help the authorities find her sister's body, but we've kept our mouths shut to protect ourselves. It's an utterly selfish act, and it was one that was easier to deal with when the family was only a name or an idea. Now she's standing here in the flesh, the reality of what we've done hits me in the chest.

I wish Reed was here, or even Darius or Cade. They'd know what to do or say to avoid this situation. A part of me just wants to turn tail and run, but my social niceties prevent me from doing so.

"Please," she says. "Just for five minutes. I've got questions no one else would be able to answer. I just want to know what my sister's final moments were like."

"We were in a plane crash," I reply numbly.

What does she think they were like? It was terrifying. One of the most terrifying moments of my life.

"Just one coffee," she pleads.

I can't say no.

I put the basket down beside me, abandoning it. "Okay, one coffee."

She places her palms together in a prayer motion. "Thank you so much."

I follow her out of the store in a daze. What the hell am I doing? My stomach is sick with guilt. What if I blurt out something I shouldn't? What if I get everyone in trouble?

We enter a coffee shop across the street.

Stephanie gestures to a small round table in the corner. "Sit down, and I'll get the coffees. What are you drinking?"

"Iced latte for me, thanks." My voice doesn't sound like my own.

She offers me a small smile and goes to order. I take a seat, choosing the one facing away from the rest of the coffee shop, so I have my back to the diners. I don't want anyone else to recognize me.

Stephanie returns with the coffees and takes the seat opposite me. She pushes my drink across the table, and I take it in both hands, glad for the distraction.

"Thanks again for speaking with me," she says. "It must be hard, reliving what happened over and over."

"Everyone wants me to repeat everything, like it's going to change."

It could change, though—maybe it even should. I'm lying with every breath.

"I'm sorry for your loss," I add.

This is something I'm supposed to say, expected to say. It's safe ground.

"Thank you. Same to you. You lost your mom right before the crash, didn't you?"

I nod, not wanting to speak.

She presses her lips together. "I can't imagine what you've gone through."

I just want her to get on with it. "You said you had some questions?"

"About Kirsty, yes. How was she during the flight? Did she seem happy?" Stephanie searches my eyes for the truth, desperate to be reassured. My cheeks flare with heat, and I want to shrink in my seat, to slide under the table and melt into the floor.

The truth was that I didn't pay much attention to Stephanie's sister. I was too busy grieving my mother, and fighting with Cade, and trying to figure out what the hell had happened to my life.

"She seemed happy. She was laughing and smiling with the other passengers. She was professional with it, though. The moment it looked like something was going wrong with the plane, she gave us all instructions, and then buckled herself in."

Stephanie swallows and blinks a couple of times. "How much time was there between things going wrong and the actual crash?"

I take a sip of the coffee through the straw in the lid. It's ice-cold, and sweet, but I still struggle to swallow.

"Honestly, I don't know. I blacked out."

"Minutes? Seconds? Do you know if she was frightened? Was she screaming?"

I remembered the screams, mine as well as her sister's. I hear them all the time, especially at night when I'm drifting into sleep.

"I don't think so," I lie. "She seemed very calm and in control. A professional, right up until the end."

"Kirsty loved her job. It was all she ever wanted to do growing up."

"Then she died doing something she loved." It's a platitude.

In my head, all I can see is Kirsty's body, punctured by the tree branch, hanging there—the smell that had been in the air. I swallow hard and try to dispel the image that is startlingly bright and clear in my mind. Time hasn't faded it at all.

Stephanie swipes at her eyes. "Yes, she did. I just wish the authorities could locate her body. Our parents are devastated, as I'm sure you can understand. All we want is to be able to bury her. The thought of her rotting—" Her voice breaks, and she snatches a breath. "I'm sorry, but it's just too awful to stand."

I tighten my hands around my coffee. "I'm sorry, we've told them everything we can. If we'd known some coordinates of where we were, it would be easier, but it's not as though we had a map or a compass or anything like that. Everything looks the same out there, and we were exhausted and starving and dehydrated."

I'm repeating what I'd said to the authorities. This part isn't a lie. It's not as though we could give anyone exact directions to the cabin, and then to the plane.

Tears stream down her face. "No, I know, but you must be able to remember *something*. Some kind of landmark. Anything that would help bring Kirsty home."

"Like I said, everything looks the same. It's just trees and more trees."

I'm growing panicky in the face of this woman's grief. I only want to get out of here, get away, run!

"I don't believe that." She grows more agitated with every word. "There has to be something! A rock or a river or a goddamned hill. Something!"

I can't deal with this anymore.

152

"I'm sorry, I just—"

I stand up too quickly, almost knocking the chair over. I swing around in an effort to prevent it toppling to the floor, and instead of saving the chair, I catch my coffee with my elbow and send it flying. Milky coffee and ice splatters everywhere. Everyone is staring now. Do they know who I am? Do they recognize me?

"Laney?" Stephanie says. "Are you okay? I'm sorry. I—"

I don't even pause long enough to hear the end of the sentence. I run out of there, knocking into other tables and people as I go. I burst into the warm sunshine, gasping for air, but instead of feeling better about being out of the coffee shop and away from Stephanie, I feel even more exposed. People on the street eye me curiously, and those driving by seem to stare at me from their windows, faces pressed to the glass. Do they know who I am—a liar, a whore?

Needing to hide, I duck down the alley beside the coffee shop. With a trembling hand, I take out my phone. I can't do this alone. I'm trying, but I can't. My fingers tremble, but I manage to swipe the screen to call Reed. He'll be at the hospital, but it's not as though Cade is at death's door, thank God.

Reed answers. "Hey."

It's so good to hear his voice, even that one syllable, that tears well and a knot binds my throat.

"I—I—"

I can't even fully articulate what's happening.

"Laney, what's wrong?"

"Please, I need…"

"Where are you? I'm coming to get you."

I drop a pin in a map on the phone and send it to him. It's easier than trying to explain. I press my back to the cold concrete wall and sink down onto my haunches. I'm shaking all over, the phone clutched in my hand. What if Stephanie follows me? I don't think I can handle that.

I'm so pathetic. That poor woman lost her sister, and I ran away from her and hid. She deserves so much better. Are we doing the right thing by making it harder for them to find the plane? What if something was wrong with that type of plane and another one goes down, and more people die? Their blood will be on our hands.

I don't know how much time passes. I zone out, lost in my head, as I seem to be doing so often these days. Sometimes it's the safest place to be, even though I'm torturing myself there.

Footsteps approach, a heavy thud on the ground, moving at a fast pace. I jerk up, my breath catching, adrenaline flooding my system yet again.

"Laney?"

Reed stands in front of me. He's real and solid, and I'm so relieved to see him. I put my arms out to him, and he hauls me up and wraps me against his chest.

"Oh, baby-girl, it's okay. You're safe."

Then why don't I feel safe? I let myself go and sob against him, my shoulders shaking. He doesn't ask any questions, just lets me get it all out. I've forgotten about my fears of people seeing us together, but we're not doing anything inappropriate. He's allowed to comfort me.

When my tears finally run dry, he separates us, holding me at arm's length so he can look into my face. I'm embarrassed now. I must look terrible—puffy and blotchy. At least I wasn't wearing any mascara, so I don't have panda eyes to add to hideousness.

"You want to tell me what happened?"

I shake my head. "Not here. Take me home."

"This way."

His rental has blacked out windows. I appreciate the small amount of security it brings me to be able to hide inside the vehicle.

"You should come home with me," he says. "Cade's been discharged, and Darius will want to see you, too."

I know I should refuse, that it's hard being around them right now, but I don't have the energy in me to fight. "Okay," I relent.

"Now can you tell me what happened?"

I nod and fill him in on the encounter with the flight attendant's sister.

"Do you think she found you on purpose?" he asks. "Did it seem like a chance encounter?"

"Honestly, I don't know. I don't think she meant to upset me. I mean, she's the one who has the right to be upset, doesn't she? Her sister died, and she can't even bury her body. I can't imagine if one of you had died out there, and we couldn't bring your body home."

"This isn't your fault, Laney. We all agreed…"

I press my knuckles to my lips. "I know we did, but was it the right thing to do?"

"The right thing to do?" He considers this for a moment. "Perhaps not the right thing, but it was the only thing. I couldn't risk those men surviving out there so they could find us again."

"We don't know that they'll die. They have phones. As soon as they get service, they'll call for help."

"They have to walk far enough to get that service, and they have no supplies. With any luck, they'll have tried to follow us and got lost out there. With no shelter and no food, they won't make it."

I want to believe that, but I can't. There's too much uncertainty. "They'll have turned back before then. They know the cabin and the area around it. They'll have followed the river back."

He takes my hand. "Remember the reason we decided to walk out of there? We knew we wouldn't survive over winter, and neither will they. They'll either have to hike to safety—which as we've experienced ourselves, can easily kill you—or they'll be there over winter, which will also kill them. Plus, we took their boat. We were only able to get as far as we did because of it. We'd never have managed to walk that distance."

I shake my head. "Smith was meeting someone, a person they planned on doing a deal with. That was the whole reason they were at the cabin."

"And that person didn't show up."

I let out a breath and sit back. How much does he really believe this, or is he just trying to make me feel better?

"We can't live the rest of our lives in fear," he adds.

I want to say that it's easy for him to say, that he wasn't the one who was assaulted with a weapon and raped, but it feels like a cheap shot. He suffered—we all did. But he's also a man. I'm the one lying awake at night, my heart pounding every time I hear a knock or a scratch, thinking it'll be them.

We arrive back at the house Reed has on a short-term lease. It's not home for any of them, and I appreciate that the only reason they're even staying in the city is because of me. It's a beautiful property, though, with gated walls and a swimming pool out back.

It makes me painfully aware of how shabby the trailer is. I don't need to stay there. I have money now. But it's the only place that feels even marginally like home. I'm like a fox hiding in its den.

We enter the house and Reed calls out, "I'm back. I've got Laney with me."

The two men emerge from what I assume is the living room. Cade's bruises are turning green and yellow, and his eye is still swollen, but otherwise he looks strong. But then he catches sight of my tearstained face and his expression morphs to a glower.

"What happened?" he demands. "Someone hurt you? Who do I need to kill?"

"No one, Cade. I'm all right."

"You don't look all right. I mean it, Laney. If someone's hurt you, I'll track them down and I'll rip their fucking throat out."

"You're not allowed to get in any more fights," I remind him. "Doctor's orders."

"It was the flight attendant's sister," Reed says. "She bumped into Laney and begged her for more information on where her sister's body might be. You can't blame her for being upset."

Cade's shoulders drop. I think he was looking for an excuse to go and start a fight. He has to watch himself. I get that he's angry at the world, but destroying himself won't help.

"It just shook me up," I say. "It wasn't her fault. I'd have done exactly the same in her position."

Darius places his hand to my cheek. "None of this is your fault either. Don't ever forget that. You're allowed to protect yourself."

I nod and close my eyes briefly, twisting my face to kiss his palm.

They're all surrounding me again. I've never felt loved in the way I do with them. I hope they know how I feel about them, too.

# 24
## REED

I'M WORRIED ABOUT MY FAMILY.

Though Cade is home now, Laney still refuses to come and live with us. She seems so fragile; I don't understand why she doesn't feel safer when we're around. It concerns me that she thinks we're—at least in part—responsible for what she's gone through.

Maybe we are.

When I first met her, she was a spiky teenager, but now she's a broken adult.

I think of all the moments in her life when I've let her down. There are so many that I can't help but think maybe she's right in not wanting to be around me. I left her when she was three years old, abandoning her to a life with an addict for a mother. Then, when I eventually reappear after her mother's death, I put her in a situation where she not only almost loses her life, but also suffers at the hands of those bastards.

Cade's physical injuries may be healing again, but he doesn't seem much better mentally. The doctor's words about how traumatic brain injuries can cause personality changes keep ringing through my head, but I don't think Cade's anger is down to the head injuries.

159

The director at the concert hall has been in touch about Darius. I explained how Darius must have picked up a stomach bug and he's agreed to rearrange the show. I haven't spoken to Darius about it yet, though.

I go to find my youngest son.

It's strange living in a house where he's not playing. He's always played, the rooms filled with the notes from his violin. I haven't heard him play a single song since we've been back.

I find him in the kitchen, drinking coffee while standing at the counter, his back to me.

I know he's already heard me come in, but I clear my throat anyway.

"The concert hall director called," I tell him. "He said he was sorry you were taken ill, and wanted to know if you were feeling any better. He's able to reschedule your appearance for tomorrow evening, if you are. Most of the audience has been happy to transfer their tickets rather than request a refund."

Darius presses his lips together. "I see."

I continue, "But you don't have to play, if you don't want to. People will understand. You've been through something traumatic. It's okay if you can't just step back into your old life."

Darius grits his teeth. "I'm a musician. It's who I am. It's what I do. You all rely on me for it."

"No, we don't. We might support you in your career, because we love you and we're proud of you, and we want to see you do well, but Cade and I can both get different jobs if we need to. You don't need to feel that pressure to support us, Darius. We're grown men. Besides, with the payout from the airline, money isn't going to be a worry for us for some time."

His shoulders stiffen. "Maybe not, but that doesn't change that playing the violin is what I do. It's more than that. I can't see the person I'd be without it."

"No one is saying you have to quit, Dax," I tell him. "Just take some time."

"If I take some time, I'll be forgotten. You know how competitive this industry is. Right now, I have a platform—a big one, too. I'd be crazy not to take advantage of that."

"Your health is more important."

He turns to face me and seems to think for a moment. "Do you think Laney would come watch if I asked her? Having her in the audience would help."

"I'm not sure. How would she be with the big crowds?"

He shakes his head. "I don't know."

I want to help my son, but I also want to protect Laney. I think of how fragile she is.

"It doesn't feel right to put her in that situation," I say eventually.

His lips thin. "How do you know that she wouldn't want to be invited? Maybe she's feeling excluded. How will we know until we ask her?"

I exhale a breath. I know what Darius can be like once he gets an idea in his head—he won't back down.

"Do what you want, Dax. What do you want me to say to the concert director?"

Darius picks up his coffee and takes a sip.

"Tell him I'll play."

# 25

*laney*

After the incident with the flight attendant's sister, I didn't stay at Reed's house.

A part of me wanted to, but I have a dirty little secret. I wanted to go back to my home, with the razorblade, and the blood.

I've been cutting, and I don't want any of them to know about it. I know what kind of reaction they'll have—they'll be horrified and probably never let me out of their sight again.

I also want to get back to my laptop. I haven't scheduled another appointment with the therapist—though I probably should—and have been tapping out my story on the keyboard instead.

I don't want to tell Reed or the boys about either of these things, though, so even when they practically beg me to stay, I refuse them. I try not to see the pain in their eyes.

I keep to myself, checking in on Cade every now and then to make sure he's doing okay, but otherwise just focusing on what is becoming a book.

A light rap of knuckles sounds on the trailer door, and I turn my face from the bright light of the laptop screen, wrenching my thoughts from the scene I'm writing—the one where Cade caught me in the river masturbating over Dax. Irritation at being interrupted floods through me, but I go to answer it.

It's my neighbor, Sonny.

"Oh, hi," I say. "What's up?"

I'm self-conscious in the short skirt I'm wearing and tug at the hem.

"Thought I'd come and see how you're doing," he says. " I don't know if you need help with anything."

I think of the broken awning on the front of the trailer. While I want to be independent, I also know there's nothing wrong with asking for a little help now and then. It's been driving me crazy at night, flapping and rattling against the side of the trailer. If any bad weather comes in, the wind will rip it right off.

"Actually, there is something."

His expression brightens. "Sure. Just name it."

I step outside to join him and show him the awning. "It's stuck. I can't roll it back in, and the noise is keeping me awake half the night."

I should have been used to a little noise after living in the cabin—the branches of trees tapping on the roof like skeletal fingers, the wind howling through gaps in the windows, the noises of wild animals outside. But I wasn't alone then. I'd been sandwiched between Reed and Cade and Dax, and they'd helped to keep any fears at bay.

"Give me a minute, and I'll go grab my tools."

"Of course."

He's as good as his word and returns with a tool bag. There's something attractive about a man with a tool bag. It means they're capable, and generally good with their hands. I think how much easier it would be if I was interested in someone like Sonny. He's around my age, and I'm guessing we'd have a normal kind of relationship. No worries about our group dynamic, or that I'm being shared around by a father and his two sons. It wouldn't matter if people found out about our relationship, and the press wouldn't care. There would be no story in it.

He catches my eye and gives a small smile, and I realize I've been staring while I'd been lost in thought.

My cheeks grow warm. "Can I get you something cold to drink?"

"Sounds good."

I leave him busying himself with the awning and a screwdriver and go back inside to make iced tea.

I carry two tall glasses back out for us both.

"How's this?" He uses the pole to roll the awning back and forth. It moves smoothly and without any rattle.

"That's perfect. Thank you so much."

"Just make sure you keep it rolled in if it looks like the wind is going to come up again."

"I will."

Should I offer him money for fixing it? That doesn't feel right, somehow. I guess the iced tea will have to do. I hold his glass out to him, the outside beaded with condensation. As he takes it from me, our fingertips brush.

I have a small table and chairs positioned outside. I gesture for him to sit. It's not as though I have many friends. I'd always been ashamed as a kid—of both my mom and where I lived— and so had never wanted to get close to anyone.

He takes a sip of his drink. "What was it like, being out in the middle of nowhere all that time?"

I'm always conscious that someone might be trying to get information out of me so they can sell my story, so I don't give any details other than what's already been reported.

"Scary," I admit, "and we were always hungry."

He gives a lopsided grin. "I can't even imagine being really hungry like that. I get hangry if I'm an hour past my lunch, and even then, I always know I can swing by the drive-thru."

"You kind of get used to it. It's worst the first few days, but I guess your stomach shrinks or something. To be honest, I haven't really found my appetite even since I've been back. At the cabin, we used to have all these long conversations about what foods we'd want to eat and what we missed the most, but since I've been back, I haven't even wanted much."

He eyes me curiously. "Do you think you'll ever get on another plane?"

I huff air out through my nose in a small laugh. "I had to get on one to come home again, but I don't know. It wasn't my choice in the first place. I was under Reed's guardianship, so I had to go where he went."

"Do you blame him for the crash?"

The question surprises me. "Of course not. Why would I?"

He rethinks. "Okay, maybe not the crash, but the reason you were on the plane."

"No. He took me in when I had no one else."

If I could go back and change things, would I? It would mean never having met the guys, but also never having to go through the assault and rape, or the crash. No, I simply can't imagine my life now without them in it. No one else is ever going to come close to them, the way they make me feel, the way they love me, our histories, the sex we have.

I realize I know nothing about Sonny's family, or his life. All we've talked about is mine. "Who do you live with?"

"No one—currently, anyway. I lived with my dad until a couple of years ago, but he got a job in New York state, so he took off. I didn't care. The two of us weren't exactly getting along."

"Have you never gotten along?" I ask.

He shrugs. "Maybe when I was younger, but the minute I got older and wanted to do my own thing, we started to clash. I think he always saw me as a small extension of himself, but when I didn't want to do the stuff he did, he took it like a personal insult or something."

"What sort of thing did he like to do?"

"Fishing, mostly. He'd sit for hours, just staring out across the water. Bored the hell out of me. He'd drag me along, and then complain about me being on my phone. What else was I supposed to do? Just sit there? I didn't get it."

All I can think is that it must be nice to have a dad who wanted to do something with you, to spend quality time with you. I never had that. Maybe that's why I have daddy issues.

"What about your mom?" I ask.

"They separated years ago. Mom wanted to live her own life, so I stayed with my dad. I'm not sure what she's doing now. She gets in touch every now and then."

Though his parents don't exactly sound perfect, I still discover I'm jealous he has them somewhere in the world.

"Who the fuck is this?"

I jump at the loud male voice and turn toward it.

The shape of Cade creates a huge silhouette against the sun.

"Cade, this is my neighbor, Sonny. He's just been helping me out with some stuff."

A muscle ticks in Cade's jaw. "Helping you out? *We* can help you if you need it. You don't need to ask some strange man."

"He's not a strange man." I grind my teeth. "He's my neighbor. He helped me."

"Yeah, 'cause he's probably using it as a way to get inside your pants."

"Cade!"

He jerks his chin at Sonny. "Is that what you're trying to do? You trying to fuck my little sister?"

"Cade!" I cry again.

Sonny is on his feet now, both hands held up in defense. "Hey, dude, I wasn't trying to do anything. I was only being neighborly."

"Bullshit. I'm a guy. I know no man helps a young, pretty

woman out unless they think they're going to get their dick sucked."

Sonny's eyes go wide. "I wasn't! I swear I wasn't."

"You're a fucking liar."

"What the fuck are you doing?" I demand of Cade.

"It's okay, Laney," Sonny says. "I'll go."

"You don't have to do that. Cade should be the one who leaves." I glare at him.

Cade folds his arms across his massive chest. "No chance."

"Really," Sonny continues, "it's fine. I don't want to come between family. I'll catch up with you later, Laney."

Cade stares at him as he walks away, and then turns to me. "Family? Is that what he thinks we are?"

"Aren't we?" I challenge.

"We're so much more than that, and you know it."

I angle my head and fold my arms, matching his body language. "But I can't tell people that, can I?" I lower my voice to a hiss. "What am I supposed to say? 'Hey, Sonny, this is my stepbrother Cade, who I also happen to be fucking. Oh, yeah, I'm fucking his brother and father as well.'"

His eyes narrow. "No, but you still don't need to be offering him iced tea and hanging out like you're interested in him."

"Fuck you, Cade," I say, turning away. "You are such a fucking asshole, sometimes."

He reaches out and grabs my wrist, halting me. "You make me crazy. I see red when I find you with another man. I can't stand the thought of you with someone else."

I arch an eyebrow. "Other than your brother and your father," I point out.

"That's different. They're a part of me, too."

I give a half laugh and shake my head. "You're fucking insane."

He pulls me closer. "I want you. I need you."

"Cade…" There's a warning in my tone. He needs to keep his voice down. Someone might overhear him.

"I'm addicted to you, Laney. I need to feel you around my cock. I need to taste your pussy. I need your tongue in my mouth."

I hate the way my body reacts to him, but it does. My lips tingle, my nipples tighten, and desire coils at my core.

"Take me inside," he orders. "Now. I'm going to fuck you so hard, you forget the name of that *boy*."

Already thinking I'm probably going to regret this, but deciding I don't care, I link my fingers through his and pull him inside with me. He slams the door shut with his foot, and within a split second, his fingers are in my hair, and he's kissing me, hard. He uses his body to maneuver us through the trailer and into the bedroom.

He shoves two fingers between my lips and grabs my ponytail in his other hand.

"Suck them," he commands. "Show me how you're going to suck my cock next."

I do as he says, my mouth and tongue working his fingers while holding eye contact with him. My pussy tingles, and I squeeze my thighs together, experiencing a pleasurable throb.

"Get them good and wet cause I'm going to shove them in your cunt."

I whimper. I shouldn't let him get away with this, but God, it feels good. He takes his fingers from my mouth, pushes them beneath my skirt, and hooks them inside me. He fingers me roughly, his other hand still holding my ponytail tight. I moan and grind down on his hand, my arousal building.

Before I can get too close, he slips his fingers back out of me, lifts them to his mouth, and sucks them off. I stare at them sliding between his lips.

"You taste so good, Laney. I'll never get enough of your pussy."

"Fuck," I gasp. "Make me come."

"First you're going to suck my cock."

He pushes me to my knees, hard enough to bruise, and then opens the zipper of his jeans. His hard cock is apparent in a curved line beneath the denim, but it only takes him a matter of seconds before he frees himself. He's so big, thick, and ridged with veins. The head is darker in color than the shaft, and the metal of his piercing glints from his slit. A drop of pre-cum already glistens there. I open my mouth to take him.

"That's right, pretty little girl. Part your lips so I can shove my cock down your throat."

I take his cock in my mouth and work the base with my hand. I lick and suck and lightly graze my teeth down his shaft, so he sucks in a breath.

"Deeper," he tells me.

Trying to control my gag reflex, I force myself down as far as I can go. The piercing hits the back of my throat, and I fight against my reflexes.

"Swallow."

I don't know how I'm going to do it with his cock so far back, but I do, my throat closing around him. The sensation makes me gag and tears gather in my eyes, but he doesn't pull away.

"Again," he commands, but now his voice is gravelly with desire.

I do it, and the action tears a whimper from between his lips. Fuck. I love hearing that sound coming from him. I'm sure my throat will be bruised from being used in such a way, and the metal of his piercing has probably scraped me. All I want is to please him.

"Holy shit," he says, moving back to free me. "I could come so easily like that, but I want to be inside you."

Now his dick is no longer blocking my airway, I gasp for

breath. He helps me to my feet, and then kisses away the tears from the corners of my eyes.

"You did so good, little sis. No one else has swallowed me like that before."

He pushes us in front of the mirror, positioned on the dressing table opposite the bed. "I want you to watch how sexy you are when I fuck you. You're mine. Not some random neighbor's, and I'm going to remind you of that."

I'm wearing a skirt and a long-sleeved T-shirt to hide my arms. To my relief, he doesn't try to strip off my clothes, but instead flips up my skirt. He bends me over so I can see us both in the mirror, then positions himself at my entrance. He's big, and I experience little stings of pain as I stretch around him, then he rams into me hard from behind. My tits bounce, and I give a gasp of shock. He takes hold of my ponytail again, forcing my chin up, my eyes still teary.

He takes me hard and fast. There's no gentleness in this act, no love. He's just claiming my body as his own. He moves faster and harder, slamming into me.

"Your cunt fits me perfectly," he says. "You stretch around me so beautifully."

"Oh, God. That feels so good."

It does. I'm so full with him.

"Look at me in the mirror," he commands. "Keep your eyes on me, little sis. I mean it. Don't make me angrier."

He locks eyes with me. He's dominant, controlling. He knows he's capable of breaking my heart, but, in that moment, I'm happy to let him.

"Say it, Laney. Say you love your big brother fucking you, 'cause you're a dirty little whore."

"I love it," I gasp. "I love my big brother fucking me." The words feel filthy and wanton coming from my mouth. I'm so close now. It's building and building. I'm reaching for my climax, knowing I'm balancing right on the precipice.

"Why?" He slams hard inside me.

"'Cause I'm a dirty little whore."

Can anyone outside the trailer tell what we're doing? Is the whole thing rocking? Can they hear my cries?

Using that word tips me over the edge, and my orgasm rocks through me. My pussy clamps down around him, and he gives in as well, filling me up. We're both coated in sweat, breathing hard, our heartbeats pounding.

We collapse onto the bed together.

"Holy shit," I manage, pushing sweaty strands of hair out of my face.

He pulls me close and kisses my damp shoulder. "See. I told you I'd make you forget the neighbor."

I playfully thump him on the chest. "I think I've got enough men in my life. There's no room for anyone else."

"Good," he says gruffly. "And let's keep it that way."

He pauses for a moment, clearly thinking something.

"What is it?" I ask.

"Darius is playing at the concert hall again. He needs to know that you're there for him."

The blood drains from my face. "At the concert hall? In the audience?"

"Yes."

I think of all the people, how I'll be recognized. It had been hard enough going there the first time with Reed before the crash, the first time I'd met them all. I'd felt so utterly out of place, but then I'd heard Darius play, and the rest of the world had just fallen away. I'd been mesmerized by him on stage, his bare torso shining with sweat, his hair whipping around his body with every draw of his bow. His music had brought tears to my eyes, it had been so beautiful.

I suck in a shaky breath.

"I—I just don't know if I can."

"Please, Laney. He'd ask you himself, but he doesn't want to put you in a difficult position."

I note that Cade hasn't had any trouble in doing so.

"Okay," I relent. "If it means that much to him, I'll come."

"We'll all be back together in public, the four of us."

I remember the time at the restaurant. "Yes, I guess so. I hope that doesn't mean people will gossip."

"Fuck 'em." Cade says. "If they want to gossip, let them."

It's easier for him. Women always get it worse in these situations. Men can sleep around with whoever they want and get a smack on the back in approval.

If women do the same, we're called whores.

But then I think of what people will call Reed if they ever find out about our relationship, and keep my mouth shut.

# 26

*laney*

CADE SENDS A CAR TO TAKE ME TO THE CONCERT HALL.

I've put together the smartest outfit I can find, but it's nothing like the sort of thing other people attending the concert will be wearing. Maybe I should have gone shopping for something new, but I couldn't find the energy to do so.

I find my seat, smiling awkwardly at the people sitting either side of me. They seem so much more grown up and sophisticated than me. My imposter syndrome is hitting me hard, and I shrink in my chair.

I suddenly remember to put my phone on silent. It would be so embarrassing if it started ringing in the middle of the concert. I can only imagine the sort of dirty looks I'd receive.

I'm still not sure why I'm here. It's not as though Darius will even see me in the audience.

There are too many people around. They're all confident and well dressed and look like they have their lives all sorted. I sense them glancing my way. I should have asked Cade or Reed to sit with me, but they're busy with Darius. I know he needs to be the focus now.

My palms grow clammy, and my upper lip prickles with sweat.

I can't do this. I can't sit with all these people and pretend like this is normal for me. I'm fully aware I'm suffering from anxiety and panic attacks now, and just the thought of having one in such a public place is enough to send me spiraling. What if I pass out or vomit? It's already bad enough, feeling as though everyone is staring, without nurturing that fear as well.

I know my way backstage from the last time I was here. Perhaps it'll be better if I find the others. Reed and Cade will be watching Darius from the wings. Why couldn't they just have suggested I do the same? I'd feel better then, I'm sure of it, and I'd still be able to be there for Dax.

Most people have taken their seats now, and because I'm in the middle of the row, I have to practically climb over the top of everyone to get to the exits. I notice some of them tutting at me and shaking their heads.

My mortification grows, and I fight my rising panic and the sense of claustrophobia that's taken over. The air feels too thick, as though it doesn't contain enough oxygen to allow me to breathe.

Even as I try to make my way backstage, I can tell I'm not going to make it. My legs no longer seem to belong to me, and my breath is tight in my lungs, so I struggle to draw another. I need to get out of this building. I need fresh air and solitude.

I can't do this.

# 27
## REED

I'm waiting in the wings with both my sons for the moment where Darius goes on.

"Is she there?" Darius asks.

"Yes," I reassure him. "I saw her take her seat."

"Are you sure? Check again."

I peer around the curtain. The seat is empty. Fuck. Do I lie to him? No, I can't do that. Where has she gone? A fresh worm of worry squirms inside me. God dammit. This is the last thing we need. Now I'm worrying about Laney as well as Dax.

"Well?" he asks.

"She's probably just gone to the bathroom or something. She was there a minute ago, I swear."

His expression grows stony. "But she's not there now."

"She'll be back." I sound more confident than I feel. She hadn't been keen on coming tonight, but she'd done it for Dax. I hadn't even wanted them to ask, but Cade had gone behind our backs. Maybe it was all too much for her.

Will he play if she's not there? Should I have lied?

The first notes of the orchestra in the pit fill the air. It's Darius's signal to step onto the stage. He lifts his chin, his grip tightening around the neck of the violin and the bow. He mouths something to himself, something that looks like 'This is who I am,' and then strides out onto stage. The audience erupts in applause, and he holds the violin and bow above his head as he takes center stage.

I hold my breath, my body rigid. I can tell Cade is the same beside me. All focus on Dax.

He plays the first note, and then the second, and for a moment I allow myself to think everything is fine. Everything is normal. He actually *was* just sick with a stomach bug the other night.

But then he plays the third note, and there's something off about it, and he falters. His whole demeanor changes.

He tries to get back on track, but he's rattled. Even from this distance, I can see his hand shaking as he plays.

He might not be able to see, but his face is still turned toward the space where Laney was supposed to be.

I know all he can picture in his mind is that empty seat. *Fuck, Laney, where did you go?* But this isn't fair to her, either. She's had enough to shoulder without having to worry about being Darius's fucking muse, or whatever it is he's decided she is. She doesn't need that kind of pressure or responsibility. I know he's not doing it on purpose, but that won't stop her feeling the burden of his entire career on her back.

Darius tries to play, but the violin screeches like a cat when someone's stepped on its tail. He lowers the instrument, a broken man.

"I'm sorry," he manages to say to the audience before he turns and stumbles off stage.

He's gone the opposite direction to where his brother and I are standing. He drops his violin and bow and hunches in the corner.

*Fuck.*

I exchange a glance with Cade.

"Still think it's a stomach bug?" he says.

Darius has been fine all day. It definitely isn't a stomach bug. My youngest son has a new case of stage fright. It isn't something I've ever seen in him before. From the first moment he'd picked up a violin when he'd only been a boy, it had transformed him. The instrument had made him stronger, somehow, given him a new confidence. It had made his shoulders go back and his chin lift. The violin had lit him from the inside. Now it seems to be doing the opposite.

"I'm going to check he's okay," I tell Cade. "Can you speak to the concert director? Explain and apologize."

"He's going to have hundreds of angry people on his hands. Once was bad enough. Twice is a fucking disaster."

"There's nothing we can do about that. Darius is more important."

The curtain comes down, and I use the cover to cross the stage to where Darius is still bent over.

I place my hand on his back. "You okay, Dax?"

"Where's Laney?"

Hundreds of people are all expecting to see him play, but the only thing on his mind is his stepsister.

"I don't know," I say honestly. "She was in the seat one minute, and the next time I glanced out, she was gone. I'll call her."

I take my phone from my pocket and swipe the screen to bring up her name. I hit call and place it to my ear.

"Shit. She's not answering."

"We need to find her," he insists. "Something might have happened to her."

"I'm sure she's fine." Was she, though? Why had she left? Had she really gone to the bathroom? If she was all right, she would have been in her seat at the start of the performance.

"Don't worry, we'll find her."

"Go. Now," he insists.

There is little point in arguing with him. While I don't want to leave Darius, he's a grown man. Laney's vulnerable. My heart punches the inside of my ribs. What if something has happened to her? My brain flips me back to when we'd been with Smith in the cabin. As men, what we'd gone through was nothing compared to Laney, but that still didn't stop it being traumatic. Being forced to listen to Smith assault her with the gun, while being at gunpoint ourselves, listening to her cries coming from behind the door, and being unable to do a single thing about it, had been a special kind of torture. Getting my brains blown out wouldn't have helped Laney, but doing nothing hadn't helped her either.

Is that why Darius is so focused on her now? He's terrified of us ending up back in that situation.

Now people are starting to realize Darius won't be coming back on stage, there's movement in the audience. Pretty soon, the auditorium is going to be filled with people, and finding Laney is going to be even harder. That's assuming she's even still in the building. She might have caught a cab home, though I thought she'd let me know if she wanted to leave.

The first place I check is the bathrooms. I don't even care that I'm entering the women's bathroom, though I suspect any women in here might have different ideas.

"Laney?" I call and check the stalls.

Thankfully, the place is empty, but that also means it's empty of Laney, too. I try the door of the unisex bathroom, but she's not there either. I don't bother with the men's. She's got no reason to be in there.

The minute the thought crosses my mind, it's wiped out by another. What if someone forced her in there? A man might be attacking her right now, but I walk right by because I assume she's not in there. Adrenaline spurts through my veins, and I shoulder barge the door.

"Laney? You in here?"

The space appears to be empty, but I check the stalls anyway.

She's not here. I exhale a breath of relief, but just because she's not being attacked in the bathroom doesn't mean she's not hurt elsewhere.

I try my phone again, but it rings out. Why isn't she answering?

I check everywhere I can think of in the concert hall and come to the conclusion she's not here.

With nowhere else to go, I race outside into the balmy Los Angeles evening. Frantic, I look around for her.

I spot her on the other side of the street, sitting on a bench. Her head is down, her hair falling over her face, so she doesn't see me.

"Laney!" I shout. "Laney?"

# 28

*laney*

I LOOK UP AT REED'S SHOUT.

He runs across the road toward me, not seeming to care about the vehicles speeding in both directions. My heart is in my mouth, and for a horrifying moment, I think he's going to go flying over the hood of one. Horns blast their disapproval, but then he makes it and stops in front of me.

He scoops me up in a hug and holds me tight. I bury my nose in his chest. He smells so good. I wrap my arms around him, my fingers gripping the muscles in his back.

"Thank God you're okay," he says against the top of my head.

I don't want to let go of him, but I'm also aware of the people around us. We could be snapped by the paparazzi or just by a member of the public. I don't want questions to be asked.

"I'm sorry. I didn't mean to worry you. I just couldn't be in there with all those people. I felt like everyone was staring at me. Like they knew who I was, and exactly what I'd been through. It was too much."

"You're right, it was too much. We should never have put you in that situation." Lines appeared between his eyebrows. "Why didn't you answer your phone?"

"Shit, sorry. I put it on silent because of the show. I didn't know you were trying to call." I take my phone out and check it now. It's showing several missed calls.

"You worried us," he says.

"How's Darius? He didn't play, did he?"

I can tell from all the people leaving the building, the way they're shaking their heads, and talking from between lips pursed with irritation.

"No, he didn't. He tried, but I guess it was too much for him, too."

I dip my chin. "That's my fault. He would have played if I'd been there."

"We don't know that, and it's not your fault. You're not responsible for him, Laney."

My chest is heavy with guilt. "He needed me, and I ran."

His tone hardens. "Laney, stop it. This is *my* fault. I should have listened to Cade, but I didn't. I should never have booked Darius to do the first show, never mind try again tonight."

A tear slips down my cheek. Why does it feel like all I do is cry lately? He swipes it away with his thumb.

"Don't cry. We're all going to be all right."

I nod. I hope so.

"I should go and see Dax," I say. "Make sure he's okay."

"I'll come with you."

I shake my head. "Is it all right if I see him on my own? I think he'll appreciate it being just the two of us."

It dawns on me how little time Darius and I have had together recently—especially one on one. I've spent time with both Cade and Reed, but Darius hasn't had the opportunity. It's not as though we haven't seen each other, but I'm sure he'll be missing *us*.

"I'll go and find Cade," Reed says. "Let him know you're safe."

We cross the road together—safely this time—and enter the building. Reed gives my hand a quick squeeze, and then we part.

I don't need to explain to the security detail who I am. They recognize me and allow me to go backstage to where the dressing rooms are located. I find the one with the name Darius Riviera on it.

I knock lightly on the door and then open it a crack.

"Hey," I say. "Is it all right if I come in?"

He sits up straight. "Laney. Of course it is."

My stomach churns with nerves at seeing him, and I have to remind myself that this is just Darius. *Our* Darius. Sometimes, when I see the number of people who pay to come and see him, and when I see the way he pulls in the photographers and the reporters, it's hard not to put him on a pedestal. But he's a man, just like the others, and though he normally exudes confidence and sex appeal when he's on stage, he hurts just the same.

I'm worried he's going to be mad at me for running off. Would he have been able to play if I'd stayed? Does he blame me?

"Everything all right?" I ask.

He twists his lips ruefully. "What do you think?" He covers his face with both hands. "I think my career might be over."

I pull up a chair opposite him and wrap my fingers around his forearm, pulling one hand down so I can see his face. "No. You don't believe that."

"If I puke every time I go on stage, I don't think people are going to want to pay to see that."

"It's still new. You've been through a lot."

"You think anyone else is going to take a gamble on me? What if I wait six months, and someone else books me, and then it happens again?"

"So, start small? People would love you to do some smaller, more intimate gigs. See how you get on with those first before trying to take on a performance of this size."

He lets out a breath, but his head is still hung, his long, wavy hair falling around his face. "It's a good suggestion, but what am I supposed to do about Reed and Cade? They've built their careers around me. If I'm not playing, they're not working either."

"You don't need to worry about them. They're both grown men. They can sort out their own careers. Besides, it's not as though they need the money, do they?"

"Working isn't only about money," he says. "It's about having a sense of purpose, of giving structure to your day. It's about the people you meet, and the connections that are forged."

I understand what he means, though for me, working has always been about the paycheck.

"We were okay in the cabin, weren't we?" I remind him. "I mean…before."

He nods his understanding so I don't have to give voice to what 'before' means.

I continue, "We didn't have jobs to go to then, but we were always occupied."

"We were occupied with trying to survive," he comments.

I repress a smile. "And with each other, too."

He must hear the tease in my voice. "Laney…" he warns. "You know it's been too long."

"Maybe I can do something that'll take your mind off the violin?"

I drop to my knees in front of him.

"What are you doing?" he asks.

"What do you think?"

I pop the button of his jeans and then the zipper. His cock seems to know exactly what's coming, 'cause it springs out to meet me. I wrap my fingers around the base and, looking up at him to watch his expression, lick the length of him with one long stroke, and then surround the head with my mouth.

"Ah, fuck," he gasps.

I want to give him pleasure. I owe that much to him. I tongue his slit, and then sink my mouth down on him, as far as I can go.

"I want to come in your mouth," he groans, "but don't swallow. Kiss me after. Share my cum with me."

Holy shit, that's hot.

I keep sucking him, and he keeps talking.

"You know I see the world through my other senses. The taste of my cum on your tongue is a fantasy to me."

I hum around his dick, hoping he understands that the idea is turning me on, too. I squeeze my thighs together, enjoying the thump of pleasure at my core.

The noises he's making grow guttural, and he thrusts his hips from the chair, fucking my mouth. I sense his urgency and suck him harder, trying to do clever things with my tongue. I'm no expert at this, but the men always seem to enjoy what I'm doing.

A knock suddenly comes at the door, and I freeze, Darius's cock still in my mouth.

"I'm busy," he yells.

The knock comes again, followed by a female voice. "Mr. Riviera? I do need to speak to you. It's urgent."

He's right on the brink, I can feel it. I want him to come, so I don't ease up.

The door cracks open.

Darius quickly pats the surface of the dressing table grabs a towel that he must have known was there, and throws it over his lap and my head. At almost the same time, he jams his cock right down my throat. His fingers are knotted in my hair, and he holds me in place so I can't move. I can't breathe, and I'm silently gagging, my throat closing around him. Above me, he makes a strangled noise, then the female voice comes from the door.

"I'm sorry to disturb you, Mr. Riviera, but the concert director requests a meeting with you. It really is urgent, given the circumstances."

"Yes, of course." His voice sounds strange. He's hanging on

to control with the finest of threads. "Give me five minutes, and I'll be right there."

The door clicks shut again, and he releases me. I come up for air, literally gasping.

"Holy shit," I manage. "I thought I was going to die choking on a dick."

"When you gagged liked that, your throat was so tight, I thought I was going to lose it. Now, we've got five minutes. Let's do that again."

I lick my lips, and he guides his cock back between them. He leans back in his chair, his hands still loosely in my hair as I finish him off. His cum fills my mouth, and I keep it there, the saltiness coating my tongue. His fingers grip my hair, and he tilts my head back. He covers my mouth with his, his tongue lapping mine, so he's tasting his own cum. The thought alone turns me on so badly, I think I might just come without him even touching my pussy.

"Wait here," he says. "Let me get rid of this person, and then it'll be your turn. Touch yourself while I'm gone. I want to taste your pussy on your fingers."

Darius tucks himself away and leaves the room.

Voices come from the corridor.

God, they were right outside the door while I made him climax.

I'm not as anxious about being caught with either Dax or Cade in the same way I am with Reed. They might be my step-brothers, but we don't have the big age difference. Reed is my stepfather, and he knew me as a child, which is why people would warp what we have into something distasteful.

Darius re-enters the room. My blowjob seems to have given him some of his swagger back.

"Now," he says, dragging his hand through his hair, "where were we?"

He moves in closer, eclipsing me with his body.

I'm wearing a short black dress—one of the only dresses I own. He yanks the hem up around my waist and pushes me into the chair.

"Sit back and spread your legs."

The heels I'm wearing make my legs look impossibly long, and I wish he could see them. Instead, he runs his hands up the back of my heel and calf, pausing at the dip at the back of my knees, and then grips my thighs.

He tongues my pussy. I imagine transferring his cum from my mouth to his, and then to my cunt. He pushes his tongue inside me and fucks me with it. Then he suckles on my clit, sending sparks through me.

It feels so good, and the thought of someone walking in on us again only makes me hotter.

"Who was here last?" he asks as he slides a finger inside me. "My brother or my father?"

I take a hitching breath. "Your brother."

"Do you enjoy being shared around us, Laney?"

"Yes," I gasp.

"Why?"

"Because you're all so different. It's like you each fill a different hole in me." I realize what I've said and laugh. "A metaphorical hole."

He pushes a second finger inside me, stretching my pussy. "I don't know...I think we fill your actual holes, too, don't we? Your mouth, your ass, your pussy." Each time he mentions a particular area of my body, he drags his thumb over it, making me squirm with pleasure.

He lifts me out of the chair, swipes everything off the dressing table, and places me on it. He opens his pants to free himself. He's ready to go again already.

Darius penetrates me, hard and fast. We cling to each other, his hips slamming between my thighs. There's no finesse in our fucking. It's raw and brutal. We kiss, our lips bruising, and he bites my neck.

"Oh, God, I'm coming, I'm coming." My pussy clamps around his cock, and he lets out a primal growl, and then holds himself deep. I feel him twitching inside me, the flood of heat as he releases himself.

We take a moment to catch our breath, and then make ourselves presentable. Darius has a bathroom attached to the changing room, so I quickly use it to freshen myself up. When I emerge, Cade and Reed are in the room with Dax.

Cade raises his eyebrows at us both. "Feeling better?"

I can't help grinning. "Much."

## 29

### laney

OVER THE NEXT FEW WEEKS, THINGS SEEM TO SETTLE DOWN.

On the outside, it probably looks like I'm doing well. I'm learning how to fake being better, though some days are more of a struggle than others. Things are good between me and the guys, but I'm still hurting inside.

To ease my emotional pain, I've grown addicted to causing myself physical pain. I'm ashamed of what I'm doing, and I try my hardest not to do it, but whenever I find myself sinking into a hole that I'm not sure I'm going to be able to pull myself out of, I go back to the razor again.

It feels safer to give in to the cutting.

Darius hasn't made any plans to try to play in public again. I feel bad for him, but I think it's the right choice. I've noticed Cade is also quieter than normal, though when I ask him if he's all right, he brushes me off.

I don't think I'm the only one who needs therapy.

Though I'm putting on a good front, when I'm not with the guys, I take to my bed.

The hours seem to bleed together, and I don't even care. More and more, I find myself in this position, lying curled on my side on the bed, staring into nothingness. What happened haunts me...

A flash of cold gun metal pushing up inside me, of the pressure internally, of my body reacting....

I squeeze my thighs together and my eyes shut, willing the memory away. I don't want to replay it in my mind, but it's as though my brain wants to torture me.

A knock at the door is the only thing that pulls me out of it, and I go to find Cade on the doorstep, holding a brown paper bag filled with burgers and fries. The scent of it is enticing, but I still don't have much of an appetite.

He doesn't wait to be invited in, but brushes past me. "Have you eaten today?"

I haven't. "Of course."

"Don't lie to me, Laney. You need to eat. You're wasting away."

He grabs plates out of the cupboards and sets them down on the table, then proceeds to dish out the meal.

He grabs a French fry and holds it to my lips. "Eat."

Obediently, I open my mouth and take a bite.

"Good girl. Now sit down and eat the rest."

There's no point in arguing with him. He'll force feed me if he has to.

I sink into the chair opposite him, pick up the burger, and take a bite. Ketchup drips out of the bottom and ends up all over my sleeve.

"Shit," I say, picking up a napkin to wipe away the sauce. The movement pushes up my sleeve slightly, exposing the Band-Aid across my forearm.

Cade spots it, his brow creasing. "You're hurt."

I glance down at my arm as though I've forgotten the Band-Aid is there. "Oh, that. It's nothing. The knife slipped while I was cutting up an apple."

His eyebrows draw together. "A knife slipped, and you cut

your arm? How is that even possible? Your finger or hand, I can understand, but not your arm."

"I wasn't paying attention. It was stupid of me."

He holds out a hand. "Let me see."

"It's covered. You can't see anything."

"So I'll take off the Band-Aid."

I put my arm behind my back. "No, Cade. It's fine. You'll only make it bleed again if you start messing around with it."

Mentioning it bleeding doesn't help. He's got that fierce look in his eyes—the one that makes me think he's about to go around setting fires to people's houses if he thinks they might have done something to hurt me.

"Let me look, Laney," he growls. "Now."

"Jeez. You're making too big a deal out of it."

"Now," he repeats.

With a sigh, I hold out my arm. Carefully, he picks off the bandage. Dark blood has seeped through and dried.

He inspects the wound and shakes his head.

"You should have gotten stitches. That's going to scar," he says.

I close my eyes briefly then open them again to study his face. "Do you really think I care about a scar, Cade? Because I don't. A scar is just a scar. A white mark on skin. It's proof I was alive, that I was hurt, but that I healed. I'm grateful to my body, at least, for being able to do that."

Maybe I want to see physical marks to see the pain I'm going through. There are times when I look in the mirror and expect to find my reflection shattered like glass, only to find the same old me staring back, a little thinner, a little older, a haunted look in her eyes, perhaps, but still me.

He runs his thumb along my skin, adjacent to the cut, and all the individual hairs on my arms slowly rise, one by one, prickling across my skin.

"I care," he says softly.

"Why? Because it means I'm not perfect anymore?"

Not that I believe I've ever been perfect. Maybe when I was a little girl, still innocent and believing her mother was the most amazing person on the planet. That was until I got older and understood that normal people didn't live how we did, and, when she brought men home with her, she wouldn't protect me. I want to cry for that little girl now, how much potential she had. But the cruelness of the world tore strip after strip off her, until she became the ruined person I am now.

He shakes his head, his thumb still touching my arm. "No, Laney. Because I hate to see you hurt. Because whenever I see you in pain, it's as though I'm feeling it for myself. I'd rather cut out my own heart and stab a knife through it than see anyone or anything hurt you ever again."

I close my eyes. "Oh, Cade…"

He means what he says—at least he believes he does. I want to give in to him, to allow him to carry me, but he's so dangerous. So volatile. He could hold my heart in his hands one minute, place it on a pedestal, but if something didn't go his way, I'd be terrified he'd knock it right back down again.

The wound has started to bleed again. It trickles down my arm, winding and weaving its way across my skin, curving to my inner wrist and into my palm.

"You're bleeding," he says.

I nod, dumbly.

I did tell him that would happen.

He takes my hand and lifts my wrist to his mouth. His lips part, the pinkness of his tongue exposed. Then he flattens his tongue to my wrist and licks a smooth, deliberate line up my inner wrist, taking the trail of blood with it.

I shouldn't be turned on, but something deep in my belly tingles, and heat condenses between my thighs. He keeps eye contact with me the whole time, watching for my reaction. My nipples tighten beneath my shirt, my lips part, my cheeks flush. This really shouldn't be hot—him licking my blood—but it is.

He's dangerous. He can hurt me.

But the way I'm feeling right now, pain is good. I deserve pain.

He can hurt me all he wants.

"I want to lick every part of you," he growls. "Right now."

I can barely speak, but I manage a whimper, which he takes as consent. He yanks me to my feet and lifts me. My legs wrap around his hips, and he carries me into the bedroom, the food and my bleeding arm forgotten.

He throws me onto the bed, and then kneels at my feet. His hands go to the button and zipper of my jeans. I'm already bare-footed, so it only takes him seconds to whip me out of both my jeans and panties. Then he pushes my thighs apart and buries his face between them.

His hot, wet mouth covers me. He licks me from my asshole, right up, across my slit, to my clit. Then he hardens his tongue and pushes it inside me, as deep as it'll go, licking my inners walls, drinking my cream. He makes a low growling sound as he tongue-fucks me, sending the vibrations right up through me.

I grip his soft hair in my fist, grinding up on his face. There is zero chance of me not reaching orgasm if he keeps this up.

"Fuck, I love how your pussy tastes. I could die happy with my tongue buried inside you."

I thought I'd probably die happy that way, too.

He uses his fingers in a V to part my pussy lips and make my clit pop, then he latches on to me, suckling my clit in a rhythmical pulse.

"Oh, God," I cry, bucking my hips.

He pauses long enough to say, "Tell me how that feels."

"It feels fucking incredible," I manage, each word punctuated with a gasp.

My inner walls clench, desperate for something to grip on to.

He rams two fingers inside me, hard and fast. Then he adds a third. Cade does not have small hands, and I feel myself stretching. There's some pain, but mostly it feels good.

"You're taking my fingers like a good girl," he says. "Think you can manage one more?"

I don't know if I can, but I want to try. I want to please him.

"There's my good little stepsister. Stretch around my fist. I know that sweet pussy wants me."

I'm wet, so wet. I can smell myself on the air and hear the squelching of his fingers inside me.

I twist my face away. "Oh, God, those noises…"

"Don't be embarrassed. I love those sounds. I love how wet you get for me. You're fucking dripping, Laney. If you gush, even better. I'll catch every drop in my mouth and drink you down."

He has to pull out of me to readjust the positions of his fingers. Without him inside me, I feel like I'm gaping open. Will I be swollen and bruised after this? I don't even care.

He pauses long enough to reach into my bedside drawer, where I keep the lube. He takes out the tube and squeezes it onto his hand. Then he pushes my legs even farther apart and slides three fingers back inside me, before adding his pinky finger to the mix.

Strange mewls and whimpers escape my throat. My head is spinning. All I'm focusing on is the sensation of my pussy stretching to accommodate him.

"That's right, my beautiful girl. Take my whole hand inside you."

"I can't, I can't." The sensations are too much for me to take. I think my head is likely to explode.

"Yes, you can. Trust me."

He goes back to sucking on my clit, while he carefully edges his hand inside me. I stretch and clench around him. I buck my hips and grab for something to hold on to. My back arches, my thigh muscles tense. My whole body is a quivering mess that's centered purely on what's happening between my thighs. The noises I'm making don't even sound human, guttural and raw.

"Oh, fuck, I'm gonna come."

I literally see stars, my vision blackening around the edges. My climax shudders through my whole body, and I jerk and convulse, my eyes rolling, my toes curling. The wetness between my legs is embarrassing—did I pee myself?

I realize the cut has also made a mess of the sheets. There's blood streaked across the material.

God, I could die.

"You squirted for me, little sis," Cade says. "Now let me clean you up."

He slides his hand from my body, and his mouth is back on me, his clever tongue licking me again, but differently this time, lapping up my juices like he can't get enough.

Then he moves up my body, using his arms to hold himself above me.

"Think you can take me?" he asks, "You're not too sore?"

"I want you," I tell him.

"Good."

He kisses me, and I can taste myself on his tongue. It fires something inside me, and I kiss him harder, our tongues tangling. He rests on one arm to open his jeans, and I reach for him.

I've missed his cock. It's big, and long, and hard. I thumb the piercing through the tip, spreading the slick pre-cum I find there.

He groans, and I run my hand up and down his length, keeping my grip firm.

We're face to face, nose to nose, body to body. He pushes into me and moves slowly at first, his strokes deep and deliberate.

"Fuck, I love you so much, Laney. You're everything to me. I don't want anything or anyone else."

"I love you, too."

He speaks to me as he moves inside me. "You're my whole world. I don't ever want to be apart from you. If things change between us…"

I wonder where all this is coming from. "They won't," I reassure him.

He stares deep into my eyes, and I feel like he's trying to tell me something via telepathy, but then his hips move faster.

His jaw clenches, and the act of fucking me absorbs whatever it was he'd been about to say.

# 30
## Laney

THERE'S A PARADE HAPPENING IN THE CITY.

Reed wants to take me.

There will be live music, and floats with dancing girls, and stalls selling street food and booze.

I want to make him happy, and I also don't want to give him a reason to be worried about me.

"Come on, Laney," he insists. "It'll be fun."

"What about Darius and Cade?"

"I was hoping we could spend some time it being just the two of us."

I'm not sure how it can just be the two of us when we'll be in big crowds of people, but I understand what he means. It's important I spend quality time with each of them. One of the things Reed was worried about back in the cabin was that I'd come between them, cause jealousy and a rift, and I'll do whatever I can to ensure that doesn't happen.

"I'm not sure…"

He takes my hand. "Is it the crowds you're worried about?"

"Pretty much," I admit.

"They'll give us some anonymity, though," he insists. "There will be so many people there that no one will pay us the slightest bit of attention."

It's been weeks now since we were rescued, and the heat has been dying down. I haven't seen anything online about us. The press has even stopped talking about Darius's disastrous comeback performance.

Flight Crash Investigation teams are still trying to find the plane. I feel terrible for the families of the people who died in the crash, that we hadn't been able to help them more, but this is our survival we're talking about. It doesn't need to be forever, just until after winter, so we know if Smith and the others are still out there, they won't have made it either. One day, we'll work harder to help the investigation teams find the location of the plane and then we'll help them return the bodies to their loved ones.

"Okay," I relent, "but if it gets too much, we can leave, right?"

He kisses me. "Absolutely. Just say the word and we'll get out of there."

I'm still unsure, but I agree.

We arrive downtown shortly after eight p.m., and the party is in full swing. I have to admit it seems like fun. The energy from both the people and the music lifts my soul, and, once we've grabbed food and drinks—fish tacos and a virgin margarita for me—I find myself dancing along with everyone else, my arms lifted in the air. The signs of my usual panic attacks haven't arisen, and I'm feeling good.

Reed leans into me. "You having a good time?"

I grin up at him. "Yes, I am. Thank you for bringing me."

"You can't hide away in that trailer forever, baby-girl."

"I know."

One of the girls on the floats throws some beads our way, and Reed catches them and strings them around my neck.

"Perfect," he says.

I'm surprised to find I'm having a good time.

"Laney!"

The male voice catches my attention, and a moment later, an arm is flung around my neck. Panic rises inside me, but then I realize who it is.

"Sonny," I say. "You nearly gave me a heart attack."

A wave of booze floats off of him.

"Sorry, Laney. Just wanted to say hi." He glances over at Reed. "This must be your dad," he says.

My cheeks burn. "My stepfather," I correct him.

"Can I borrow her to come and dance?"

He grabs my hand, dragging me through the crowds. I throw a backward glance to Reed. It's not that I mind dancing with Sonny, but my gut tells me this isn't going to end well.

Reed's expression has taken on a hardness I've never seen in him before.

He storms after me, shoving people out of the way, ignoring their cries of protest. He reaches the spot where Sonny— completely oblivious to what is going on—is still trying to dance with me. His hands are on my hips, but he's not making any other contact with me. I almost feel sorry for the guy. He's trying to have fun, but he's completely misread the situation.

Reed reaches us and shoves Sonny in the chest.

Sonny's eyes widen, and he stumbles back in surprise. "What the fuck?"

"Get your fucking hands off her."

"It's okay, Reed," I say. "He wasn't doing anything. We're just dancing."

"You only dance with me."

Reed twirls me away from Sonny and jams his hips against mine.

Sonny stares at us. "Your family is fucking weird."

He can sense there's something going on, his gaze flicking between us. His expression goes from confusion to under-standing dawning.

"Oh, shit. You're *with* your stepfather?" Then he must remember Cade back at the trailer. "And your stepbrother, too?" His disgust at the situation is written all over his features. He throws up both hands. "I don't want to get in the middle of *that*." And he turns and walks away.

I glare at Reed.

"Do you see what you did then? You overreacted. He knows something is going on between us. Something more than a stepfather and stepdaughter."

"I don't give a fuck. I'm not having some boy thinking he can take you from me."

He catches up my hand and pulls me away from the main drag where the parade is happening, and into a small parking lot.

We're fighting now.

"He wasn't taking me away. He's a friend. We were just dancing."

"You don't get to dance with anyone else. You're ours. Got it?"

"Fuck, Reed. I'm allowed to be my own person."

"No. Your mouth is ours. Your pussy is ours. Your ass is ours. No other kid is thinking he's got a chance with you. Now, turn around."

"What?"

"I said turn around."

He spins me around so I'm facing the car, bends me over the hood, and yanks up my skirt. He drags my panties to one side and roughly plunges two fingers inside me. I cry out, the force of him shoving me forward. I'm instantly wet.

"Take it, baby-girl. This is Daddy's pussy."

He fingers me roughly, his digits curled to apply pressure to the spot on the inside of my walls. I whimper and moan.

Then I hear the clink of his belt buckle. He reaches over the top of me and uses the belt to cinch my wrists together.

I'm splayed across the hood, half-naked, exposed. He kicks

my feet apart. A cold night breeze kisses my wet skin, and I can smell myself on the air.

"I'm gonna fuck you now."

Maybe I should protest more—fight back—but I'm fully into this. Seeing this possessive, dominant side of Reed had made me forget all about what happened with Sonny.

"Take me, Daddy. Fuck me hard."

The head of his cock presses to my opening—hard and smooth and hot. He barely pauses long enough for me to snatch a breath, then rams in deep and hard.

"Oh, fuck," I cry out.

He's not taking any prisoners. He grabs both of my hips and fucks me hard and fast.

My head is spinning; my brain has gone into meltdown. We're both chasing the high of a climax and giving no thought to anything else.

"Ah, fuck, baby-girl. I'm coming. I'm filling your tight little pussy with my milk."

The noises that leave his lips are some of the hottest sounds I've ever heard—so raw and primal.

I come with him, my body shattering around his cock.

I lay slumped on the hood of the car, breathing hard. My hands are still bound with his belt. My heart thumps in my chest.

Suddenly, Reed pulls away from me, tugging my skirt back down to cover me up.

"Shit," he curses.

I lift my head and chest. "What's wrong?"

"Someone was over there."

"You think someone saw us?"

I realize how stupid we've been. How incredibly reckless. What had we been thinking, having sex out in the open like this? Yes, it had been incredibly hot, but no orgasm was worth the risk.

"I'm sure it was no one," Reed says.

I don't believe him.

"We shouldn't have done that." I hold out my arms. "Quick. Untie me."

He does and threads his belt back through his jeans.

"Do you think it was Sonny?" I ask.

He shakes his head. "No, I don't think so, but it was hard to get a good look."

"Is this going to cause us problems?"

"No, I'm sure it'll be fine." Despite his words, his expression is troubled. His forehead is furrowed, his lips thinned.

He places his hand on my lower back. "Let's get you home."

# 31
## *Laney*

I WAKE THE FOLLOWING MORNING TO THE RINGING OF MY PHONE.

I'm back in my own bed in the trailer, and I feel around for my cell. I locate it and check the screen. Cade's name flashes up.

"Hey," I answer, half sitting and brushing my tangled mess of hair out of my face. "What's up?"

"Have you been online?" he asks.

"What? No. You just woke me."

"I tried to think of a way to protect you from it, but the truth is there isn't one."

My stomach drops. "Protect me from what?" As so often is the case, the first thing my mind jumps to is Smith and his men. "Have they been found? Are they being brought home?"

His confusion is clear in his tone. "What? No, Laney. It's not that. It's you and Reed."

*Fuck.*

My heart clenches, the air in my lungs freezing. I don't even tell Cade to hang on, I just pull up a social media site and search Reed's name. Sure enough, there's a picture of Reed bending me over the car. The angle of the shot means no intimate part of either of us is exposed, but it's obvious what we're doing.

"Oh, God."

With the photograph is the headline: *Reed Riviera in intimate cinch with barely of-age stepdaughter.* Accompanying it is the by-line: *What really happened in the wilderness?*

"No, no, no," I mutter.

I pull up a different site.

*Did Reed Riviera groom his underage stepdaughter?*

It's exactly what we feared.

I put the phone back to my ear. "Where is Reed? Is he okay?"

"What do you think, Laney? What the fuck were you two playing at?"

There is nothing I can say to make this better. "I...*We* weren't thinking..."

"I can see that. The pair of you have ruined everything. We'll never recover from this."

"*We'll* never recover? Your name isn't even mentioned, Cade. Mine is, and Reed of course, and Darius for being Reed's son, but not yours. You're nothing!"

I speak out of anger and self-defense, but he didn't deserve that.

"I'm so—" I start, but the line is already dead. Cade has gone. Will he ever want to speak to me again? Tears stream down my cheeks. I wish I could go back and change what we did last night, but it's impossible. What's done is done.

Someone would have found out eventually. Were we supposed to keep our relationship a secret forever? No, it wasn't supposed to be forever, just until the media storm surrounding the plane crash went down, and I hadn't even been able to do that.

I think of something and go to my window. I crack open the drapes and peer out. My breath catches. Sure enough, several strange vehicles are parked outside. People I don't recognize hang out beside the cars and vans. A couple have large professional cameras hanging around their necks.

Shit. Reporters.

Fresh tears fill my eyes. I'm too hot and my heart beats fast. I swallow down a wave of sickness. What am I going to do? I can't hide out in the trailer forever, but the moment I try to step outside, the reporters are going to swamp me.

It was one thing having to deal with them when they only wanted to talk about the crash and how we survived, but this is something else entirely.

What am I supposed to say?

I can hardly deny there is anything between us considering they have photographic proof. Should I stand up for Reed and tell the press that nothing happened between us until after I'd turned eighteen? Would they believe me? Or is it something a groomed victim would say? I have no idea. But does staying silent make him look worse?

For the moment, I can't face doing anything. I want to climb back into bed and pull the covers over my head. I can't deal with this. It's all too much.

What about Reed? This is going to be a hell of a lot worse for him. Does he hate me now? Does he regret ever getting involved with me? He must rue the day he received the phone call to say my mother had died and he was my only living relative. They're making him out to be a weirdo, a pervert, even a child abuser. Nothing could be further from the truth.

If Reed hates me, then Darius and Cade are going to utterly despise me. I'll have singlehandedly destroyed their father.

Would it be better or worse if the whole world knew I'd been sleeping with Cade and Dax, too?

I don't know what to do. One thing I do know is I won't be stepping outside of the trailer door anytime soon.

Instead, I do what I'd planned and climb back into bed. I pull the covers over my head. I still have my cell phone clutched in my hands. I will for a message or a call from any of them, but my phone taunts me with its silence.

Despite my better judgment, I torment myself by going back

through all the social media articles. There are so many, it's over-whelming. All the stories have a similar theme and wording. It's as though one member of the paparazzi has gotten hold of the information and sold it to anyone who'll take it.

Then I make the mistake of reading the comments.

**< Why does the stepfather get all the blame? I bet she's just a whore who'll spread her legs for anyone.>**

**< Little slut. Bet she screwed her two brothers as well.>**

That someone has guessed the truth punches me in the gut.

**< Bet the stepfather is a pedo. Should be stoned to death IMO.>**

**< Dirty old man. Needs locking away>**

**< I'll never listen to Darius Riviera again. I bet he's as bad as his father!>**

I'm shaking all over, my hands trembling. This is awful—so much worse than anything I'd imagined.

All I can do is hide away. My appearance to the press will only stir up more of a media frenzy. If I hide for long enough, maybe everyone will forget about this.

It's early, but I need a drink. I have a bottle of vodka under the sink. I've watched my mother destroy herself with drink and drugs and her bad choices of men, and for the first time in my life I understand how she felt. It's what I want to do now—destroy myself. I don't deserve any happiness or kindness in my life. I'm just that girl with her legs spread on the beach while a man who hated her fucked her. I'm the girl on the bed with a gun pushed inside her.

I'm disgusting, repulsive.

I ruin people. I ruin lives.

Getting out of bed, I find the bottle of vodka, unscrew the cap, and take a swig. It burns down my throat, and I grimace. I suck in a sharp breath and drink some more. I keep drinking, seeking oblivion. It doesn't help my sadness, though, and I continue to cry. I drink again. I don't care that it's first thing in the morning and I haven't even had breakfast yet.

I've lost everything.

I glance up at the urn containing my mother's ashes still sitting on my shelf, and stagger to my feet and lift it down. Then I sit back on the floor, hugging what remains of my mother.

The mother I'd railed against all my life, but who I'm more like than I'd ever known.

# 32

*laney*

I CAN'T SLEEP.

It doesn't matter how much I lie on the bed, staring at the walls, my brain simply refuses to switch off. The people I want to be with more than anything are the same ones I can't go anywhere near. If I even try, the press will be on me like a swarm of locusts.

Destroying me and the men I love.

I remember the medicine cabinet in the bathroom. My mom was forever popping pills—uppers, downers—I'm not sure even she knew what she was taking half the time. If I can find something that will turn off the world, if only for a little while, then it will help.

Maybe it's a slippery slope to head down, but I don't even care. What's going to become of me now, anyway? What possible future can I have? If it's one that doesn't have the guys in it, then what's the point? I'll never have their kind of love again. I'll never have people in my life who truly know, who completely understand and get what I went through. Our shared experiences and trauma have bonded us like nothing else. I simply can't picture a future without them in it.

I don't *want* a future without them in it.

I'm nauseated and light-headed as I make my way to the bathroom. My legs don't seem to belong to me, and acid burns up my throat. I've never experienced jetlag, but I guess this is what it feels like. My lack of sleep means I've completely lost track of the day and my regular sleep pattern.

In the tiny bathroom, the final resting place of my mother, I open the small cabinet. It has a mirrored door, and I pause half-way, catching a glimpse of my reflection. I don't look eighteen years old. If I'd had to guess, I'd have said at least late twenties to early thirties—and a rough early thirties at that. My hair is a bird's nest, my skin pale and blotchy, dark circles under my eyes. I think I'd looked better at the cabin.

I experience a sudden pang of longing to go back there, but as swiftly as that sensation hits me, the memory of what Smith and his men did to me arrives on its tail.

We can never go back. What good memories we had there have been ruined. Now it's tainted with pain and violence.

I gulp back a sob and reached into the cabinet. Multiple bottles of pills are within reach, so I pick up the nearest and check the prescription. I have no idea what the pills do, but I tip a couple into my palm. Then I take down another bottle and do the same. It should be enough to knock me out.

But what if I want more?

I shake the thought from my head.

The razor blade on the side draws my attention. It would be easy, wouldn't it? Just a few handfuls of pills, a couple of good drinks from the bottle of vodka, then some cuts up my wrist—vertically, not horizontally—and I could close my eyes and not have to worry about waking up. It would be relatively painless, except for the razor, but if I drink enough and take enough pills before I do that part, I'm sure I won't feel much.

Besides, the pain of a razor cut is nothing compared to the

pain in my heart. My whole chest feels as though it's opened up and become a yawning chasm, and now I'm exposed and raw.

I'm not strong enough to handle this.

For now, the pull of oblivion releases its grip, and I take the pills back to bed with me.

# 33
## REED

I<small>T'S BEEN TWENTY-FOUR HOURS NOW SINCE THE SHIT HIT THE</small> fan, and the press still haven't given up.

They're camped on our doorstep, the road crowded with them.

Should I contact a lawyer? No criminal charges have been brought against me, but I'm wondering if I'm going to need to protect myself.

I want to phone Laney, check if she's all right, but I'm worried our phones might have been tapped. Will it only make things worse for her if any of us try to contact her? If we leave her alone, will the reporters leave her be, too?

She doesn't deserve this. She's been through so much already.

"What are we going to do?" Cade asks. "We can't hide away inside this house forever."

Darius drags his hand through his hair. "What choice do we have? If we go out there, we're going to be hounded."

Cade shakes his head. "We should never have let Laney go back to the trailer. She should be here with us."

I hold up a hand. "First of all, we don't get to decide what Laney does or doesn't do. She's an adult, and she gets to make her own choices." I take a breath, painfully aware of how hypocritical I'm being right now considering how I'd acted when that boy had tried to dance with her. "Secondly, how do you think it would be better for her to be here with us? What would the press do if they knew she was locked away in this house with us? What would the cops do? They'd probably decide she was in some kind of danger and raid the place. Imagine the media showdown if that happened?"

"But she's alone," Dax says. "It's not right that she's alone."

He's right. It suddenly hits me how little I know of Laney's life outside of us. I know she used to work, but I couldn't say where. She's never spoken of any friends who might have been missing her. The only person I knew was in her life was her mom, and she's dead.

"Fuck." I knot my fingers in my hair. "What are we going to do?"

I'm normally the one with the answers, not the one asking the questions.

My two sons stare at me, but no one provides a solution.

---

LATER THAT AFTERNOON, my concerns about the police showing up are proven to be real.

A cop car pulls up in front of the house, and two uniformed police officers knock on my door and then ask that I come with them. They don't put me in cuffs, but they do pat me down for weapons. The press have an absolute field day snapping photographs of me being put in the back of the car.

Within an hour, I find myself in an interview room.

The room is bare, apart from a table in the middle of it, and chairs on either side. In the corners of the room are cameras, and I'm fairly sure it's rigged with recording equipment, too.

An officer in his late forties, who introduces himself as Detective Knox, is there to interview me.

"I'm not under arrest?" I check.

"No, Mr. Riviera. You're simply helping us with our enquiries."

"I see. I'm fairly sure I know what those enquiries are about."

I can't lose my temper. As frustrating and insulting as this is, it won't look good for me if I come across as hot-headed or violent. I've always known this would happen. It would come out at some point. I could kick myself for being so stupid, though. What the hell had we been thinking, having sex out in the open like that? We hadn't been thinking; that was the problem.

On a laptop, Detective Knox pulls up a still image. It's clearly me, with my fucking pants open, and Laney bent over the hood of a car. My chest tightens, but my cock also tingles at the sight. It's not good timing to get an erection.

"Can you identify the two people in this photograph, Mr. Riviera?"

"Yes. That's me and Laney Flores."

"As you can see from the photograph, it's been brought to our attention that you have a sexual relationship with your step-daughter."

From the look of disgust on his face, it's clear what he thinks of me.

"That's right. There's no point in me denying it. We're not related by blood, and she's eighteen. We're both adults. Legally, we haven't done anything wrong."

The detective clears his throat. "See, that's what we have to figure out. Laney Flores came into your guardianship when she was seventeen years old. We need to know the nature of your relationship while she was still underage."

"There was no nature of our relationship. We barely had one

back then. She didn't come into my life until shortly before she turned eighteen."

"You have to understand, Mr. Riviera, that Miss Flores was trusted into your guardianship when she was an emotionally vulnerable young person. Did you and your sons take advantage of that?"

I grind my teeth. "I don't believe so."

"Did your sons have a sexual relationship with your stepdaughter before she turned eighteen?"

I hate that he's brought Darius and Cade into this. He has no proof that there's anything between them.

"No, they did not."

"Three adult men and a vulnerable girl, all trapped together in the wilderness. She had no one else to turn to. You can understand how this looks from the outside."

A horrible thought occurs to me. What if he's already spoken to Laney, and she's said that we hurt her?

"You're saying that we groomed her?"

I hate the suggestion. Is it because there's just a tiny part of me that worries he might be right? I remember seeing Laney for the first time, how it had been like a punch in the chest. She'd had a physical impact on me from the moment I'd laid eyes on her. But I'd done my absolute best not to cross any boundaries that would have been considered inappropriate, at least until she'd come of age. Had Cade and Darius done the same? I couldn't say for sure. It wasn't as though I'd been with them every second of every day. Besides, Cade had acted as though he hated Laney, at least at first, and I didn't think Darius was like that.

"You're putting words in my mouth, Mr. Riviera," the detective replies curtly.

I turn the questions back on him. "Have you ever been in a plane crash?"

"No, I'm fortunate enough to say that I haven't."

"What about any other survival situation?"

"Again, no."

"Let me tell you that the absolute last thing you're thinking about is grooming someone. We were focused on our survival, on finding shelter and food. We were focused on not getting sick or injured, because if we did, it could kill us. Yes, over time, our relationships changed, but none of us did anything wrong, and I am one hundred percent certain that when you speak to Laney, she will say the same."

Am I one hundred percent certain, though? Do I truly know Laney's mind? What if she looks back on events and sees things differently? She'd been traumatized by the assault and rape, and by the struggle to survive. Maybe that has warped things in her mind. What if her insistence to stay at the trailer was actually a way of creating some distance between us so she could unravel what had happened?

Time is a strange thing. It has the ability to warp memories. The stories we tell ourselves solidify themselves in our neural pathways to the point where they become real to us, even if the actual events played out differently.

But I remember the morning she came to me, when she had me take her virginity, but I hadn't even known she was a virgin. There was no way that was me seducing her. She had wanted me, and she'd made it very clear that she wanted me. I hadn't misread that.

The detective nods and scribbles something down. "I'll make sure our records are updated to show I've spoken with you. Assuming Miss Flores' account of events match your own, we won't be proceeding any further."

"That's good to know." I get to my feet. I want out of there.

"Oh, Mr. Riviera, how *did* you survive out there all that time?"

"We had each other to live for," I reply.

# 34

## Laney

I STARE AT THE IMAGE ON MY LAPTOP SCREEN.

The police have arrested Reed. It's all over the internet.

I want to scream and cry, to claw at my face, and tear out my hair. I was the one who first instigated things with him. I was the one who seduced him back in the cabin, despite knowing he was trying to do the right thing and behave himself. I'd practically torn off my panties and forced myself on him.

I've ruined his life.

I pick up the vodka bottle beside me and take another swig. I've almost finished it, and so I throw a couple of pills into my mouth as well. I'm desperate for oblivion, but so far all it's given me is a cloudy mind, heavy limbs, and a headache.

In a rush of adrenaline and certainty, I jump to my feet and go to the bathroom. I find the razor blade, still sitting beside the sink. The sharp edge of it is dark with dried blood, and I pick it up and rinse it beneath the faucet. The crusty dried brown turns red, and my breath catches as it swirls down the sink.

The first cut is hesitant, almost experimental. It's just a nick on the inside of my wrist. How much will it bleed?

I only want to close my eyes and for this to be over.

The guys will be better off without me. I'm just a nuisance to them. Without me, they can get on with their lives. No one will be able to accuse Reed of anything if I no longer exist. Maybe I'll even see my mom again on the other side.

My chest clenches with pain, and it dawns on me how much I've missed her.

Was that the reason I'd insisted on returning to the trailer? It hadn't been as much about me needing my space and independence as it had been about wanting to have some time to be close to her again. She hadn't been the best of mothers, but she'd still be the only one I'd ever had. The only *parent* I'd ever had. While Reed might be my stepfather legally, he'd never been a dad to me in any way. He'd raised Cade and Darius, though. They'd been important enough in his life for him to sober up and get clean. He'd never done that for me.

I thought I'd gotten over that pain during the change in our relationship, but clearly it has always been there, simmering beneath the surface.

Blood trickles from the wound. I like seeing it. It comforts me, like an old friend. All I want is peace. A rest from the whirling torment of my thoughts and the pain in my heart.

I've always believed I'm not strong enough to deal with all this. I guess I'm right.

I take the blade to my bed, picking up the bottle of vodka and a couple of containers of pills on the way.

I have no idea how much vodka I've drunk or the number of pills I've taken, but my eyes are heavy, and my thoughts are cloudy. If I want to be certain I won't wake again I need to make the cut bigger.

The razor blade grows slippery with blood between my fingers, and I almost drop it. My dexterity seems to be leaving me, my fingers feeling fat and numb.

Is it the drugs and alcohol that are affecting me? Or the loss of blood?

I'm not sure, but before it's too late, I draw the blade up the inside of my wrist once again.

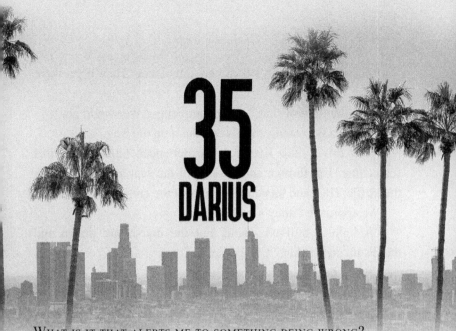

# 35
## DARIUS

W<small>HAT IS IT THAT ALERTS ME TO SOMETHING BEING WRONG</small>?

I wish I knew, but it's as though someone speaks inside my head, telling me to go to her.

I can't do that alone.

"Something's wrong with Laney," I tell Cade.

He frowns at me. "What? How do you know that?"

"I have no idea, but I do. We have to go to her trailer. Now."

I'm already on my feet. If Cade won't take me, I'll have to call a cab, but I'd prefer it if the rest of my family came. I need their eyes, especially if my instinct is right.

"Can you get her on the phone?" Cade asks.

Reed is back from the police station, so he tries. I can hear the distant ringing, the way no one answers.

"Fuck," he curses. "The press—will they follow us if we go to her?"

"I don't give a fuck if they do," I reply. "We need to go now. We're wasting time."

I sense Cade's stare.

"You think she's done something stupid," he says.

I don't know what to say, but yes, I do. I feel it in my bones.

Reed is on his feet. "I'll call an ambulance. They'll get there faster."

"You don't know that," Cade comments. "We should go."

I'm already moving. "Let's call them on the way."

Reed drives like I've never experienced before, the tires screeching. I'm thrown side to side in the seat as he negotiates the traffic. His hand hits the horn almost the entire way.

We approach Laney's trailer.

"A light is still on inside, but the drapes are drawn and there's no sign of her," Cade describes.

I know he's doing it for my benefit.

"What about the reporters?" I ask.

"No sign of them. They must have gotten a call about some other poor bastards they can tear apart."

Cade throws himself out of the car before it's even stopped moving. I want to follow, but it's not so easy for me. I hate it when I'm reliant on someone else to find my way around, but I don't know exactly where Reed has stopped the car.

"Wait," I tell my father. "I need to follow you."

He pauses long enough to let me take his shoulder, and together we hurriedly follow Cade.

The screen door swings open with a creek and bangs shut again.

I negotiate the steps to the front door.

"Oh, fuck!" Cade yells.

The iron tang of blood is in the air, combined with stale alcohol.

"Oh, God." Reed leaves me and, I assume, rushes to her side. "Laney? Wake up, baby-girl. Stay with us. Help is on its way."

I'm desperate. "What is it? What's she done?" It's easy enough to find my way around the trailer. There isn't much to it, after all. "Where is she?" I demand.

"In the bed," Reed says, his voice choked.

My blood runs cold. Are we too late? The thought of Laney

being dead opens a giant chasm in my chest, and for a dizzying moment, I think I'm going to fall into it. How will any of us continue if she's gone? Suddenly, the thought of never playing the violin to a crowd again doesn't seem the slightest bit important. I'd give it up in an instant if it meant saving her.

I follow the sound of my father's voice to be at her side.

"Where the fuck are those paramedics?" Reed says.

"Motherfucker!" Cade smashes his fist against the wall and lets out a roar of rage and pain.

I understand exactly what he's feeling. I want to do the same. How have we let this happen? We should have been here with her. We never should have given her the chance to do this terrible thing.

"Should we take her to the hospital ourselves?" I wonder.

From outside comes the rise and fall of sirens in the distance.

"They're coming," Reed says, his relief clear in his tone. "Help is coming."

I go to the side of her bed, desperate to make contact with her. I drop to my knees on the floor and reach out to her.

She's still warm to the touch. I lower my cheek to her mouth and feel the heat of her breath. She's still breathing. I take her wrist, my fingertips meeting with wet stickiness. In my mind, I'm building a picture. She hurt herself. How could she do that? Doesn't she know that she'd take all our hearts with her if she died?

I turn my head away from her to address the others. "We need bandages, to stop the bleeding."

"I know where she has some," Cade says.

His footsteps slowly fade as he disappears into one of the other rooms.

I hear the brush of material on skin as Reed pulls up her sleeve. The breath of horror on the air as he curses once more. "What the fuck?"

"What is it?" I demand to know.

"There are other cuts. She's been hurting herself."

I cover my mouth with my hand. We've failed her so badly.

Cade returns with the bandages, and he nudges me out of the way so he can wrap her wrist.

"I thought we were doing the right thing by staying away," Reed says. His voice is broken. I hear the anguish in his tone. He's blaming himself, too.

We all are.

The sirens grow louder. I hear Cade's footsteps as he rushes out to them.

"This way!" he yells. "She's through here."

Strangers are in the trailer now. Paramedics. They're brusque and efficient, moving us out of the way with requests of "Give us space, please." There are too many of us in this small space.

They're taking her to the hospital.

"I'm going to ride with her," Reed says. "Cade, can you drive you and Dax? I'll meet you there."

"Yeah, of course." He sounds stunned.

Then they're gone, and it's just me and my brother left in the blood-soaked trailer.

# 36

## Laney

THE ROOM IS TOO BRIGHT.

Sunlight presses against the backs of my eyelids, telling them to open. I don't want to. I hadn't ever wanted to open them again. From somewhere nearby comes a steady beeping. A hospital monitor of some kind. I remember what happened almost instantly, and my heart sinks. It didn't work. How could it not have worked? Did I not press deeply enough? Was the cut not long enough? Had I not taken enough pills?

Before I've even opened my eyes, I feel the wetness of a tear slide down my cheek.

A male voice comes from near my head.

"She's crying. Why is she crying?" His tone changes, directed toward me now. "Laney? Baby-girl? Are you awake?"

It's Reed. Maybe I should be happy that he's here, but I'm not. I don't want him to see me like this. Does he know what I did, or tried to do? He must, if he's here. Someone must have called him—he's my next of kin, after all.

I'm embarrassed, humiliated, and the sadness residing deep in my soul hasn't gone anywhere.

Someone takes my hand, the grip firm and warm.

It's Darius. "Laney, can you hear us? Can you open your eyes?"

But I don't want to. More than anything, I just want to vanish. This is even worse than before.

Are all three of them here? I've let them down so badly. Did the press follow them? God only knows what they'll be writing about us now. I can't bring myself to open my eyes because then I'll have to look into theirs and see the pain and disappointment I've caused. I already have so much pain inside me. I'm not strong enough to bear their load, too.

I hear a doctor or nurse's voice, speaking in low tones. I pick up on a couple of words. *Suicide risk.*

Yes, I guess I am, and I can't even find it in me to care. Why didn't they let me die? It would have been easier that way.

As much as I might want to, I can't lie here with my eyes shut forever. I have to face them.

I force open my eyes, squinting against the bright light.

"She's awake!" Cade shouts.

Reed squeezes my hand. "Christ, Laney. You gave us one hell of a scare. How are you feeling?"

I feel like shit—mentally, emotionally, and physically.

"Water?" I ask. "I need some water."

They spring into action, probably happy to have something practical to do. Reed lifts a small paper cup to my lips. It's blissfully chilled and helps to soothe my sore throat and wet my lips and tongue.

I push the cup away and fall back onto my pillow. "Thank you."

Darius takes my other hand and lowers his head to press his forehead against it. "Don't ever do that again."

I don't reply. Reed and Darius are seated on either side of me, but Cade hasn't even sat down. He doesn't even seem to be able to bring himself to look at me.

"You were going to leave us?" Cade paces back and forth

past the window. His jaw is clenched, the muscles ticking. "How could you do that to us?"

"I was doing you a favor."

"No!" he rages. "No, you fucking weren't. What would we all do without you? You think our lives would be better, somehow? Fuck that. How could you ever think such a thing?"

"It's true."

"No, it fucking isn't. Would you say the same if I tried to kill myself, or Darius? Would you say any of us were better off?"

I shake my head against the pillow. "It's not the same thing."

"Yes, it is. I never took you for a fucking coward, Laney."

"Cade, that's enough," Reed warns. "She doesn't need this."

"No, he's right. I am a coward. I'm not brave, or anything else you think about me. The person you've built me up to be in your mind is not the same person I am in real life."

Reed brushes my hair away from my face. "You're *you*, Laney. That's all we ever want you to be. Just for you to be who you are, one hundred percent. The good, the bad, and the ugly. No matter what struggles you might be going through, if you're at your strongest or your weakest. It doesn't matter to us. We love you. We will always be here for you, no matter what's going on in the outside world. You are the most important thing to us."

"I've let you down so much."

"No, you haven't. *We* let you down. We should have seen how much pain you were in and stepped in sooner. We should never have stayed away."

"He's right," Cade says. "I'm sorry. I'm angry with myself as much as anything."

The three of them crowd around my bed.

They bury their faces into me—my neck, my chest, my stomach. I reach for them, making sure to touch all of them, running my fingers through their hair, feeling the solid muscle of the backs of their necks, the breadth of their shoulders. My chest swells with emotion, and fresh tears slip down my cheeks. I don't know what I've ever done in my life to deserve these three, but I'm so grateful to them.

"You're not alone in this world, Laney," Reed continues to reassure me. "Not anymore. It doesn't matter if you depend on us, because we depend on you, too. That's what happens when you love someone, when you need someone. There's nothing wrong with that."

"What are we going to do about the press?" I ask. "They're going to keep coming."

"They won't," Darius says. "They'll get bored of this story soon enough, I promise."

I choke back a sob. "It doesn't feel that way. There must be more interesting things going on than us."

Cade gives me a rueful smile. "Maybe not right now, but there will be."

Reed sits up straight. "They know now, so there's no point in trying to hide away. I'm going to tell the world the truth—that I love you, and we're both consenting adults who can do what they want. I'll stand on the top of the Hollywood sign and shout it to the whole city if that's what it takes. No one is ever going to make me feel like I have to hide our love again."

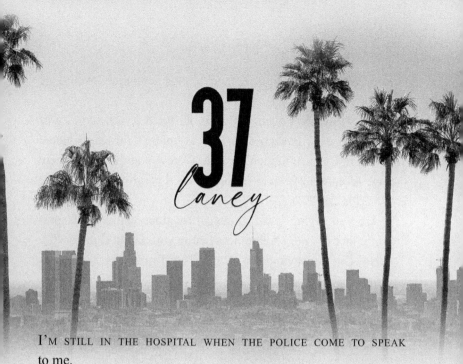

# 37
## *Laney*

I'M STILL IN THE HOSPITAL WHEN THE POLICE COME TO SPEAK to me.

The officer in charge introduces himself as Detective Knox. I've never been good with authority figures, and having this man in my room makes me want to hide under the bed.

But I remind myself how much our future relies on me making sure the police know that Reed did nothing wrong, so I force myself to sit up straight and make eye contact with this man.

"Miss Flores," he starts, "I realize this isn't easy to speak about, especially after you've been through so much already, but you understand that we have to follow through with these things when complaints are made."

"Complaints from whom?" I ask. "Not from me."

"It's been brought to our attention that you have what some might consider…" he clears his throat… "an inappropriate relationship with your stepfather, Reed Riviera."

I hold my chin high. "Is something being considered inappropriate also illegal now?"

"No, you're right about that, but if this relationship began before you turned eighteen, then it most definitely would be considered illegal."

"But we weren't even in California for the vast majority of the time we were in each other's lives before I turned eighteen. We were in Canada, though we didn't know it at the time, where the age of consent is sixteen. Surely we'd be governed by those laws in this case?"

"Are you saying you had sexual relations with your stepfather or either of your stepbrothers before you turned eighteen?"

"No. I'm not saying that at all. What I'm saying is that you have no reason to be here, Detective. No crime has been committed. I'm an adult. I can choose to be with whoever I want."

I wish I was as confident as I'm making myself sound.

"We will be speaking with both your stepbrothers as well."

"Speak to whoever you want. Like I said, no crime has been committed. You're wasting your time. It's not as though Los Angeles doesn't have enough real criminals to chase after. I'm sure your time would be better spent elsewhere."

He sucks in a breath and nods, then flips his folder shut. "Unfortunately, high profile cases tend to take priority, and as I'm sure you've seen from the amount of newspaper and social media coverage, your case is definitely considered high profile."

"I understand," I say, though I don't. Not really.

Cases that make the newspapers and social media will always get more police attention than those that don't, and often it means the cases that aren't properly investigated are the same ones that aren't newsworthy enough. It's the reason most people can name white serial killers but can rarely mention killers who are people of color. People tend to kill within their races, and the media doesn't seem to care about men or women of color who are murdered. There's even a term for it—Missing White Woman Syndrome. They're the stories that will sell papers. I watched a documentary about it before the crash.

Detective Knox continues, "I know this must be hard, but I understand that you tried to take your own life a few days ago."

I'm still ashamed about what I did. "Yes. I made a mistake. I can see that now."

"Did your reason for wanting to take your own life have to do with any abuse you might have suffered at the hands of your stepfather?"

My jaw drops. "No! It absolutely did not."

I can't tell him about the abuse I did suffer, the rape by one man, and sexual assault by another. As far as the police are aware, those men don't even exist. Maybe they see something in me. Do victims of a sexual assault act in a certain way? Do we subconsciously say or do certain things that give us away to those who have experience dealing with victims? I find it hard to believe that to be true. I imagine some women would be triggered by sex, where I haven't been able to get enough of it. It's been like each time one of the guys has fucked me, it's taken me one more step away from the assault. It's given me control of my body again, allowed me to reclaim it as my own. We're all individuals and deal with things in our own way.

"It was the press I couldn't handle," I tell the detective. "What they, and everyone on social media, was saying about Reed. They were trying to destroy him, and I felt responsible. I just felt like if I no longer existed, they'd all go away and leave him alone."

Except now they'll blame him for this as well, will probably claim he drove me to it, just like the police are doing now. I hadn't even considered that, but then I hadn't considered much except my own pain.

"Please," I say, "just understand that Reed Rivera would never hurt me. He loves me, and I love him. Neither of us are doing anything wrong, no matter what everyone else is saying."

He nods and closes his notebook. "Thank you for speaking

with me, Miss Flores, I'll be sure to update my report with your statement. As far as I can tell, no further action will be taken."

I let out a sigh of relief and drop back against my pillows, suddenly exhausted. It probably won't make any difference to the press that the police agree we've done nothing wrong, but it's something. It feels good to have someone in authority on our side.

# 38

## *laney*

I STAY IN THE HOSPITAL FOR THREE DAYS.

The guys make sure I'm never alone. They take turns sitting at my bedside, holding my hand, getting me whatever I need, doing their best to make me smile. I don't know how much of their attentiveness is because they're too worried to leave me alone, in case I do something stupid again, or if it's just because they like being with me, but I appreciate it either way.

The consultant agrees to discharge me on the promise that I will make regular visits to my therapist. He wanted to put me on antidepressants, but I've resisted for the moment. I'm not going to say I'll refuse them forever—if I need them, then I'll take them—but I want to see how my brain is coping first.

It's as though I've been a slowly simmering pot that finally reached the boiling point, and then the suicide attempt allowed everything to overflow so that now I'm back to simmering again. The pressure has been released.

Or maybe it's simply that I've allowed myself to give in and let Reed and the boys support me. I'm able to breathe again.

When the doctor announces he's happy to discharge me—assuming I agree to stick with seeing my therapist—Reed takes charge.

"No more trailer, Laney. You're coming home with us."

I opened my mouth, but he holds up a hand to silence me. "I won't hear any argument about it. I'll get Cade to bring your belongings over to the house. Don't worry, you'll have your own room there, so you'll get your privacy, too. We won't watch over you all the time. I know it's only a short-term rental, and not exactly home, but you'll be with us."

"Wherever you are is home," I say, grateful to him for taking the choice out of my hands. I wanted to prove I could hack it on my own, that I could stand on my own two feet, but I guess I can't. I need them more than I ever realized, and is there anything wrong with that? Is there something wrong with needing the people you love to be in your life? Surely that's just natural at the end of the day.

I think of something. "What about the press? If they learn I'm living with the three of you, they're going to have a field day. I don't even want to think about the sort of stories they're going to write. They're going to make you look like a villain in a fairytale."

"Fuck 'em," Reed says. "Let them say whatever they want. We're not doing anything wrong. I love you, and so do the boys, and we'll shout it from the fucking rooftops if we want to. I won't let anyone else make us feel ashamed for what we have, okay?"

My chest swells with love and pride...and even hope. Maybe everything will be all right. I'm sure we're going to get called some names in the press and online initially, but the noise will quieten down eventually. It has to. Some celebrity will do something wrong, and they'll all turn their attention toward them, and away from us.

I hold his hand, lift it to my cheek. Drink in the warmth of his skin, the familiar scent of him, and close my eyes.

"Thank you, Daddy," I say softly enough that no one else will hear.

He leans down and presses his lips to my forehead. "Anything for you, baby-girl."

I give a little sigh of happiness, and for the first time in as long as I can remember, something akin to peace settles in my soul.

---

LATER THAT DAY, they take me to the house. I've been here before, of course, but never with the thought that this will be my home now, for however long we choose to be here. In typical Riviera style, the place is gorgeous—all thick plush carpets, high ceilings and chandeliers, and granite kitchen tops. The living room alone is about the size of my trailer. I try not to feel any shame about the more than modest roots I've come from, but it's not easy. No wonder they wanted to get me out of there when I could have been staying here.

"We'll show you to your room," Reed says. "The boys have done it out for you."

I open the door and snatch a breath. "Oh!"

Aside from the furniture, they've brought everything from the trailer here. The lamp is mine, the rug and throws are mine, the pictures on the walls are mine. All the little knickknacks from my childhood have been displayed on the dresser. The bedding is from home as well. I have my own bathroom, which now contains all of the toiletries from the trailer—minus the pills and razor blade, of course.

Sitting on a shelf is the urn containing my mother's ashes— the ashes I still haven't been able to bring myself to scatter.

The room blurs as my eyes well. I clap my hand to my mouth, trying to hold back my emotions.

"Do you like it?" Cade asks worriedly.

Darius thins his lips. "Fuck, I knew it would be too much."

I manage to find my voice, though it's squeaky because I

have to speak through the lump closing up my throat. "I love it. Thank you so much. I don't deserve this."

"Yes, you do," Dax says. "You deserve the entire fucking world, if we could give it to you. The moon and stars, too. This is the least we could do."

I turn to him and wrap my arms around his neck. His arms slide around my waist, and we squeeze each other tight. I only let go so I can hug Cade, and then Reed in turn. They've all done this for me, and I appreciate them all.

"I don't know how I'm going to repay you."

Cade throws me a wink. "I can think of a few ways, but we'll let you get your strength back first."

That evening, we eat around the dining room table. Reed has made a lasagna from scratch and served it with a big Cobb salad with ranch dressing. For the first time in what feels like forever, I seem to have gotten my appetite back.

Reed nods approvingly at my empty plate. "That's what I like to see."

I let out a sigh and place my hands across my now bulging stomach. "I needed that."

There are still photographers lurking outside the front of the house. I don't want to speak to them, or even see them, but I also hate that they're making me feel as though I have to hide. Like Reed said, we haven't done anything wrong—at least not rela-tionship wise. While society might judge us, we're all consenting adults, and it's not illegal.

We love each other, and what could be better than that?

# 39
## *laney*

IT'S BEEN A COUPLE OF WEEKS SINCE I LEFT THE HOSPITAL, AND I'm feeling much better. I'm not going to pretend that sometimes getting out of bed in the morning isn't a struggle. I still have to fight the darkness clawing at my soul, threatening to drag me down, but its hooks have released somewhat. I'm finally able to picture a time when my memories and thoughts about what happened back at the cabin don't control my life.

Each time I catch sight of my arm, my stomach knots. Cade had been right—I don't want to see my scars. I'm ashamed of what I did, of what I almost achieved. If they hadn't come to the trailer when they had, I probably wouldn't be here today.

"How did you know to come when you did?" I ask them one day.

Reed glances at his youngest son. "Darius knew. An instinct, I guess. He just sensed something was wrong."

I take Dax's hand. "You saved my life."

"We all did. I wouldn't have been able to reach you in time if it wasn't for Reed and Cade."

That's the truth of it. We work as a team, the four of us. One of us without the others just doesn't make sense. It had been stupid of me to try. I'd put my own life at risk, and I'd have destroyed the others if I'd succeeded.

"How about I cook tonight?" I suggest.

No one answers, but they exchange glances with each other, eyebrows raised, lips tensed.

"Hey," I protest. "I want to cook for my men. What's wrong with that?"

"Nothing's wrong with it," Reed says. "It's just that..." He trails off.

"Just that what?" I insist.

"Do you even know how to cook?"

My jaw drops in mock incredulity. "Do I even know how to cook?" I parrot back. "Did you forget that I practically raised myself? Of course I know how to cook."

He throws up both hands. "Okay, okay, I was only asking."

"Didn't I make a killer rabbit and random root stew when we were at the cabin?"

Cade grimaces. "Killer would be the word for it." He wraps his hand around his throat and pretends to choke.

I slap him with a hand towel. "Asshole."

"Keep that up, and you won't be standing long enough to cook."

I know he's threatening sex rather than violence.

"I just want to cook, okay? It's no big deal." I go to the huge refrigerator and open the door. The shelves are stacked with food. With three adult men living here, they can put away a decent amount, anyway, but they're also still feeding themselves up after going without for so long. I have no idea what the grocery bill is like, but it must be huge.

I rifle around and make sure I've got ingredients to make something tasty. I do.

"Okay, you can leave me to it."

They do that same glance again, and I roll my eyes and shoo them out of the kitchen.

I've already decided I'm going to cook them something substantial. They're all big men and take a lot of feeding, so something fancy and tiny like you might see in an expensive restaurant isn't going to cut it. I don't want my men to still be hungry after they've eaten.

I settle on making beef steak burritos, filled with black beans and rice, chopped tomatoes and lettuce, cheese, sour cream and spicy jalapenos. I'm going to sear the steak to give it some flavor on the outside, while still keeping it pink in the middle, and then finely slice it.

I get to dicing and slicing and chopping. I use multiple ingredients and sauces, and use countless pans to cook the steak and rice and beans, and then to warm the tortillas. Getting everything ready at the same time proves a challenge —I normally only have to worry about myself—but I manage it.

I dish everything up, and then call to them, "It's ready!"

One by one, they step into the kitchen, but it's not the food on the table that catches their attention. Their gazes drift past me, to the kitchen counters behind me.

Reed's jaw drops. "Laney, baby, you are one seriously messy cook."

I glance around at the chaos I've caused. Every packet is open and still sitting on the countertop. Sauce is splattered every-where. A million dirty utensils sit in the sink.

Cade lifts his eyebrows. "Umm, yeah. You've used every pot in the house."

Dax pulls out the nearest chair and casually drops into it. "For once, I'm glad I can't see, 'cause I don't know about the mess, but this smells fucking fantastic."

"Thank you, Dax," I say. "Now, the rest of you sit your butts down and eat your food before it gets cold. I can clean up the mess."

Reed catches me around the waist and plants a kiss on my

neck. "No way, baby-girl. You cooked for us. We clean up. That's how it works."

"Even when it looks like a bomb has exploded in here?"

He kisses me again and laughs. "*Especially* when it looks like a bomb exploded."

We join Cade and Darius at the table. I take a big bite of my burrito. I made the guys two each, but I only have one. It's huge, though, and plenty for me. The steak melts in the mouth, and there's just the right combination of the cooling sour cream and cheese, and hot sauce and chilis.

I speak with my mouth half full, so the words come out muffled. "See, told you it was good."

They're all devouring their food and nod in agreement.

# 40

## CADE

I'M LYING ON A SUN LOUNGER, WATCHING LANEY SWIM.

My ears have been ringing all morning, and I've just tossed back a couple of painkillers in the hope they'll ease the thumping in my temples. I'm in need of a distraction, and Laney seems like a good choice.

She's sun-kissed again now.

The last few weeks of being here, lazing around the pool, swimming and eating well, have done her good. She should have done this from the start. I'm kicking myself that we allowed her to persuade us that her going back to the trailer was the right thing to do. Reed would argue she needed the time to figure out that being here with us was what she really needed, and she would have only resented us if she hadn't had that time. Maybe he's right, but I'm not sure I'll ever get over finding her in the trailer that day.

The thought that we'd almost lost her had been like a punch to the chest. I don't think I've ever been so fucking terrified in my whole life.

Laney lifts herself out of the pool, water droplets glistening on her long limbs, her hair dripping down her back.

Sex has been off the menu since she got back—we wanted to

give her some time to recover before we all pounced on her—but seeing her soaking wet and dressed only in a skimpy bikini which clings to her curves is making me hard.

She senses me staring and glances over her shoulder at me.

"Why are you watching me?"

"Because you're the most beautiful thing I've ever seen."

"I'm a thing now, am I?" she teases.

"You know what I mean. How am I supposed to not look at you when you're standing there with barely anything on?"

She pouts. "I'm wearing a bikini."

"That's still too much for me. Take it off."

She raised her eyebrows. "What? Here?"

"I want to see you. All of you."

She turns to face where I'm lying on my back on the lounger. I'm only in a pair of swim shorts, and my growing erection is beginning to tent them.

Her gaze travels down my body, lingering on my shorts. Her tongue flicks out and swipes across her lower lip. I recognize the hunger in her eyes, and my cock jumps, my balls growing tight.

"If I have to take off what I'm wearing, then you should, too," she says. "I want to see you touch yourself. Masturbate for me."

She's flipped this around on me, and I like it.

I push my shorts down my thighs and shins and kick them onto the tiled ground. I'm completely fucking naked in the sun now, my cock sticking up at a right angle from my body.

"Touch yourself," she says.

I take my dick in my hand and flick the piercing with my thumb. The vibrations make me even harder. My cock is big, but then so is my hand. I smear a little precum around as lubrication, and then slowly run my fingers down my length and back up again.

I keep my eyes on Laney. She's completely focused on my

cock, her pretty lips parted. Beneath the thin, wet material of the bikini top, her nipples have pebbled.

"Take off the top," I tell her. "Touch your tits."

She gives a coy smile but follows my instructions, dropping the bikini to the ground and then cupping both breasts in her hands. She uses her thumb and forefinger to pull and roll her nipples, and I get even harder.

"Do it faster," she tells me.

"First, take off the bottoms and put your hand between your legs."

The bikini bottoms are held on by strings at her hips, and she pulls them apart, first the left side, then the right. The wet material drops away.

"Fuck, you're so sexy," I growl. "The hottest thing I've ever seen."

"I thought I was the most beautiful thing you've ever seen," she says as she steps her feet apart.

"Sexy... beautiful... my little stepsister is fucking perfect. And I'd really like to see her riding my cock."

"Not yet." She gives a combination of a sigh and a whimper as she pushes her hand between her thighs. She rubs her clit with her middle finger, and then slides it down and pushes inside herself.

Movement comes from the house, and we both glance over to see Darius approaching the pool.

"What are you two up to?" he asks.

"Laney is about to ride my dick," I say with a grin.

The corners of his lips curl. "Well, that's not fair."

"She's got her fingers in her pussy right now," I describe to him. "She's standing by the pool completely naked, her legs spread, one hand feeling up her tits, and the other between her thighs. I bet she's wet and tight, and just waiting to be fucked."

Darius runs his hand across his mouth. "Jesus fucking Christ."

"Hang on a minute," Laney says. "I want to watch you, remember? Keep touching yourself. I want to see and hear what you look like when you make yourself come." She turns her head toward my brother. "Now, Darius, get over here and fuck me from behind while I watch your brother climax."

Dax is already stripping off his clothes. Mindful of the pool, Laney takes his hand and carefully guides him toward her.

She's still facing me, only now my brother is behind her. His hands are all over her, one on her breast, the other between her smooth, slim thighs to rub at her clit. He licks the water droplets from her shoulder and neck. Her expression changes, contorting, as he pushes his cock inside her.

It might be my brother's cock inside her, but it's me she can't take her eyes off. Her gaze is completely focused on my hand running up and down my length. I stop to pay attention to the piercing tipping the bell end. I build my momentum to match with theirs.

The noises she's making are out of this fucking world, getting me even harder. I know it won't be long. She wants to watch me come, but I have a better idea.

"How about you take both of us?" I say. "Come sit on my cock, and Darius can take your ass. I bet he'd like that." I pick up a small bottle of coconut oil from beside the sunbed. "I think we can make use of this."

Darius is still pumping into her from behind. "Ah, fuck, I don't think I can stop, bro."

"Not even for her tight ass?"

He lowers his forehead to her shoulder, his teeth clenched. "Fucking hell."

I can tell it's taking every ounce of self-control not to come inside her.

"What do you want, Laney?" he asks her, before ramming into her one more time, making her cry out.

"I love feeling both of you inside me," she gasps.

"What Laney wants, Laney gets," I say.

The two of them part, but Laney takes Darius's hand and guides him over to the sun lounger. She straddles me, positioning her pussy right above my cock, and then sinks down. Darius is right. Her pussy feels incredible. My hands find her hips, and then I sit up slightly to catch one of her nipples in my mouth. I suck and lick and bite, and she slowly lowers herself onto me.

Her eyes slip shut. "God, you feel so good." She reaches back for my brother. "Your turn, Dax."

The sun loungers are large and wooden, and solid—strong enough to hold all our weight.

I place the coconut oil into his hand. "Use this."

It's warm enough for the oil to be in liquid form, and he positions himself behind Laney and pours some over her ass.

"How does that feel?" he asks, using his fingers on her asshole, pushing the oil inside her and stretching her.

I can tell exactly how it feels because her inner muscles clamp down around me and pulse as though she's trying to get herself off on my cock with barely any movement.

"Oh, God," is all she manages.

Dax applies the oil to his cock and grips himself. "Breathe, Laney, slow and steady. I'm going to fuck your ass now."

# 41

## Laney

DARIUS'S COCK NUDGES AGAINST MY ASSHOLE, AND THERE'S A sting of pain as he stretches me. My pussy clamps down around Cade, and I can tell by his expression that he's doing everything he can to hold still and let his brother work his way inside me.

Nothing feels sexier or more wanton than being taken by more than one man at the same time.

"Ah, fuck, Laney," Darius gasps. "Your ass is so tight. Cade's cock makes it hard to fit."

"Keep going," I tell him. "You feel so good."

It does—hedonistic and filthy.

Cade joins in. "She can do it. Our little sis loves fucking both her brothers at once."

I gasp and whimper as Dax edges deeper. His hands are around my waist, his fingers digging into my skin.

"Shit, it's so intense," he groans. "I'm sliding deep. I wish I could see what your ass looks like all stretched around me."

"It's hot," Cade says. "So fucking hot."

He sucks on my tits and rubs my clit. I'm so sensitive, I think I might explode. Tremors of pleasure spark through me, and, almost out of nowhere, an orgasm hits me.

"Oh, shit…I'm coming…oh, fuck, yes."

The guys haven't even moved yet, but they hold themselves deep as I climax around them. I squeeze my eyes shut, my body bucking on them, my toes curling.

I'm left gasping for breath. "Oh, God. That was too soon. I'm sorry."

"Never be sorry," Cade says. "That was hot as fuck. I swear I almost blew my load."

Darius speaks from behind me. "I love hearing you come. Let's do it again."

They give me a minute to come back to Earth, and then, together, we start to move. The sensation of two big cocks sliding in and out of me is insane. I want to capture this moment, so I can relive it whenever I want. I'm so swollen from my climax, blood filled and sensitive.

Their movements get faster, until they're both pounding into me.

I'm so into it, I almost don't hear the voice that comes from the house.

"I'm interrupting," Reed says.

"No," I manage to cry. "Get over here."

For a moment, I think he's going to refuse, but then he approaches, his hands going to the front of his pants to free himself.

His eyes are solely on me. It's my body, my noises, my arousal that's turning him on.

"I've got one more hole," I tell him, opening my mouth so he gets the hint. "Fill me up."

To bring myself to the right level, I go onto all fours, one hand on Cade's shoulder, the other on the edge of the sun lounger. I angle my upper body toward Reed and twist my head to bring me face to face with his cock.

I gaze up at him. "I want you all to come inside me. Flood me with your cum. Wash away everything else."

"You're such a good girl," Reed tells me, lifting my chin with two fingers. "Such a special, beautiful girl."

Love blooms in my chest at his words. "I want to please you, Daddy."

"You do, baby-girl, every fucking day. Now, take my cock in your mouth."

Obediently, I part my lips and he slides his cock over my tongue. He grips a fistful of my hair to hold me in place. It's not easy when I already have my ass and pussy filled, the two brothers carefully fucking me while we get into a rhythm that involves me sucking their father off.

I'm so full of cock, it's absolute heaven. The way they all want me, treating me like I'm the most desirable person on the planet, nurtures my soul. I feel utterly safe with them. I know if I didn't like something, it would only take a single word, and they would stop.

It's a sensory overload, the air filled with the sounds and scents of us fucking.

Eventually, I lose all control. I can't even think straight. Reed fucks my mouth, hitting the back of my throat with every stroke. My ass is stretched full by Dax, and my pussy and clit are all about Cade. My body is just a vessel for them to use, and I love it that way.

Another orgasm builds inside me, and I know I'm going to reach my second climax soon. I'm hovering on the brink, reaching for it...

Cade comes first, jamming himself hard inside me. It's all I need to tip me over the edge. I feel his cock pulsing as he fills me up, and I cry out, shuddering and shaking around him. Then Darius loses it, flooding my ass with hot, wet cum, and my orgasm stretches on. As they both grow soft inside me, their father swells in my mouth and holds me down on his cock by my hair as he fills my mouth with salty fluid.

I fall onto the lounger, utterly spent and exhausted. Cade

edges over to make space for me, and I lie there, thinking I might never be able to move again.

Cum dribbles from my pussy and ass and runs down my chin, but I don't even care.

"Look at you, little sis," Cade says. "Daddy's little cum slut."

He spreads my legs and pushes his fingers inside me. "Keep all that cum safe in your pussy."

Then he rubs my clit, and I don't think I can handle a third time, but then it hits me all over again. My body bows from the lounger, my vision practically blacks out, but what I can see are stars. I practically scream my release.

As my orgasm ebbs away, and I slump back down again, I wonder what the hell the neighbors will think.

# 42
## REED

M<small>Y FAMILY IS HAPPY, AND THAT'S ALL</small> I'<small>VE EVER WANTED.</small>

Cade still doesn't seem quite himself, and Darius still hasn't played a note, but considering everything we've gone through, I'm trying to focus on the positive.

They're both much happier since Laney has been here, as have I.

The short-term lease on the house will be up soon, and I have to speak to them all so we can figure out what we're going to do next. Do they want to stay in Los Angeles? The world is literally our oyster. We can go wherever we want.

I keep my ear to the ground about how the investigation into the crash is going. The more time that passes, the safer we are. I know the fear of Smith and his men hasn't gone away completely, but I've taken steps to make sure my family is safe.

I've arranged to have additional security cameras placed around the property, but since it's a rental, I can't have anything that's wired in. All it'll take is for our Wi-Fi to go down, and the place will be unprotected.

My cell phone rings. The number on screen isn't one I recognize, but I answer it anyway. It might be someone inquiring about Darius and whether or not he's playing for the public again. While obviously the answer to that question will be no, currently, things might not always be this way. I want to keep the lines open in case he decides to return to work.

"Reed Riviera," I answer.

"Mr. Riviera," a voice says on the end of the line. I vaguely recognize it but can't quite place it. "It's Sergeant Moore."

I still can't quite put a face to the name, and he seems to sense this.

"We met in Ottawa shortly after you were rescued."

Recognition dawns. "Yes, of course. I remember now. What can I do for you, Sergeant?"

I listen to what the detective has to say, while barely hearing a word.

"Are you sure?" I ask.

My ears are suddenly full of bees, and a gaping void has opened up inside my chest. All I can think is, 'How am I going to tell Laney?'

# 43
## *laney*

REED HAS JUST TAKEN A CALL, AND, FROM THE WAY HIS FACE HAS grown so rigid it appears to be carved from stone, it's clear something serious has happened.

I creep closer to listen in.

"Okay, thank you, Sergeant." A pause, and then he adds, "Yes, of course. I understand. Whatever you need."

He ends the call.

I step into the room. "Who was that?"

His mouth opens and shuts, and then he closes his eyes and runs his hand over his face.

I harden my tone. "For fuck's sake, Reed. Just tell me what the call was about."

"They found the plane. The cabin, too."

The world drops out from under me, and I'm not sure I'm even still standing. I put out a hand to steady myself, but there's nothing there to catch me. "Oh, God. Smith…"

That one syllable is enough for Reed to understand what I'm asking. "They didn't find anyone in the cabin. No one alive, anyway. They found the body that we also found."

Smith had called the body by a name, but I struggle to recall it.

Reed continues. "The police are getting forensics in. They're going to find our DNA and prints all over that place. They'll know we found the body, too, and they're going to want to know why we didn't say anything."

"We're going to have to tell the truth."

He presses his lips together. "We could be charged—obstructing justice or something."

I don't even care if we end up in prison, though the thought of us being separated breaks my heart. It's still better than the alternative of Smith finding us and killing us all. I'm quite sure he won't just kill me either. He'll have his fun with me, take his time. I expect he'll pass me between his friends and let them do whatever they want. With any luck, he'll have killed Reed and Cade and Darius before that happens rather than forcing them to watch.

"If they didn't find Smith and the others, does that mean..." I trail off, unable to give voice to my worst fears.

"It doesn't mean they're alive. It doesn't mean they made it to safety either. They could easily have tried to hike back and died along the way, or they got lost, and are *still* lost out there."

"Or they used their phones to make contact with other criminals and got help."

It's a very real possibility, and the thought is terrifying. What if they find us?

Cade and Darius must have overheard us talking, as they enter the room.

"What's going on?" Darius asks.

Reed fills them both in.

"We should leave the city," Cade says, his hands on his hips. "We have passports, we have money. We can go anywhere in the world."

I widen my eyes. "You mean start over?"

I can't imagine living anywhere other than America. Up until recently, I'd never even been out of the United States, and the trailer was the only home I've ever known.

"What about Dax's career?" I ask. "The moment he tries to play for an audience again, it'll be publicized, and then they'll be able to find us."

Darius shakes his head. "Fuck my career. It might have been important to me once, but not so much now. All that matters is we're all safe."

"Are you sure, Dax?" I ask.

I can't imagine giving up something I've worked my whole life for. He's always said that his music is who he is.

He pulls me in and gives me a hug. "I'd give up the whole world for you, Laney, if it meant you were safe. Besides, I think I've probably fucked up my career, anyway, after the last couple of performances. Who wants to bring in sell-out crowds, only for the star of the show to puke in the wings? I'm not saying I'll stop playing—I don't think I ever will—but playing for an audience..." He shrugs. "It doesn't feel like that big of a deal."

He smiles, but I know this can't be easy for him. The possibility that we might be running for no good reason, too, is like a shadow hanging over me. Reed is right when he says Smith and his men might not have made it out alive. They could easily be dead—eaten by bears, or drowned in the river, or killed by a snake bite. They might have simply starved to death. It's been weeks now since we were rescued, and while the temperature might not have changed a whole lot in California, it will have up north. We left because we'd known we wouldn't survive the winter. Why would Smith and the others fare any differently?

Darius always said he'd play for me when we were safe, but he still hasn't. Is that because in his soul he always knew we hadn't truly made it yet?

"Pack some things," Reed says. "Whatever you can fit in carry-on. We can buy anything else we need when we get there."

"When we get where?" I ask.

"Wherever it is we end up. Let's get to the airport first, see what flights are leaving soon, and take it from there."

Our futures are going to be resting on the toss of a coin.

My stomach flips at the thought of being on a plane again. Though I've only been on a big commercial flight once, I know they're safer than a smaller aircraft. It's still going to be a nerve-wracking flight, though, and not only because of the previous crash. We'll be heading to a life we don't even know, to a strange country, and we still have the worry that Smith will be after us.

I have no idea what to pack. How do you condense your whole life into a bag big enough to fit in an overhead compartment? Clothes can be replaced, so I only pack my absolute favorite items. I think the same about toiletries. Instead, I fill my bag with photographs, the few items of my mother's jewelry I have, the silly mementos I've collected during my time with the guys.

I'm packing my memories.

There's one item I won't be able to take—my mother's ashes. I could try to take it with us, but I'm worried it'll attract questions. I imagine I'd need specific paperwork or something to get it on a plane and into a different country, and since we don't even know where we're going yet, it adds an extra layer of complication that we just don't need.

The urn sits on the shelf, accusatory. I should have scattered them by now, but I haven't been able to bring myself to do it. Now I have no choice but to abandon her here, and it leaves me sick with guilt.

The future is a great gaping chasm of the unknown in front of me, but at least now I have a future. It wasn't so long ago that all I'd seen ahead of me was darkness, and I hadn't even wanted to fight for my life. Now I know with one hundred percent certainty that I want to live. I want a future with the three of them, building a home together, maybe even having a family one day.

I've got my story to finish writing, too. My therapist was right when she said writing everything down would help. It feels like I'm purging my soul. I'm not sure I'll ever let anyone read it, but I do know that I want to be able to give it an ending, and not only an ending, but a happy one. After everything we've been through, we deserve that much.

With that thought in mind, I also pack my laptop and the charger.

A light knock sounds at the door, and Reed sticks his head around it. "You ready?"

I look around the room. "I think so."

A wave of nostalgia sweeps over me, but it's not for this house. It's for the cabin we left behind, the version of it that didn't include Smith and his two friends. I'd felt this way when we'd left that place too, the thought 'we'd been happy here' echoing through my head.

We hadn't been in this house for long, but yes, we'd been happy here, too.

Reed seems to read my mind. "We can be happy wherever we are, as long as we're together."

"You're right. Let's go."

I give the urn a final glance. Maybe I can get it shipped to wherever we end up, though that'll mean giving someone my new address, which might be too dangerous.

As well as a small rucksack, Darius has his violin case. I'm pleased to see it. I never want him to give up on music entirely. Like he says, it's who he is. He's also tucked his hair up into a baseball cap. It's not much of a disguise, but it's something. He's too easily recognizable, especially after all the recent publicity.

The car has blacked out windows, and for that I'm grateful. We can hide from the world, at least until we get to the airport.

"I'll leave the car in the airport parking," Reed says, "and get the rental company to come and pick it up. We'll have to hope no one thinks to look for the keys under the hubcap."

Just as we're pulling out of the street, the air fills with the wail of sirens, and suddenly the road is no longer clear. Black and white response cars screech into our path, turning sideways to block the road.

"Fuck," Reed curses, slamming on the brakes to prevent driving into the side of the nearest police car.

We're all thrown forward, the seatbelts snapping across our chests. I see Reed glance in the rearview mirror, perhaps considering if it's worth hitting reverse and trying to drive the other way, but then his shoulders drop and he glances away. It's not worth it. A car chase won't achieve anything. We'll never get to the airport with the cops on our tail, and we'll definitely never make it onto a flight. A car chase will only result in shots being fired, and someone getting hurt. It's better that we face what's coming.

We only lied, maybe not even that much—we omitted the truth, a part of the story. We're not criminals, not like the men who raped me. The police are going to have to see that.

Uniformed police climb out. They're armed but haven't pulled their weapons on us. We're not armed or dangerous, only a flight risk.

I recognize the detective who dealt with our case, the one who came to the hospital to interview me.

"Get out of the car, slowly, and put your hands on the roof of the vehicle," he says.

We don't have any choice. We each open the car doors and climb out.

"Keep your hands where I can see them," the detective shouts.

"Why?" Reed throws back. "Are we being arrested?"

"Too damn right you are. Until we know you had nothing to do with the body in the cabin, the four of you are murder suspects."

The air is snatched from my lungs. "We didn't kill anyone!"

"Save that for the interview room." He spots the bags in the car. "Were you trying to run? You understand how guilty this makes you look?"

I can't believe this is happening. Panic builds. Of course, the cops know nothing about Smith and his men. They don't even know they exist. The existence of the body is bound to be blamed on us. I'm sure that with an autopsy and forensics they'll be able to see that it was there long before we were, but I assume those kinds of tests take time, and right now we are their only suspects.

"Please, you don't understand. The men who killed that person are criminals and they're dangerous. If they're still out there somewhere, still alive, they could send people after us. We were lucky to get away from them the first time."

"We won't let anything happen to you," the detective says, far too confidently. He turns to his colleagues. "Now cuff them. I want them all in separate interview rooms."

I realize they're going to put us in different cars. "No! Please, let me stay with them."

The thought of being alone now I know Smith and the others might still be alive is overwhelming. I'm terrified. The detective takes my upper arm, but I'm not going to go willingly. I try to pull out of his grip, but he pushes me up against the car, wrenches my hands behind my back, and cuffs me.

Cade realizes what's happening. "Let go of her! Leave her the fuck alone!"

Two uniformed policemen are on him, cuffing him, too. He manages to swing back an elbow and catches one of the officers in the chest.

The officer shakes his head and grabs Cade again, wrenching his wrists into the cold silver cuffs.

"Now you'll be charged with assaulting a police officer. Keep going, and you'll have resisting arrest on top of that."

"You fucking assholes," Cade snaps. "You'll get us killed."

"It's going to be okay," Reed calls back to us as he's led toward a cop car. "Just tell the truth. We haven't done anything wrong."

That's not completely true. We lied—or at least omitted the truth. I'm sure they'll figure out that we're not responsible for the dead body, but it's going to take time.

I'm pushed into the back seat of one of the cars. I want to cry, but my eyes are dry. I'm in shock.

Within an hour, I'm processed and brought to a stark interview room down at the station.

Someone has fetched me a coffee, but I haven't touched it. The top has formed a film, and I stare down at it.

"What do you know of the body found at the cabin?" one of the sergeants asks me.

I tell them everything. There's no point in hiding it now. I tell them how I thought they were going to kill Cade, how Smith assaulted me, and how Axel raped me down on the beach. My voice is coming out of my mouth, my tongue shaping the words, but I'm distant from it all.

"Why didn't you tell us this before?"

"Because we knew you'd find the cabin, and if Smith and his men were still there, you'd rescue them."

"If your story is true, then we'll have to send a search team out to find them. If they're in the forest somewhere, they're most likely dead. You know that, don't you?"

"So everyone keeps telling me."

Why can't I bring myself to believe it? Because men like Smith don't just die. They're like a bad penny, always turning up again.

I feel as though I've been catapulted back to the start. All the healing I've done over the past few weeks has vanished, and suddenly I'm the Laney from straight after the rape and assault. The scab has been torn right off, and I'm left raw and exposed once again. If we have to spend time in jail, will Smith have people he can contact in there? Will we find ourselves shanked in the showers one day?

I don't know if I can do this for a second time.

If they find us, they'll kill us.

## 44
### REED

WE'VE ALL BEEN CHARGED WITH OBSTRUCTION OF JUSTICE, BUT not for the murder of the man in the roof space.

It's a relief, but we're not out of the woods yet.

Because everything happened in another country, we might also still be facing charges to do with concealing the body from the Canadian authorities. It's all complicated, and I bring in the best lawyers I can think of.

I want to get away from Los Angeles, but we've been warned that the cops will probably need to speak to us again. Plus, we're on bail and have to report in, and the judge has ordered us to surrender our passports, as we're considered a flight risk. I can't say he's wrong on that. If we had our passports, we'd be gone within the day.

The whole thing is fucking bullshit.

They're not taking our fears about Smith catching up to us seriously. The detective insists that these men are in a whole other country, and we have nothing to worry about, but that's crap.

Besides, even if Smith is still in Canada, it doesn't mean he hasn't got friends nearby. I imagine a gun-smuggling ring would have widespread contacts. All it would take is a phone call and a promise of payment or perhaps a favor owed to send someone with a gun to our house.

Mostly, I'm worried about Laney. The lightness we've seen in her over these past few weeks since she got out of the hospital has vanished again. Those fucking asshole detectives kept her in an interview room for hours, and then had her locked up again.

The thought makes me so angry, I want to destroy something. She's the fucking victim, not the criminal. How dare they treat her like that? She never touched the body, so I'd hoped she'd think to say that she knew nothing about it, but Laney had probably been so desperate to get everything off her chest that she told them every detail.

Even the rape and assault.

Where's their fucking compassion? Sure, we may have omitted some of the truth, but we did it for good reason.

I don't give a fuck what happens to me, but seeing Laney like this makes me want to rip my heart out of my chest. I'm terrified she's going to do something stupid again, and I know the boys feel the same. We're following her around like lost puppies, and we're all back to sleeping in the same room. It's comforting, knowing we're all in the same place, should something happen.

Of course, this new development has also got the press all stirred up again. Once more, they're asking questions about exactly what went on in the wilderness. None of us have spoken to the press, but that doesn't stop them making shit up.

We try to get back into some kind of routine, but it isn't easy. As the days pass with no appearance from Smith and the others, I try to find some breathing space. Maybe we don't have anything to worry about. Maybe they are really dead.

Until we get the hell away from the city, I'm going to keep my wits about me.

# 45

## *laney*

I STEP OUTSIDE OF THE POLICE STATION.

The detectives had wanted to go over my side of the story again. I went alone, not wanting to upset Reed and the boys. They've been even more overprotective of me than usual since the arrest, and I worried that telling them would only get them in trouble.

There's no physical evidence of what I went through now, so it's our word against the word of men they haven't even been able to locate. If our plan worked, then Smith and his men are already dead out there somewhere, hopefully starved to death or eaten by animals. I'm just thankful they haven't made an appearance.

I'm immediately surrounded. I'd been so lost in thought about what had been said inside the interview room that I hadn't even considered the reporters.

"Laney, did you hide a body at the cabin?"

"Did your stepfather assault you when you were underage?"

"Do you know the identity of the body that was found in the cabin?"

"Miss Flores, Miss Flores. Did your two stepbrothers join in with the abuse? Is Darius Riviera guilty of grooming you, too?"

"Did you have a sexual relationship with your stepfather before the plane crash?"

Their words overlap one another, creating a cacophony of sound. I consider turning around and going back inside the police station, but no one there is my ally either.

Camera lights flash, and I angle my head away. By remaining silent, am I only making us seem guiltier? But I'm terrified if I say something, they'll only twist my words and make things worse. I can't win with these people.

I spot a waiting cab and put my head down and go straight to it. I have to knock people out of the way with my shoulder, to ignore the fluffy booms of microphones shoved in my face. I picture the sort of shots they'll be getting of me, the same ones they run online and in the papers. Of me, too thin and pale, clearly stressed and anxious, looking every part like a victim, but now also possibly considered a killer.

Of course, I *am* a victim, just not of the men they're accusing.

I climb into the back of the cab. The driver glances with a frown at the reporters about to surround him.

I give him my address. "Just go," I beg. "Please."

Thankfully, because this address is also a short-term rental, the press haven't found us here yet, though I know it's only a matter of time. But as I approach the house, I realize the cops are here, too.

My heart sinks.

Had the request to interview me just been a ruse? Had they been trying to get me out of the way?

I pay the driver and jump out.

"What's going on?" I ask no one in particular.

I spot the detective who interviewed me at the hospital, along with a number of his colleagues. All four doors of the car Reed has leased stand open, as does the lid of the trunk, and officers appear to be rifling around inside.

"Stay right there, Miss Flores," he says, holding up a hand.

I look to the guys. Cade's jaw is tense. Reed is shaking his head. Darius just seems confused.

What now? When are we ever going to be able to get a break?

"Got it," one of the officers shouts and straightens holding a large bag of white powder.

My jaw drops.

Detective Knox takes out a pair of cuffs, as do his colleagues.

"Cade Riviera, Darius Riviera, Reed Riviera, you're all under arrest for the possession of a class A drug with intent to supply."

My jaw drops. "What? No! That can't be right. They haven't done anything."

"We'll find that out in the interview room, won't we?"

I suddenly realize that with them arrested, I'm going to be left here alone. "No, wait. Arrest me, too. Whatever they did, I would have been involved. We do everything together."

There's desperation in Reed's eyes. Cade is going crazy, and I'm worried he's going to get himself Tasered if he's not careful. Or worse, shot. Darius is frozen in place, his whole body rigid. How much harder this must be for him. Do they have someone in jail who'll help him navigate the place, or will he just be expected to manage on his own? The thought of him inside, getting pushed around by actual criminals, breaks my heart. I hope they'll at least be kept together so Cade can watch out for his brother.

The police officer looks at me like I'm crazy. "You want us to arrest you? Don't waste police time."

Maybe I should hit them? Then they'd have to arrest me, but I'm just a girl faced with armed men. What kind of damage can I even do?

It must dawn on Reed what I'm afraid of. "Don't stay here,

Laney. Go to a hotel. Pay cash if you can. Don't let anyone follow you."

Tears fill my eyes. I can see myself holed up in some crappy motel, the door locked and chained, while I sit on the bed, staring at it, and praying Smith and his friends don't bust through it.

"It won't be for long, Laney," Reed says. "We'll clear up whatever mistake this is fast and come and find you."

Will it be too late by then?

My heart breaks in two as the men are hauled away by police officers, their wrists once more cuffed behind their bodies, and are pushed into the backs of the police cars.

I stand, my feet glued to the ground, as they're driven away.

With my heart pounding, I convince my feet to move and run into the house. I go to my room. I never unpacked the bag I'd taken to the airport. There hadn't seemed to be any point. Though the judge had made us surrender our passports, we'd known we wouldn't be staying in Los Angeles. It wasn't safe for us here.

I pick up the bag and wonder where the hell I'm supposed to go.

# 46
## laney

I'M AT A COMPLETE LOSS ABOUT WHAT TO DO NEXT.

I can order a cab, but I don't know where I'm going. Reed said to stay at a motel, but which one? How will I know that somewhere is safe?

A part of me just wants to shut my bedroom door and hide away. Surely, it's safe here? Going out into the big wide world, alone, feels like a worse option. The police will get this cleared up soon enough, won't they, and release Reed and the boys again? Or will the fact they're already on bail go against them?

I wish I knew more about how the system worked. They do all have one phone call, though, and I make sure I have my cellphone with me in case they try to make contact.

I need to be brave. If Reed told me to go to a motel, then that's what I'll do. I glance around my bedroom, and then grip the bag on my shoulder a little tighter. I leave the room and run down the stairs to the entrance hall.

I draw to a halt, the air punching from my lungs.

A man is standing in the opening of my front door.

A part of me had hoped this moment would never happen, but deep down, I've always known this day would come. As

273

much as I wanted to convince myself that I was unreasonably paranoid, I've now been proven right.

I've never wanted to be wrong about something so badly in my life.

"Hello, Laney."

With a gasp, I step back, only to collide with a solid body directly behind me. I spin to come face to face with Axel. Close behind him is Zeke.

"No!" I cry and try to dart away, but Axel is too fast.

He grabs my shoulders, pinning me in place. My bag falls to the floor. I struggle, but he's holding me tight.

Smith approaches, his footsteps slow and deliberate. "Where are your boyfriends?" he asks. "Wait, don't tell us—the cops busted them for possession, right?"

My eyes widen. "How do you know that?"

"How do you think?"

It dawns on me that this was a setup. They'd planned it all to get back at us.

I can't go through this again. I just can't. It almost killed me last time, and I'm simply not strong enough to survive a second time. Not that it'll matter. They're probably going to kill me, anyway, once they've taken what they want from me.

I picture Reed, Cade, and Darius being released, free to come find me, only to discover my body instead. It will utterly destroy them. They'll forever question if there was something they could have done differently. Not that it will matter. If Smith and his men are lying in wait for them when they get back, they'll also end up dead.

In the afterlife, will we still get to be together?

Maybe we should have told the truth when we'd first been found. Lying clearly hasn't helped—in fact, it made things worse. If we'd told the police all about the body, and Smith and his men, they wouldn't have had a reason to arrest us and take our passports away. We could have left the country—gone to

Europe, maybe—and gotten lost on the Spanish beaches or in the French countryside, or maybe the lakes of somewhere like Finland. Smith would never have bothered to look for us there.

But it's too late for wishes now.

Axel shoves me over to Smith, so I end up in his arms.

"Let go of me!" I struggle again. "Don't you fucking touch me."

I'm so angry. I'm fucking furious. I don't deserve this, I realize. Nothing I've ever done has brought me to this moment. All I've ever tried to do is live my life, to love the people in it. Even though I've been knocked down, over and over, I've gotten back up. I don't deserve this. I don't fucking deserve it.

"How did you get here?" I ask in desperation.

Maybe if I get them talking, I'll buy myself enough time to figure something out.

"Here, as in L.A.?" Smith cocks an eyebrow. "Or out of the wilderness, after you stole our fucking boat, and left us stranded in the middle of nowhere with no supplies? I bet you thought you were being clever, huh? Hoping we were going to die out there. Well, you forgot that we were going to meet someone. They were delayed, but then when they couldn't get hold of us to rearrange, assumed something must have happened. They knew the exact location of the cabin. Admittedly, it did take ten days, so we were pretty fucking pissed by the time they arrived, but as you can see, we made it out, safe and well." He purses his lips and shakes his head. "I was surprised you didn't send the cops after us. That was what I'd been expecting—to find our names and faces plastered all over the internet under some kind of 'most wanted' list. I couldn't believe it when I realized you'd kept your mouths shut about us. At first, I couldn't figure out why. After what we did to you, why not tell the cops? But then it dawned on me that you didn't want them to come looking for us. You wanted us to die out there, didn't you? What a cold-hearted bitch. You act like a little princess, but actually you were perfectly happy to let three men die."

There's no point in me saying anything. It won't make any difference. He's venting. I hope it'll make him less angry, by getting it off his chest, but I doubt it.

I think of something. If the cops hauled the guys away on drug charges, doesn't that mean they'll search the house as well? It would only make sense for them to do that, and if they do, they'll find these assholes here.

Maybe the cops are waiting for a search warrant to come through for the house. I have no idea how long these things take, but perhaps they figure there's no rush since they've got Reed and the boys in custody.

I don't understand why the police aren't more suspicious. We told the detective about our fears of Smith and his friends, or even someone associated with them, coming after us. How can they not see straight through this setup? It's clearly been done to separate us.

Smith seems to know what I'm thinking. "Don't expect the cops to come back here any time soon."

I'm terrified, but I do my best to hold my shoulders back and jut my jaw. "Why not?"

"You know that detective who just had your boyfriends hauled away? He also happens to be a friend of mine. It's handy to have members of the police force on the payroll. Means they hide evidence when needed, or even plant it places where you do need it."

Understanding of what happened sinks in. "Fucking bastard."

"He'll give us a heads up if it looks like this place is going to be searched, or if any of your family are going to be released." He shrugs. "So we can take our time with you. Enjoy ourselves a little."

"You set them up."

"They're getting quite the reputation for themselves, aren't they? First lying to the police, and now this." He tuts his tongue against the roof of his mouth. "And we're supposed to be the criminals."

"You *are* the criminals."

"Maybe so, but right now it's your stepfather and step-brothers who look like the bad ones. No one even knows we're still alive, and that's the way I'd like to keep it. It's amazing the number of people who stop looking for you when they think you're dead, and that can definitely work to our advantage."

They must have used fake passports to get into the country, or else they know some illegal route to have gotten them from Canada into the US. I wouldn't put either possibility past them.

"How have things been between you and your stepdaddy since he fucked you?" Smith asks. "I see you both decided you liked it, and did it again. I saw the stories all over the papers."

My face burns, a furnace raging inside me. He studies my expression, and interest sparks in his eyes. "You fucking him now on the regular?"

"Fuck you," I spit.

"What about your stepbrothers? Are you spreading those long legs for them, too? Sucking their cocks? Tell me how the dynamics work. Do you take them all at the same time? One dick for each hole? Or do you let them take turns?"

"You're fucking disgusting."

"Maybe so, but am I wrong? And anyway, I don't think you've got any right to call me disgusting when you're the one fucking your daddy and big brothers, all at the same time. You really are a little whore, aren't you?"

The things he's saying cut me to the core, confirming every-thing I've feared about myself.

"We love each other," I say, but it's barely a whisper.

"Sure, they love that tight young pussy of yours. What man wouldn't?"

I manage to hawk up a big globule of saliva and spit it right in Smith's face. The next thing I know, his hand cracks around my cheek, sending my head rocking.

"Don't be a stupid cunt." Smith holds up his gun. "Remember your old friend?"

"Fuck you."

"Don't pretend you didn't like it. You're nothing but a whore. I was there, remember? I sucked your swollen little clit while I fucked you with my gun, and I heard the noises you made. I watched your pussy clench around the barrel as you came, and how you arched your hips up to get better contact with my mouth."

My face burns. The worst part is that what he's saying is true. It did make me come, but that didn't mean I wanted it. My body just did what it's supposed to.

*It's not my fault,* I tell myself. *It's not my fault. It's not my fault.*

But if that's true, and I haven't done anything to deserve this, then why does this shit keep happening to me? Ever since I was young, men have wanted to hurt me this way. It's getting harder and harder to believe I haven't done something—maybe in a previous life—for God, or fate, or whoever, to want to punish me.

Axel grabs the front of his jeans. "She liked my cock, too. Dirty little slut."

Zeke looks between them. "So, I'm the only one who didn't get to fuck her? How's that fair? I should get to go first this time."

Smith jerks his chin toward me and addresses Zeke. "Come and get a feel, then."

I'm lightheaded with panic. "No!"

Smith and Axel hold me in place. Zeke approaches and shoves his hand down the front of my jeans and into my panties. He roughly pushes two fingers inside me. I balk at the contact, twisting my face away and squeezing my eyes shut.

"Nice and wet," he says approvingly. "Just how I like them."

"Wait 'til she really gets going," Smith says. "She gets so wet, she's practically squelching."

I'm humiliated and mortified. Zeke's thumb finds my clit, sending sparks through me, and I let out a sob. I don't want this —I've never wanted these men's hands on me. How will I cope if they rape me again?

"Let's tie her up," Smith instructs. "Get her naked first, and then we can have some fun. Make her see what a dirty little slut she is, and how much she enjoys this. I wonder how many times we can make her come."

I want to die.

Dying will be better.

# 47

## REED

I'M SITTING ON THE OTHER SIDE OF AN INTERVIEW TABLE, MY hands in cuffs—but in front of me now—the chains linked through a metal loop on the table. I assume this is to prevent me from attacking either of the detectives interviewing me. This isn't something I would do, but they obviously think it's a possibility.

Everything is moving with a frustrating lack of urgency.

I don't know where Detective Knox has gone—possibly in with one of my sons—but I have a different detective interviewing me.

"I'm Detective Stanner," the plain-clothed police officer tells me. "Do you wish to have a lawyer present? If you do not have one, we can provide one for you."

Getting a lawyer involved is only going to slow the process down.

"No, I don't want a lawyer. All I want is to get the hell out of here. This whole thing is a mistake."

I hope the boys are okay. I don't like the way Cade was lashing out at the arresting officers. He needs to be careful. Police brutality is a thing, and if Cade does something that makes them hurt him, he could end up with serious lasting injuries from it, or even worse.

Darius is calmer, but being in a jail cell or an interview room with cops when he's visually impaired is going to be even more challenging for him. I don't even know how it'll work—if they'll make exceptions for him, or treat him like anyone else. That he's also a celebrity will probably work against him. The cops like to bring people down a peg or two, if they think they're too big.

"Finding a kilo of cocaine in your car means you're not going anywhere any time soon."

I blow out a breath and shake my head. "Why the hell would I just leave a kilo of coke sitting in plain sight?" I think of something. "How did you know to search the car in the first place?"

"Detective Knox received an anonymous tip."

Warning bells ring. He's the same one who questioned me about the allegations about Laney. I'd picked up then that the guy didn't like me much. Would not liking me really make him plant drugs in my car, or is there more to it? Because I think he might have planted them, or he got someone else to do it. One thing I know with one hundred percent certainty is that the coke has nothing to do with us. Someone is setting us up, and they must have a reason to do that. The only reason I can think of is Laney.

"What do you make of Detective Knox?" I ask. "Is he a good cop?"

"This is supposed to be me interviewing you, not the other way around."

"Maybe I wouldn't need to if you were asking the right questions. Now, is he a good cop?"

The detective's features tighten.

His lack of response is all I need.

The car had been in the garage ever since last night, and I know full well that there wasn't a big bag of coke in it when I parked it. That means someone—quite possibly Detective Knox

—planted the coke during the night. Of course, one thing the detective didn't know was that I was already paranoid about security. That paranoia might have served me well now.

"I believe those drugs were planted, and I think the detective may have had something to do with it."

Stanner's eyes narrow. "How could you possibly know that?"

"Get me access to a phone. I can show you."

"You'll get your phone call when we say you do."

I lose my temper. "I don't want to make a call, asshole. I want to show you footage from the hidden security cameras I've got placed around the property." I can tell he wasn't expecting me to say that, so I press on. "I thought the police were interested in evidence. I'm trying to hand some key evidence over to you. I guarantee you won't find a single fingerprint or sample of DNA on those drugs that belongs to either me or my sons. You want proof about whose drugs those are? I can get you proof, and I promise you they're not mine or my sons'. All I need is access to a laptop or a phone."

Detective Stanner hesitates, appearing to consider my offer. "Fine," he relents. "I'll get you what you need, but I'll watch what you're doing in case you try to delete evidence rather than showing it to me."

I grind my teeth. "I don't want to delete anything. That goes against exactly what I'm trying to achieve."

He leaves the room for a few minutes, and then returns with a laptop. I quickly log in to the security footage from the house. I'd paid extra to not only ensure the cameras are recording twenty-four-seven, but that the footage is also stored on a cloud for ninety days.

The footage onscreen is in black and white—as I suspected, the crime was committed during the night—but it's still clear enough to make out any details. The white flit of a moth crosses the camera, the scurry of something small—most likely a rat, on the far side of the screen.

But then the side door opens on the garage and a man in a baseball cap slips inside. I hate that someone got onto the property while we were all sleeping and we didn't know anything about it. Maybe we should have gotten a dog as well as the cameras.

The man on screen unwittingly turns his head and looks directly at the camera.

Detective Stanner sits back. "Oh, fuck."

Time is running out. Smith and his asshole friends could easily have found Laney by now. The possibility that they already have and are hurting her makes me want to tear the walls of this place down.

"You can see who that is, can't you? It's clearly not me. It's Detective Knox."

The detective seems to remember himself. He frowns and zooms in to get a better image. "I'm going to need to get this sent off to Digital Forensics, get facial recognition software on it."

I slam my fist down on the table, as much as the cuffs will allow. "Bullshit! You know who that is. Look at it. It's clearly Knox. You might not want to believe that one of your own is bent, but he's planting the drugs in my fucking car. That's why he knew about it. It wasn't some anonymous tip who sent the police our way. It was him. What reason would he have for doing that if it isn't to get me and my sons away from the house? Away from Laney Flores. She's out there on her own now, and some very bad men are most likely trying to find her. We knew if they made it to safety, they'd come after us, and something tells me that's exactly what's happening here."

No matter what he says, there's no denying that it's Knox on the security cameras and he's clearly putting something inside the vehicle. Why the fuck hadn't I thought to lock it? I guess it doesn't even matter. If he hadn't had access to the car, he'd have put the drugs somewhere else.

"Please." I'm aware I'm begging now, but I don't even care. I will stomp all over what remains of my pride if it means Laney is safe. "Just find Laney Flores. Make sure she's safe. I don't give a fuck what you do to me."

The detective looks between me and the laptop.

I want to grab him by the collar of his suit and shake him until his teeth rattle, but I clench my fists and hold back my building frustration. Every minute that ticks past is another minute where Laney might be being hurt.

Detective Stanner replays the footage.

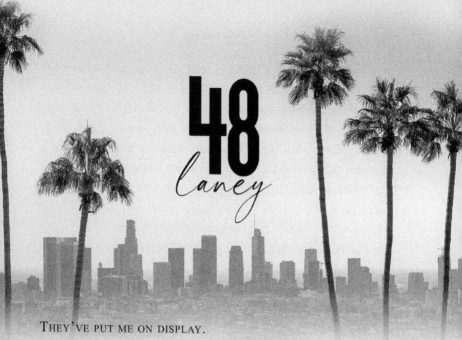

# 48
## *laney*

THEY'VE PUT ME ON DISPLAY.

Despite my best attempts to fight back, they stripped me naked. Now I'm hogtied with a gag in my mouth to stop me from screaming and alerting the neighbors. They've suspended me from a beam in the ceiling, ensuring I'm exposing every part of my body to them. The strain on my muscles is huge, but that's not the part of this that makes me most uncomfortable.

These assholes are having their fun.

They push their fingers inside me, slap my tits hard enough to sting, smack my ass so my skin burns. I sob against the gag in my mouth. I wish they'd just kill me already, but they clearly want to have their fun.

I can't believe I'm back in this position again. I want to curl up and die. The guys have been taken away by the police, so there's no chance of them coming back to save me. This is how my life is going to end, and maybe it's better if I accept it instead of trying to fight.

These bastards.

"I say we take every hole," Smith threatens. "We've got a few hours, so I think that'll give us enough time to try each one. I want to see her a fucking mess. Our cum pouring out of every orifice, dripping off her eyelashes, matted in her hair. She needs to look like the little slut she is." He takes out his phone. "Then I'll take some pictures and send it to her stepfather and stepbrothers—well, not directly, because they won't have their phones in prison—but we'll make sure they see it. Maybe even a short video clip would be better. You never know, they might get off on watching their little princess getting railed by all of us at the same time."

"Dirty little whore," Axel comments.

Smith shakes his head. "Did you really think you'd get away with running from us? That we'd just let it go? You're more naïve than you look."

I try to take myself away from this, to do what I had on the beach when Axel raped me, and picture myself somewhere else. While my body might be here, my mind doesn't need to be. I can take it to somewhere I was happy.

To my surprise, the place my brain conjures for me—my happy place—is the cabin and the river. I'm on the beach again, but not with Axel this time. Instead, I'm with Reed, Cade, and Darius, and it's my birthday. Cade is teaching me how to skip stones, and we're enjoying the last few items of food and drink that we'd taken from the plane.

I don't need to know what's happening to my body.

I don't need to feel.

I just—

My thoughts are suddenly torn back to the present.

From outside comes the screeching of tires on asphalt as several vehicles are brought to an abrupt halt, and with it sounds the blast of a police siren. The air is filled with shouts of men, and doors opening and slamming shut.

Men burst in through the back door, and then moments later emerge from the front of the house as well. Armed police wearing protective vests, all with their weapons aimed at the three men who'd been only moments away from raping me.

"Down on the ground!" the police shout. "Hands behind your head."

I know they're not talking to me.

"Jesus Christ," one of the officers comments. "Someone get the girl down, and untie her. Find her something to cover her up."

I'd almost forgotten I'm completely naked, now in front of several armed police as well as Smith and his men.

One of the officers grabs a knife to cut the rope that suspends me from the beam, and carefully lowers me to the floor. Another picks up a throw from the nearest couch. He goes to wrap it around me, but I must flinch, as he puts up both hands.

"It's okay, I'm not going to hurt you. Let's get you untied, and then covered up, okay?"

I nod my consent, my face streaked with tears.

Around me, Smith and his men are being handcuffed and then hauled to their feet.

"You're under arrest for sexual assault, gun trafficking, and one count of murder," a detective I don't recognize says.

I have no idea how they got the tipoff to come back here, but I'm so relieved they have.

"Where's Reed Riviera?" I ask the officer who's untying me. "And Cade and Darius, too?"

"Laney?" I turn at my stepfather's voice. Cade and Darius flank him on either side.

"Oh, God." With my hands and feet finally freed, I clutch the throw around my nakedness and run to them. They form a circle around me, holding me tight.

"Did those bastards hurt you?" Cade asks. "Did they touch you?"

"No, I'm okay." It's not the whole truth, but what good would come of them knowing all the details? Maybe Reed will decide to watch everything back on the security cameras, but perhaps he doesn't want to know either. I feel like it would kill Cade, for him once again to be unable to stop them.

But they've saved me now, and that's all that matters. With what's just happened, combined with our statements about the events at the cabin, Smith and his men will be going away for a very long time.

# 49

## *laney*

I†'s been a month since Smith and his men were arrested. We've all given our statements, and were warned we'll most likely be called upon to testify in court. It's not something any of us want to do, but it's the agreement we came to in order to have the charges against us for obstruction of justice dropped.

It's not been an easy time, but knowing Smith is behind bars gives me some comfort. I'm still fearful he'll send someone else after us, but so far, everything's been quiet. I'm back in therapy again, speaking to Sharon Tharp, only now I'm telling her the whole truth—every sordid detail. I'm sure she's horrified at parts of it, but I don't hold back.

Speaking about it all does make me feel better.

Once the trial is over, we'll get out of the city. I don't know where we'll go yet, but we all want a fresh start.

I've made myself a fresh coffee and carry that and my laptop into the living room with the intention of writing some more. It's been surprisingly addictive, watching the words add up into paragraphs, and the paragraphs into chapters. How I've created something from nothing. I'm determined to finish the story one day, though I'm not yet sure how it ends.

I walk into the room and pull up short.

Cade is sitting in one of the armchairs, his elbows on his knees, his head in his hands. He doesn't even glance up. Right away, it's clear something is wrong. An atmosphere radiates from him, but it's not his usual anger.

This is something else.

"Cade?" I say with hesitation. "What's wrong? What's the matter?"

Still, he doesn't respond, and my heart lurches. I put down the items I'd been carrying, take the seat next to him, and reach out to touch his shoulder.

The contact appears to have an effect. He falls to his knees from the chair, so he's on the floor at my feet, and then buries his face in my lap. I've never seen him like this, and my adrenaline spikes in alarm. His shoulders shake, and he clings to the skirts of my dress, his fingers knotted in the fabric.

I try again. "Are you hurt?"

He still doesn't reply. All I can do is try to comfort him, to stroke my fingers through his soft hair, to lower my face to the back of his head. Does this have something to do with me? Has he done something? Hurt someone? Seeing this big, strong man literally on his knees in front of me fills me with a combination of awe and fear. But with it also comes love. I can't stand to see him hurting. I'll do anything I can to take away whatever is behind this.

"You're frightening me, Cade," I tell him.

"I'm frightened, too," he finally admits. His voice doesn't sound like his own. It's strangled with emotion.

"You are? Of what?"

"My head hurts. It's been hurting ever since the cabin. That's not all. I've got ringing in my ears, too. The doctor said I could have lasting brain damage. What if these are signs that I have it?"

"But you were checked over. You had the scans, and they couldn't see anything wrong."

He tightens his fists. "Something is wrong. I know it. Why else would I be in pain?"

I want to look for an answer that doesn't include permanent brain damage. "It could be stress. Maybe they're tension headaches. You've been through a lot lately."

*We all have...*

I place my fingers beneath his chin and tilt his face up so our eyes meet. I hold his gaze steady. "And if it is something more serious, then we've got money to get you the best doctors and the best treatment, okay? And you've got us."

"They say with this illness you can change. Your whole personality can change. I might get violent and irrational."

I risk a smile. "How would we know the difference?"

His lips tweak, but the expression doesn't meet his eyes. "They say a person can stop loving what they loved most in the world. What if that happens to me, Laney? What if I stop loving you? I can't ever do that. I won't."

I squeeze his hand. "No, you're right, you won't." My tone is fierce. "I won't let you. And if something happens, then I'll love you hard enough for both of us, okay?"

"I'd never want to be a burden on you."

"You're not, and you won't be. How many times do I have to tell you that? I love you, Cade. You'll do anything to protect me, right? Well, I'll do the same for you, and so will your brother and dad. We all love you."

I put my arms around his neck, and he pulls me off the seat so I end up in his lap. We wrap our arms around each other and hold on so tight, it's as though we're trying to crush our bodies into one being.

I part from him and stroke his face and place kisses to his mouth. "And in the meantime, we go to the doctor's and tell them about your symptoms. No hiding from it or pretending it's not happening. That's not going to help anyone."

He exhales a breath, and, for a moment, I think he's going to give me an argument, but then he nods.

"Okay. Thank you, Laney. I'm glad I told you. The fear has been eating me up inside. I don't know what I'd do without you."

"You never have to know, because I'll always be here for you. I swear it. In sickness and in health."

I kiss him again, and our kiss grows deeper.

He rolls me onto my back, pushes up my dress, and makes love to me fiercely on the floor.

# 50

## *laney*

"I WANT TO SHOW YOU SOMETHING," REED SAYS.

Cade and I have filled both Reed and Darius in on the conversation we had. They both needed to know, so we're all aware of things to look out for regarding Cade. He doesn't want to be taken care of, but that's what we'll do, if necessary. We're a family, and families watch out for each other.

"What is it?" I ask.

He hands me a brochure, and I frown down at it. On the front is a cabin, only it's nothing like the one we lived in after the crash. This one is worth almost five million dollars, according to the brochure, and has five bedrooms, a home cinema, and a pool. It's also set within twenty acres of forest and has its own lake.

"It's beautiful," I say, flicking through the pages. I take in the real hardwood floors, the full-length panoramic windows, the huge bedrooms with attached bathrooms and dressing rooms.

"It's ours," he replies, "if you want it."

My jaw drops. "You bought it?"

"I've put an offer in, yes, but if you say it's not right for you, then I'll pull out. It's far away from any other neighbors. The land is private, so no one can come on it without our permission.

I know it's not exactly roughing it, like we did at the cabin, but I thought it's got that same kind of vibe."

"Where is it?"

I ask the question, but honestly, I don't even care. I'll go wherever they are.

"A place called Hocking Hills in Ohio."

"Sounds perfect," I say. "What about Darius and Cade?"

"They're up for it," he says with a smile. "Cade's better off out of the city, and Darius can still travel when he's ready to start performing again. It would be the four of us, living as we want to, without having to worry about the judgement of anyone from the outside."

My eyes fill with tears.

His expression furrows in concern. "Do you hate it?"

"No, I love it. It's perfect. Can we get a dog? I've always wanted a pet."

He grins. "We can get two dogs, if you want. It'll be good for you to have something to keep you occupied, other than us." He throws me a wink.

I also have my writing to keep me busy, but I realize I haven't told any of them about that. While I haven't finished our story yet, I'm over fifty thousand words in, and it's taking great shape. I never thought it would be something I'd enjoy, but I've loved writing every word—well, maybe not every word. Some of it has been unbearably painful, but my therapist was right. I have felt purged of many of the negative feelings I've been carrying around for so long.

But it's not only my story to tell. The guys have all played their part, too, and if anyone other than us is ever going to read it, the men need to know about it and give their consent.

Darius and Cade both come in to the room. Cade draws up short, Darius almost colliding with him.

"What's going on?" he asks.

"I told Laney about the house." Reed grins. "She loves it."

"That's fantastic news," Dax says.

Cade takes a step forward and scoops me up, swinging me around. "The best news."

I laugh and smack him on the shoulder to put me down. Before we can all more forward, I have a confession to make.

"I—I have something to tell you." Nerves swim inside my stomach. How will they take this? Will Reed be angry that I've written everything down? Will Cade hate how I've portrayed him? Will I have made Darius seem weak in any way because of his sight loss when he's anything but?

"What is it?" Reed asks.

"I *will* have a way to occupy myself," I admit. "I've been writing our story."

Darius's brow furrows. "What do you mean?"

"It started as a project my therapist encouraged me to do, to write down what happened to me—to *us*. So, I started at the point where I found my mother's body and have been writing down everything that happened from there. Don't worry, I changed all our names and some other details so it's not so obviously us." I hesitate, and then add, "The thing is that I think it's good. I might even be able to get it published one day, but obviously I wouldn't even think about it if you thought that was a bad idea, and I'd publish in a pen name, too." I'm getting ahead of myself. "That's even if anyone wants to publish it."

Reed takes my hands. "Laney, I think that's an amazing idea."

I'm bursting with happiness. "You do? I've so enjoyed writing it. I never thought I would. I might even start a new story, once I've finished this one. A completely fictional one next time, of course. I don't think a story like ours ever happens twice in one lifetime."

"You're right, Laney," Dax says.

Cade nods in agreement. "A *love* like ours only happens once in a lifetime."

# 51
## Laney

I STRIDE THROUGH THE WOODLANDS TOWARD HOME, MY ARMS swinging, inhaling the fresh, clean air.

Bounding along the path ahead of me are two sleek black Labradors.

Their names are Luna and Kyra—two female pups. I'd decided I could use a little female company, since I was outnumbered, three to one. Now I've evened up the stakes a little. We're making sure each of the girls is trained separately to avoid the chances of them forming littermate syndrome, but also because they focus better when they're on their own. Having a playful sibling beside you when you need to focus on training isn't a good idea.

They look almost identical, but I can tell the difference, much in the same way I imagine the mother of twins can always tell who is who.

The dogs are still young, and they chase each other as much as they do any unsuspecting wildlife that happens to stray in their path.

I enter the cabin, with its high-beamed ceiling and panoramic windows. I love this place. Right away, I can see that something's afoot. The men are all sitting around the living area, like they're waiting for me.

"What's going on?" I ask, hanging up the dogs' leashes, though I rarely use them, unless we come across some wildlife.

"It's time, Laney," Darius announces.

"Time for what?"

"Time for me to play for you again. Do you remember what I told you when we were in the cabin?"

I do. "That you wouldn't play again until we were back in civilization."

"That's right. The crazy thing is that I always thought civilization meant a city somewhere, with people, and stores, and cars. But actually, I was wrong. It had nothing to do with places or things, but how we felt in our hearts. We've made it now. This is our home. No one is ever going to touch or hurt you again."

He's beautiful, and my heart swells with love for him. The dogs are for Darius as well, and we're training them both to give him even more independence when he's both on and off our property.

Just as he always is on stage, Darius is bare-chested, his hair loose.

He's utter perfection.

One day, he'll go back on stage and wow the audience like he used to. We've all needed time to heal from our experience, but it's been almost a year now since the plane crash, and we're all doing better.

Cade isn't showing any signs of permanent damage, which is a relief. The headaches that plagued him after the first head injury have subsided, as has the ringing in his ears. There's no way of knowing if it might return, and, of course, he must do everything he can to make sure he doesn't get hurt again. It's unlikely that he will out here, away from the bars and the gambling and the booze.

He's turning into a regular outdoorsy kinda guy, spending all his time maintaining the acres of woodland around us, chopping firewood for winter, and doing what needs to be done to prevent forest fires. The outdoor life looks good on him.

I've sent off the first few pages of my completed book to publishers, too, and a couple of agents. I don't know if anyone will pick it up, but we'll see. It might be a little too spicy for them. I think the 'based on a true story' part will grab the attention of some of them, though. Not even having an offer yet still doesn't stop me dreaming, however. I'm picturing myself attending book signings and flying off to conferences around the world.

While I wait, I've started a new story. This one is about a woman whose boss turns out to be a man who hires himself out to bring women's fantasies to life—and he just happens to have brought the main character's fantasy of being taken by a man who breaks into her home to life the week before she starts the job. It's a fun, dirty story, and I'm enjoying writing it. Reed, Darius, and Cade are also enjoying me writing it, as they get the benefits of how it gets me all worked up.

Darius stands, framed by the floor-to-ceiling windows, the woodland that belongs to us as his background. He places the violin beneath his chin and raises the bow to the strings.

I hold my breath, unsure if he's going to play or not, or if he'll get stage fright like before. I know we're not much of an audience, but it's still possible when he hasn't played for so long.

The first note he plays vibrates through the air and snatches the breath from my lungs. Then he draws another from the instrument, and another, and another, building on the sound.

Hot tears prick my eyes, and I clutch my hand to my chest.

He plays just like he did that first night I saw him, putting his whole body into it. I can tell his brother and father are equally captivated.

Darius comes alive with the music.

# 52

## *Laney*

THE MORNING OF MY NINETEENTH BIRTHDAY DAWNS BRIGHT AND warm.

I open my eyes and stretch out luxuriously in our huge super king-sized bed. I'm disappointed to find I'm alone.

Where is everyone?

I use the bathroom and throw on some clothes, and then make my way downstairs. The two dogs are the first to greet me, licking my bare legs and acting as though they haven't seen me for a week. I make a fuss of them, scratching their solid, silky heads and ruffling their fur. They never fail to make me smile.

I find the guys in the kitchen, standing around the marble island.

"Ta-da!" the three of them say together, a chocolate cake sitting on the kitchen counter between them. "Happy birthday, Laney."

"You got me cake!" I exclaim. "My favorite."

"You mean we *made* you a chocolate cake," Cade says. "We waited until you were asleep and stayed up half the night baking."

"You did?" I laugh. "Thank you, Cade."

"And we got you this." He holds up a bottle of icy champagne.

"For breakfast?" I ask.

"Absolutely. Champagne and homemade chocolate cake. What more could you ask for?"

"Coffee?" I suggest hopefully.

Reed slides a mug toward me, the aroma filling the air. "Already done."

I smile. "This is perfect. Thank you."

"What would you like to do today?" Reed asks. "Just name it."

I think for a minute. There *is* something I want to do, but I don't know how well it's going to go down with them all.

"There is one thing…"

"Anything," he says. "The day is yours."

I hesitate and say, "I think it's time to say goodbye to my mom."

He studies my face. "Are you sure? It's your birthday. Won't that make you sad?"

I twist my lips as I think. "Maybe a little, but it also feels right, too. I've been holding on to her, clinging to her as a part of my old life. It's time to move on."

"If that's really what you want, you know we'll support you," Dax says.

I touch his hand. "Thanks, Dax."

"Do you know where you want to spread her ashes?"

I nod. "Overlooking the lake. I kept trying to think of somewhere that was special to her, but I couldn't think of anything. Then I realized it doesn't need to be somewhere special to her. She's gone. She's not the one who'll be saying goodbye. The place needs to be somewhere I can remember her, and it doesn't need to be somewhere she's been. It just needs to be somewhere peaceful and beautiful, and that belongs to me." I look around at the three men. "Belongs to *us*."

"I think that's a perfect idea," Reed says.

I smile. "Let's get it done, and then I can get on with enjoying my birthday."

"I'll get her for you, Laney," Cade offers.

"Thanks."

I've been keeping my mother's urn in my bedroom. Maybe it's strange to have her sitting on my shelf, but I haven't been able to let go of her yet.

Today is the day.

Cade returns, carrying the urn, but I put my hands out for it.

"Are you sure?" he says.

"I want to carry her," I insist.

It'll be the last time I get to hold her.

If my mother had lived, would I have ever grown to understand her? I don't know, but I do know that now is the time to forgive her.

For a while, I'd been frightened that I'd become like her. I pictured a future alone, with a drug and alcohol problem.

The reality couldn't be farther from the truth. I'm nothing like her, and I'm grateful for that. I have a future, and I'm loved, and I respect myself and my life too much to ever throw it away.

I could have gone on hating her, but what would be the point? The only person I'd been hurting was myself. She's gone now, and it's time to move on.

We leave the dogs inside the house. We'd could have taken them with us, but I don't know how they'd have reacted to the ashes being scattered. I could just imagine them thinking we were throwing a ball, and landing in the middle of the lake, covered in my mother's remains. The image is both funny and horrifying.

The sky is a perfect blue as we weave our way between the trees, following a well-worn natural footpath. A light breeze rustles the branches overhead.

It doesn't take us long to reach the lake, and we draw to a

halt at its bank. Bright sunlight reflects off the water. Insects skim the surface. Birds twitter nearby and swoop down over the lake for either a meal or a drink. There's nothing around us but trees. When we'd been at the cabin, the surrounding trees had felt almost imposing—suffocating—but now I feel the opposite.

It's freeing here. I can finally breathe.

"Are you okay?" Reed asks. "Still ready to do this?"

I nod. "Yes, I am. It's time to say goodbye."

I think part of my wanting to go back to the trailer was about saying goodbye. Even though the drugs and alcohol made her sick for a really long time, her death still hit me out of the blue. And then there was the crash and everything that happened, and I still hadn't had the chance to say goodbye.

Maybe that is the reason I've held onto her ashes for so long, too. I needed that time to process everything.

I open the lid of the urn and look down into the gray grit inside. I reach in and take a handful.

"Bye, Mom," I say as I throw the ashes out toward the water. Tears choke my voice. "I forgive you. I hope wherever you are now, you're at peace."

The ashes land on the surface and drift away. A tear slides down my cheek, and I use my shoulder to wipe it away.

"Let me," Reed says, taking the urn from me.

Between them, Reed, Darius, and Cade scatter the remaining ashes on the lake, while I silently cry—not only for the loss of my mom, but for everything we've all been through.

I watch the ashes drift away and eventually vanish.

Together, we crouch at the edge of the shore and rinse our hands in the water.

"Come on," Reed says, putting his arm around my shoulder as we stand. "I think you deserve some of that cake and champagne now."

I sniff and nod. "I think you're right."

We walk back through the forest. I draw the clean air into my lungs and release it again. I'm feeling lighter, as though a huge weight has been lifted off my shoulders. The house comes into view, the glass glinting in the sunlight, and a smile spreads across my face.

I've been through hell, but I've come out the other side. I have a beautiful home, and three incredible men by my side who want to support me.

I couldn't be luckier.

The dogs greet us as though we've been gone for an entire day rather than an hour, and we play with them, laughing at how goofy they are.

We head into the kitchen, which is open plan, with the same floor-to-ceiling windows as the rest of the house, allowing the light to flood right through the property.

Cade takes the champagne from the refrigerator, and Reed finds plates and a knife for the cake.

"Before we open the champagne," Darius says, "I think we should give Laney her present."

My heart lifts. "You didn't have to get me a present. I have everything I could ever need right here."

"I think Dax is right," Reed says. "It feels like the right time."

"Yeah, it does," Cade agrees.

I look between them, feeling as though they're up to something. "What's going on?"

All three men drop to one knee, and I gasp.

"We know it'll never be a traditional kind of relationship," Reed says, "but we still wanted you to have something that shows our commitment to you."

He produces a dark blue velvet box from behind his back and opens it to reveal a stunning diamond ring with a white gold band. It's classy and beautiful and must be worth thousands.

"Oh, my God." I clap my hands to my mouth.

"So, will you be ours?" Cade asks.

Darius adds, "Forever?"

"Yes! Of course. I always have been."

I don't need a ring to know that, but I have to admit it is absolutely gorgeous.

Reed slips the ring onto my finger. It's a perfect fit. He rises and kisses me.

"Save some for us," Cade teases and pulls me away from him to kiss me as well. I sink into him, only to be whipped away by Dax.

"Let me show you how it's done," he says and then kisses me like we're in a movie, tilting me back, so I squeal and laugh. The dogs think something is wrong and bounce around us, wanting to join in.

I wipe tears from my eyes, but now they're tears of happiness.

My heart is full.

We made it through the wild, the darkest of times, and now, finally, we're home.

THE END

———

WANT to read a dark cut scene that never made it into the final book? Click this link to download the scene and join my newsletter! You'll get all the latest news, free books, and I promise to never spam.

———

IF YOU LOVE dark reverse harem, you won't want to miss out on the brand new omnibus of my co-written, dark, primal, CNC, reverse harem series, *Primal Limits*.

It contains all three books in *The Limit* series, and the paperback contains gorgeous formatting as well as a stunning new cover!

Order from Amazon today!

***Experience** the thrill of the hunt, where mistaken identity adds a seductive twist to the ultimate game of chase...*

When I take on the job as a maid for four wealthy men on their private island, they mistake me as their plaything.

Quickly, I realize they have a twisted game in mind: they want to chase me across the island and, if they catch me, they can do whatever they want.

They offer me a million dollars if I can last until the end without begging to leave, but I'm not the naïve victim they think I am.

As the game unfolds, secrets are revealed and power dynamics shift, leading to a thrilling and unexpected finale.

*Don't miss out on this dark, why choose, primal romance.*

*Contains:*
*Blurred Limits*
*Brutal Limits*
*Broken Limits*

*Order from Amazon today!*

# ACKNOWLEDGMENTS

There's always such bitter sweetness that comes with finishing a series, and this one has a particularly special place in my heart. I've absolutely loved writing about Laney, Reed, Darius and Cade. The words have flowed from my fingers and it's honestly been a pleasure to write. I'm sad to leave these characters, but I hope I've done them justice.

As always with my books, I have a lot of people to thanks.

First of all, huge thanks to you for reading. I wouldn't have this amazing career without the readers, and I'm grateful every day for being blessed to do my dream job. If you've taken the time to review the books, or post to social media, or even just tell your friends, extra, extra thanks to you. Nothing beats word of mouth when it comes to spreading the word about my books, so go and tell the world (or at least anyone you don't mind knowing that you're reading tab00, smutty books!).

I also need to thank my brilliant team of editors and proof-readers—Lori Whitwam, Jessica Fraser, and Tammy Payne. I love how you never flinch at the craziness of my books.

Thanks to Wander Aguiar for the gorgeous photograph on the cover, and Daqri at Covers by Combs for the fantastic typography.

And last but not least, thanks to Silla Webb for her formatting. Thank you for squeezing me in at the last minute—it's appreciated!

Until next time!

Marissa

# ABOUT THE AUTHOR

Marissa Farrar has always been in love with being in love. But since she's been married for numerous years and has three young daughters, she's conducted her love affairs with multiple gorgeous men of the fictional persuasion.

The author of more than forty novels, she has written full time for the last eight years. She predominantly writes dark reverse harem romance, but also writes dark m/f, paranormal romance and fantasy as well.

If you want to know more about Marissa, then please visit her website at www.marissa-farrar.com. You can also find her at her Facebook page, www.facebook.com/marissa.farrar.author or follow her on TikTok @marissafarrarwrites.

She loves to hear from readers and can be emailed at marissafarrar@hotmail.co.uk. To stay updated on all new releases and sales, just sign up to her newsletter!

# Other Dark Contemporary Books
# by the Author

**The Limit Series: Dark Contemporary**
**Reverse Harem**
Blurred Limits
Brutal Limit
Broken Limits

**The Bad Blood Trilogy**

Shattered Hearts
Broken Minds
Tattered Souls

**The Monster Trilogy:**
Defaced
Denied
Delivered

**Dark Codes: A Reverse Harem Series**

Hacking Darkness

*Other Dark Contemporary Books by the Author*

Unraveling Darkness
Decoding Darkness
Merging Darkness

## For Him Trilogy

Raised for Him
Unbound for Him
Damaged for Him

## Standalone Novels:

No Second Chances
Cut Too Deep
Survivor
Dirty Shots

Printed in Great Britain
by Amazon